Matriarch of the Witch Clan

Book One

John Stormm

Matriarch of The Witch Clan

Double Dragon Press

Published by
Double Dragon Publishing, Inc.
PO Box 54016
1-5762 Highway 7 East
Markham, Ontario L3P 7Y4 Canada
http://www.double-dragon-ebooks.com
http://www.double-dragon-publishing.com

ISBN-10: 1-55404-660-2
ISBN-13: 978-1-55404-660-7

A DDP First Edition March 26th, 2009
Book Layout and
Cover Art by Deron Douglas
http://www.derondouglas.com

PROLOGUE

Ella's Story August, 1939

"Let me tell you a story about an ancestor;" Ella Mae began, her conversational tone belying the storyteller's magick that made the teller and the told all one.

Although Emma had heard this family tale a thousand times. She gazed on her mother's aging form, how she held the tea cup, closing her eyes and drawing up the tale. The humble enamel topped kitchen table faded and from the shadows emerged an ancient court, the linoleum floor transformed into the thresh strewn flagstones, the window that offered a glimpse of the backyard garden melted into the heraldry of the court that Emma knew as well as she did her well tended kitchen. She closed her eyes, succumbed to her mother's magic.

"A king, the High King in Ireland," she went on, "in Tara, the seat of the Earth. Had no male heir, but three daughters. Three cherished daughters."

In Emma's mind's eye the daughters emerged, resplendent in green and yellow kyrtles, one with hair of raven's wing, one of henna red and the last the palest blond, gleaming from the powder of limestone she had washed it with. Emma never knew why they looked that way, her mother had never said such a thing, but it was how she always saw them.

"So you may imagine the relief when the prince of foreign court came visiting," she continued, "professing his love for the youngest of the damsels and how the King, knowing the true measure of love, granted them to wed. It would be some time, they would be long married, before they found just how foreign this prince truly was."

Emma always had a hard time seeing the prince, the older she got, the more shadowed his face, first a dark and swarthy youth, reminiscent of Clark Gable, but no, a lad, hair pale and blond and eyes that at a flash of thunder went from gray to blue to gray again.

"In the course of married life, the prince's secret was found out. He was not fully human, as his mother was foreign royalty and his father was even more so, of the court of the ancient Tuatha Danaans. These were a supposedly divine race of beings that the early Celtic settlers displaced in the land, mostly at sword point," she said taking another sip of tea.

"As it happened, the prince was not a bad sort of fellow. He genuinely loved his princess bride and they raised children. To be precise, they raised daughters. His contribution to the royal family line was no small affair, as these were very wise and talented women, to be sure. But as the number three is a potent number in Celtic magic, it also happens that every third generation produces an adept of exceptional craft and power.

Thus, a tradition of matriarchal succession has come down to us in this clan. The reigning matriarch usually being an adept born with this inherited trait."

"Our next matriarch will probably be born of one of your daughters, Emma," she concluded. "If we're wise, we'll prepare for her to improve our clannad's station in the world."

"Are you proposing we marry one off to a foreign prince?" Emma laughed.

"Not exactly..." Ella Mae said. "I'm saying we should consider the things that make us what we are, and do all we can to enhance our chances. At several points in our lengthy family history, our clan was all but wiped out by witch hunters. But, in this liberal modern country, where women vote for presidents and own property, the right woman, in the right place, at the right time can change the world. With the right mate, we can insure that our next matriarch comes out perfect in every way. Just imagine the effect of an alluring, blue eyed, vision of loveliness, with the power to move men whither so ever she will, in a country with all the promise of modern America," she expounded. "Imagine, one day, colleges formed, where men and women go to learn not just knowledge, but wisdom. Imagine the changes they make to their worlds, when they take it home with them."

It was late August of 1939 as Ella Mae sat at her daughter's kitchen table having this discussion while making jam and canning tomatoes. Emma's youngest daughter, Lorry, was helping her mom and grandma by sweeping the kitchen floor.

"Be careful so near the stove with that broom handle," Emma called out.

On top of the wood burning, kitchen stove, a variety of pots bubbled with grape jam, and tomatoes stewing for canning. As six year old Lorry looked up at her mom, the broom handle she wielded hooked the handle of a pot of boiling grape jam, and it toppled over, spilling its entire contents over her. The women gaped and jumped as Lorry shrieked her pain and danced hysterically around the kitchen in front of the stove.

Ella Mae, as matriarch, was quick to take matters in hand, and with a stern word to Emma, she did the unthinkable.

"Do as I do, and the child will be fine," she said. "I know this."

She took Lorry by the shoulders and began turning her in a widdershins circle and blowing on her, chanting between breaths. Taking her cue, Emma did likewise while speaking words of comfort to her daughter. It seemed an eternity, and they were getting light headed from all the puffing. As her grandchild's sobs subsided, she pulled off Lorry's shift and took a cool damp towel and began daubing away the sticky jam from her face and body. The skin beneath was a healthy pink and completely unblistered.

"Mom, I was so afraid she'd be horribly disfigured," Emma sobbed.

"Her kind of beauty doesn't fade or mar easily," Ella Mae said thoughtfully, looking at her granddaughter.

Ella Mae Shaw was a lovely, green eyed, red head with a white forelock. Her husband, Robert, was away much of the time on council business as an Iroquois chieftain. During these excursions, she would stay in her own room at her daughter's home. Her daughter, Emma, got her iron black hair and dark eyes from her father. It seemed that adepts were incapable of passing their superficial traits on to their offspring. No matter, it was the deeper things that really counted.

Words like "witch," or "coven" were never used in this household, even though it was the enlightened Twentieth Century, the persecution was sure to follow. Christian terms were used instead. A witch was a herbalist, a healer, or a midwife, and in place of a coven was the women's circle. Every parish had one of those for bake sales and ladies' auxiliaries and such. Outsiders never had a clue, though close kin and friends might have suspected these women were a bit too knowledgeable to be rank amateurs. In fact, husbands rarely suspected their spouses, and were content to leave women things to the women. Dinner was good, the children were well cared for, and the house was clean. What more could a man want to know?

Of her three daughters, Emma remained the closest to Ella Mae, to learn her craft.

A fine rural midwife and still called often in emergencies. She had a singular gift for the healing arts. Emma idolized her.

Emma had four daughters and two sons. Mary, Margaret, Evelyn and Edward Junior had their mother's dark, native features, while Johnny and Lorry were blond haired and blue eyed, the spitting image of Emma's husband, Edward Senior.

Little Lorry doted on her father and had little time or inclination to learn the family craft. She was a tomboy and a heartbreaker, and enjoyed fitting in her own social circles.

Ella Mae watched her carefully, considering what traits a non-adept like Lorry might pass on to an adept daughter.

Over the span of the next decade, Lorry blossomed into womanhood. When she dressed to go out for the evening, everyone remarked how she looked so much like the actress, Loretta Young. She would have the young men eating out of the palm of her hand like tame birds, but the only man in her life she really loved was her father. He was diabetic and had suffered a stroke that had paralyzed his left side. Lorry was there to faithfully administer his insulin shots. All the time, Ella Mae watched and noted her granddaughter's progress as a woman.

It was the time of the summer solstice when she confided to Emma about her full plans for Lorry.

"I think Lorry will be the mother of our next matriarch," she said.

"But Mary, Margaret and Evelyn are so much more active in the craft, " Emma pointed out.

"True," she said, "but we need a matriarch with the Anglo features, so sought after by men, to be able to wield the kind of influence we'll need to move into the circles of power and effect change for our kind in the world. A woman, a president would not hesitate to marry for fear of what some might say. Every bit of charm we can add to the mix, will only advance our cause that much more."

"Lorry certainly has those," Emma conceded. "How will we insure that she bears the next adept, and one of that kind of strength?"

"We've been making progress getting contacts of the Sidhe in the Otherworld, through the use of our gazing bowl," Ella Mae said. "From this well is where our traits originated, and from this well we will find Lorry's husband."

"How will you cause a Sidhe prince to cross over?" Emma asked, wide eyed.

"Isn't that dangerous to cross worlds like that?"

"Leave that to me," she said smugly. "There are some of them, in the Otherworld, who have been misplaced by humanity and feel their true heritage lies here. This and my own blood gives them a link to this plane. A human wife of Lorry's caliber will give them an even better foothold in this world. Actually, we only need him here long enough to conceive a child."

"An unwed mother and bastard child won't be an easy obstacle to surmount," countered Emma.

"The clan can take care of Lorry, my dear," she explained, "and men don't think of girls as bastards. No matter, I was planning on an actual marriage and joining of worlds. A golden age of witchcraft and wizardry to dawn yet again on this world."

"Won't they try to overrun the planet," Emma asked, referring to her favorite radio program, "like in 'The War of the Worlds'?"

"No, my sweet." Ella Mae laughed. "There will be only one of them, and his lot will be best thrown with those of fae blood, like ourselves. Our goals will be in their best interest. There may be a price for this crossing, but I don't see much chance for failure, and everything is to be gained by it. I'm prepared to pay for my dreams."

She noted the look in her daughter's eyes. Emma loved her, and had no reason to doubt her capabilities. Still, somehow, the mention of a price, seemed to trouble her daughter deeply.

"Don't be such a worrywart, my dear," she admonished. "You'll be right by my side when we make our parley this Midsummer."

At this, Emma brightened. It was just before sunrise on Midsummer's Eve of 1952. Ella Mae was gathering her walking stick and belting a witch's long knife under her apron. She and Emma had fasted since the day before and they would not break that fast until business was concluded later that day. Even then, it would be only a light meal before the real feasting began at Lughnasadh on the morrow.

The sun was barely peeking over the horizon as together they made their way into the forest at the edge of town. Ella Mae picked her way down a trail to a clear, north running stream with a large white oak on its banks. Emma was carrying a small iron cauldron with some coals from the stove, and a parcel wrapped in a cloth napkin tied to her apron strings. Where a game trail crossed the stream was a roughly rectangular stone about two feet high and three feet long. Ella Mae chose this spot to begin her calling ritual.

She crushed some rock salt with a fist sized stone from the stream on the crude altar. Emma scraped the resulting powder into a five inch circle filled by a cross aligned at the four cardinal directions. They set the cauldron at its base, on the altar, and sprinkled sandalwood onto the burning embers within. They centered themselves as the smoke from the incense arose. Raising her staff, Ella Mae spoke the agreed upon words of calling.

Over the crude altar a light sprang into existence.

"You have an offer for us, wise woman?" An androgynous voice called out in the Old Language.

"I have a fair bride, of my own children, to a worthy husband," Ella Mae responded.

"And your expectations?" Queried the voice.

"My clan requires a daughter of fae blood to lead our next generation in prosperity. The husband sought, would have a prominent place in our clan and in our world," she intoned.

"And your bond to this end?" Came the voice.

"The honor of a witch of the blood," she said. "As my word, so mote it be." With this she unsheathed her long knife and drew its razor edge across her left palm and squeezed a few drops of her own blood into the smoking cauldron on the rock.

"You will have your Sidhe husband for your daughter," said the voice, "and you will have your fae child of this union. By the next equinox you will know him by the storm in his eyes."

The light winked out over the altar. Ella Mae and her daughter cleaned up the evidence of their visit and returned home before the day was in full swing.

PART TWO

Sidhe Prince

Late September of 1952, she and Emma sat out on the front porch doing their needlework. It was a balmy autumn day, the foliage on the trees had not even begun to turn to their fall colors, when a tall, dark haired stranger came striding up the sidewalk to the house.

"It would appear that Lorry has yet another gentleman caller." Ella Mae nodded in his direction.

"He looks every bit like Jimmie Dean, the folksinger," Emma remarked. "Where does she find all these men?"

The gentleman in question stopped and placed one foot on the front steps and bowed at the waist as he extended one arm.

"Good day to you fine ladies," he said in a mellifluous voice. "My name is Lee Shamblynn. I met Lorry at her job at the dry cleaners, and she said it would be fine if I came over today to take her to the matinee.

Emma stared, struck dumb. Clearly, she was smitten by the charm of this visitor. It was Ella Mae who gathered her wits and spoke first.

"We've been expecting a gentleman caller since midsummer. Would you know this man?"

"Indeed, I would," Lee smiled at the women as he looked up to meet their eyes, "I would be the man you were expecting." With this, a flash of light arced in his eyes and the distant rumble of thunder punctuated his sentence.

"Is that rain, I hear?" Startled out of gawking at the stranger, Emma looked around. "And it looked as if it was going to be such a lovely day. Do be careful not to get caught in it."

"I promise to have your daughter in the theater before a single drop of rain can touch her lovely hair." Lee smiled broadly, as Lorry was coming through the front door. "What's this about rain?" Lorry asked, stepping onto the porch.

"We thought we heard a little thunder in the distance, dear," Ella Mae said.

"Nothing to worry yourself about. You and Lee have a fine afternoon."

"I take it you've met then," Lorry said.

"We've met your fine young man." She smiled at her granddaughter. "Now you two get along now. Your mother and I have plenty to occupy our time."

"We're going to see that new James Dean movie," Lorry said as she kissed her mother and grandmother on their cheeks. "I'll tell you all about it when I get home. I just gave Daddy his insulin. I should be home before he needs another injection." She and Lee rushed off hand in hand.

"Is it Jimmie Dean or James Dean?" Emma sighed watching the pair leave.

"It's both, and it's neither." Ella Mae chortled at her daughter's puzzled frown.

"Jimmie is a singer. James is an actor, and Lee is dating our Lorry," to which she and Emma broke out laughing themselves to tears.

Lorry saw Lee steadily for the next several weeks, so much so, that Emma and Ella Mae had taken to administering Edward's insulin shots more and more in Lorry's absence. This was taken as a good sign by all, including Lorry's father, who said it was fair time that Lorry should have her own life to live as a wife and mother. It was apparent that Lorry was very much in love with Lee.

Summer turned to fall. It was an Indian Summer and still quite balmy in October. Lee had bought himself a new Harley-Davidson like the one they had seen in the James Dean movie. Lee and Lorry would go on day trips on his bike almost every weekend. One night Ella Mae awoke to a thundering roar as the bike pulled up to the house. She peered through the curtains as Lorry got off and ran into the house crying. She pulled on her robe and went downstairs to see what was wrong. Her granddaughter was sobbing in the dark.

"Are you alright, dear?" She asked softly. "Can Grandma be of any help?"

"No." Lorry pulled away. "I'm fine. I'll be okay."

"No, dear," she whispered. "You are not fine. You are crying. Let me help."

"Oh, it's nothing, Grandma," Lorry sobbed. "I made a darned fool of myself and fell down some stairs."

"Here." She pulled out her basket from besides the window seat and lit the kerosene lamp in the parlor to examine Lorry. "Let me have a look at you, and we'll see if Grandma can fix you right up."

There were several nasty bruises. The first was a darkening weal on Lorry's cheekbone. She wet a towel in the kitchen and dabbed it liberally with oil of lavender as a cold compress for her granddaughter's cheek. For the ribs and arms, she smeared on an ointment made of arnica. It was obvious that the bruises encircling Lorry's arm did not come by falling down any stairs.

"Did Lee hurt you, Lorry?" She asked pointedly.

"No, Grandma," Lorry answered. "Don't be silly. Lee would never hurt me."

"I just wanted to be sure," Ella Mae replied, believing none of it. "It's just that some of these bruises are pretty bad. I've a bottle of rosemary you can rub on that facial bruise tomorrow. It will help it fade faster. I can make more, so you can use it all up. Okay?"

"Thank you, Grandma," Lorry said, gratitude shining in her eyes. "I'll be okay. Lee's taking me to the Halloween ball next week. I'll need to look my best. I'm going as a black cat, a witch's familiar."

Ella Mae winced at the reference, and they both laughed.

***

"I have a very bad feeling about this one," Ella Mae remarked to Emma that day.

"What could go wrong?" Emma asked. "They're both madly in love."

"Perhaps, madly is the problem," she replied. "I believe Lee may have hurt Lorry. Madly in love, or not, we'll need a spell to keep his darker nature in check."

"I think you're making too much of nothing," Emma retorted, clearly taken in by Lee. "But a good spell never hurt anything," she added.

What exactly could a good spell hurt? Ella Mae tamped down her feeling of guilt.

As it was, Robert had returned home from a lengthy tribal council and it was time she returned home with him.

***

It was good to be home and tend her own garden. She caught up on all the news with Robert, and spent some time working on her spell craft. The dark fae could not tolerate silver. It was like poison to them. Still, dark or light, life was about choices. All people had an affinity for one choice or another, but it was always their own choices that made them who and what they were.

"Something I had never considered," she scolded herself, "was having a fae male in the clannad. I think we'll need an appropriately masculine, silver clan medallion for our newest member. Tradition will compel him to wear it, and he'll have to make better choices or suffer the effects." It was the perfect idea. She had some money stashed in a jar in her cupboard and took it to the jeweler's.

"I'd like to commission a masculine version of this silver cross as a gift for my new grandson-in-law," she said as she handed the jeweler her own on its chain, "and I'd like it on a slightly thicker silver chain." The pendant was a Celtic cross with a tiny emerald centered at the crosspiece, and crafted with Celtic knot work round about.

"With all the Irish in the neighborhood, I've seen my fair share of these," the manager said. "I can have this made for you in a few weeks. The silver chains I have already in stock. Take your pick." He motioned to the display case.

"Here's three hundred dollars cash in advance." Ella Mae pushed the money at him.

"A silver pendant won't cost nearly so much as this, madam." The jeweler's eyes widened.

"If you would be so kind as to make this effort your priority," she explained, "I have no idea how soon I may have to present this gift."

"Oh,...OH!" The jeweler said, catching the hint. "I'll get to it, right now.

Check in with me in a few days."

"Thank you, ever so much." She said, putting the money in his hand.

***

It was Halloween, and Ella Mae took the trolley across town to visit her daughter.

"I have the charm being made this very moment," she told Emma excitedly. "As a clan member, he'll have to wear it, or risk casting aspersions on our family honor. He'll also have to curb his baser nature, or it will give him no end of discomfort."

"I knew you'd come up with something, Mom," Emma replied proudly. "But, if they have a child, won't she get her nature from her father?"

"I've already considered that and I have just the spell for that too," Ella Mae beamed. "I've a copy for you on this vellum. Put it in a safe place until you need it. I never know how long your father and I may be around to help or not. You may be the one to train this next adept in the craft. We have to be careful how we handle things. It's always a dangerous thing. To offend the Sidhe."

Emma tucked the folded vellum away in her sewing basket, seemingly missing the hint that she might not be around to guide the women's circle. The sound of distant thunder rumbled louder as Lee's motorcycle was pulling up to the house. Ella Mae went out to the street to speak to him as he waited for Lorry.

"Lee, you will be a welcome addition to our clan. You know this," she said. "But my family is precious to me, and you must see to it that you do none of them any hurt.

Do you understand me, son?" She stared straight into his eyes. "Neervallat. You hear me?"

"I hear you, old woman," Lee rumbled, eyes flashing as he revved the mighty engine and called, "LORRY!"

Lorry came bounding out of the house dressed in her black cat costume, a black half mask, with cat ears and whiskers, topped off a sleek black turtle neck, matching tights with a tail, over black spiked heels. She was positively fetching as she hopped on the back of the bike and put her arms around Lee. Her tail, she tucked into the belt of her costume for safe keeping during the ride. She waved to her mom and grandmother as they prepared to ride.

"Don't wait up for me!" She called over her shoulder as they sped away.

"I have a very bad feeling about this," Ella Mae remarked to no one in particular.

She had decided she would stay for the night at her daughter's house. Just in case.

***

It was after three in the morning when the rumble of the Harley-Davidson pulling up awoke her. There was shouting and screaming coming from the street in front of the house. Ella Mae bolted up and drew on her cloak and slippers and dashed down the stairs with Emma running behind her. Coming out the front door, she saw Lorry still clinging to Lee from the back of the motorcycle. He cocked his arm and swung back with his elbow, catching Lorry on the side of her head, knocking her cart wheeling off the bike to the sidewalk. Ella Mae's fists were clenched in rage as she roared at the dark Sidhe. He had dismounted the machine and was advancing upon Lorry's dazed form.

"I warned you not to hurt any of mine, Lee. All things having their price, it will not go well for you. NEERVALLAT." She cursed him in the Old Language as her left fist shot out at him with index and pinky fingers extended.

***

Emma was helping Lorry to her feet as Lee was knocked backwards over his bike by the force of Ella Mae's curse. It was as if she had just awakened from a dream and was seeing Lee for the first time. This time, she was not so impressed with what she saw.

Lee was quickly back on his feet and raised his arms to the sky and roared. His eyes flashed with lightning that reflected in the skies overhead and struck the lamp pole he was parked under. Rain began coming down in sheets as he raised his arms again for another bolt.

Emma, bracing Lorry in her right arm, looked over her shoulder and raised her left arm in the same manner as her mother and cursed him the second time.

"Neervallat!" Emma yelled.

Lorry also, looked over her shoulder at her mother's pointing fingers, as Lee, eyes flashing brightly, was bowled end over end across the street.

"What the hell is that?" Lorry cried hysterically. "Momma, what in hell is going on? Is that Lee? What are you and Grandma doing?"

"We are putting a monster in his proper place, dear," Emma consoled. "It will be all right in the morning."

"You're damned right it will," Lorry growled and emulated the move she saw her mother and grandmother make towards Lee and shouted, "Neervallat!"

Being thrice cursed, the form that was once Lee, exploded in a shower of sparks as lightning struck out of the stormy night sky. His precious Harley lay on its side at the curb. Ella Mae and Emma helped haul the injured Lorry into the house.

Inside, they collected all the first aid supplies in Emma's cupboard and started in dressing Lorry's wounds. Emma's husband, Edward had limped down the stairs in his bathrobe to hold Lorry's weeping form close as Ella Mae ministered salves and ointments. In the kitchen, Emma brewed a tea mixture of valerian, verbena and motherwort to mix with a little brandy and soothe everyone's frazzled nerves.

"I wouldn't be mistaken, if I had observed that a great deal more than herbal cures and midwifery had just occurred on the street in front of my house," Edward said pointedly, "now, would I?"

"No dear, you wouldn't," Ella Mae replied, "though, I wouldn't speak much on it, until I had a chance to understand all of what happened myself."

A kind and patient man, Edward cradled Lorry's head on his shoulder and looked from his mother-in-law and to his wife, his eyes silently conveying that as much as he loved them all, he intended to eventually hear that explanation.

***

In the morning, Lorry's brother, Johnny, had went out and set the bike aright at the curb. He then ran some errands for his mother and grandmother, including picking up the commissioned silver cross from the jewelers.

Before that night grew old, a local street gang had stolen the motorcycle. Nobody missed it and nobody cared, except for Edward Junior. His friends called him "Sonny," and he had come into some quick and suspicious cash. Otherwise, no further sign of Lee was forthcoming.

PART THREE

Dark Heritage

Weeks went by. Lorry was healing well, with the exception of a bad case of morning sickness. Winter had set in and she craved fresh strawberries and was driving her younger brother to distraction by sending him all over town in search of strawberries. He brought back frozen strawberries, chocolate covered strawberries, dried strawberries, strawberry preserves, but no fresh strawberries to be found in November.

Just after Thanksgiving, Ella Mae's husband, Robert was killed in a automobile accident on his way back from a Six Nations council meet. The family was devastated. Robert was a kind and caring individual. He knew her as a Celtic witch woman and was completely accepting of her ways. He had hoped she might even be a Beloved Woman in his own clan for her great wisdom. One of his three daughters would, no doubt, occupy that post one day. It was good medicine, he used to say. She brought him and his tribe great luck. But she wasn't feeling very certain about that just now.

Ella Mae consoled herself by doing all she could to nurture Lorry, who was looking more than slightly pregnant by this time. She reminded herself that the child within her would be the most powerful adept the family had produced in centuries. There would eventually be no more hiding in shadows. The world could be changed and made brighter.

"Faery heart, burning bright," She crooned to the unborn child, "eyes beholding deeper light. Spirit brighter than mortal men, spirit born of faery ken. Of the unicorn, thou art the last, a magickal link to ages past. Wisdom beyond such tender years, a heart that is touched by mortal tears. Unicorns and virgins, dressed in white, seen by eyes with faery sight. Dare to withstand the power of night, O' firstborn child with second sight."

"That's a pretty song, Grandma." Lorry smiled, holding her sizeable tummy. "I think little Linda Marie likes it too."

"That's a pretty name you've chosen," she replied. "It means 'pretty.' I am very sure she will be as pretty as her mother."

"Do you really think she will be our next matriarch?" Lorry asked.

"I'm sure of it, all the stars favor it," she reassured. "She will grow to be a woman of exceptional strength, courage and talent. She will be able to charm the very birds out of the trees with her music, and men will drop whatever they are doing to obey her every word."

"Wow," Lorry murmured dreamily, and sang. "Whenever I sleep, I never count sheep, I count all the charms about Linda," and fell asleep.

It was following Beltane that year when Edward died in his sleep. Emma was heartbroken even though it was not entirely unexpected. In spite of his illness, Edward was a very strong man who treasured the heart of his wife, and she had given him nearly all of it. For weeks after, Emma had taken to drowning her grief in a bottle of wine or brandy. The family understood her sorrow, and no one begrudged her a moment of weakness. Lorry took her father's death rather hard as well, and Ella Mae did what she could to keep her spirits up for the baby's sake.

The months and trimesters passed. Ella Mae would spend odd weeks at home to tend her garden and stock her larder with herbs and medicines for the family. Emma could collect herself from her sorrows long enough to be there for Lorry and the baby. It seemed to give her something to live for. When Lorry was ready to be delivered, Johnny drove his little sister to the hospital in his new Studebaker. He paced in the waiting room with his other siblings as his mother was busy preparing the house for their return with the baby. She had given Johnny explicit instructions to come and get her when the delivery was under way.

Ella Mae was notified that night. She would be brought in by Johnny as soon as the situation stabilized with Lorry. It was hard for her to sleep that night. As worn out as she was, she knew she should be there with Lorry. It was all her fault. She should be there…

***

Lorry was exhausted from the strength of the contractions. It was a long night and the labor pains made sleep impossible. Robed nuns bustled in and out of the room to check on her, but there was really nothing to do but wait.

"Everything will turn out just fine, Lorry," Ella Mae said. "You have to believe that, dear."

"Grandma, you came!" Lorry gasped, seeing her standing at her bedside.

"Of course, dear," she reassured her. "I wouldn't miss this for anything."

The head nurse came in that moment to find Lorry was fully dilated and quickly had her wheeled into the delivery room.

"Don't leave me, Grandma!" Lorry called out.

"Don't worry, dear," an elderly nun replied. "I won't leave you."

***

It was shortly after sunrise, on Midsummer's Eve, when the doctor rushed in and delivered Lorry of her baby.

"It's a fine baby boy you have here, Lorry," the doctor said merrily.

"A WHAT?" Lorry gagged deliriously. It was a long night and she was fatigued beyond words.

"It's a boy, see?" He said holding the infant closer.

"Ugh," she said, as the child was opening his eyes. "Get that goddamned thing away from me."

"She's delirious," said a nurse. "Let her rest a while and we'll clean up the baby to present to her later. It may be just a reaction to the drugs."

The doctor however, didn't look so sure. Was it a trick of the delivery room lights that flashed across the child's stormy gray eyes? It sounded like thunder outside.

"Oh great," he said. "I didn't even think to bring an umbrella."

***

Johnny had gotten his mom as soon as he heard his sister was going into the delivery room. He had dropped her off at the hospital on his way to go pick up his grandmother. The ambulance and medical examiner had left the house and Johnny made his way back to the hospital, sleep deprived and numb from the whole night's events.

It was hours later when he arrived back in the maternity ward.

"Here he comes," Emma said to her girls. "It's about time, son. You have a nephew. We're naming him after his favorite uncle," she chortled, and then looked closer at her son's face and then down the hall for yet another familiar face, but seeing none.

"Are you all right?" She asked. "And where's your grandmother? She should be here for this."

Johnny broke and sobbed his story.

"I got to the house to pick her up." Johnny continued to weep. "She didn't answer the door when I knocked, so I went in and found her."

With this, his sisters and his mother all froze in place and stared expectantly at him.

"I found her dressed and sitting in her sewing chair," he continued. "Her eyes were closed as if she fell asleep there. Mom, she was dead. They took her body away not a half hour ago."

Emma dropped to the floor as if pole axed. The family and hospital staff rushed to help her.

***

Lorry heard the news first from her sister, Evelyn.

"It's that cursed spell, it is." Lorry insisted. "It was supposed to be a girl, but we were all cheated, and Grandma paid with her life, as well as Grandpa and Daddy."

Evelyn and the sisters agreed that the child was an abomination caused by the dark fae, and Lorry had no doubts the child should be put up for adoption as no single mother could be expected to raise it. For weeks to follow after the funeral, her mother drank herself into a stupor. For the rest of the clan, lives went on, albeit dismally.

***

At St. Brigit's convent, a blue eyed baby boy cooed and gurgled merrily at something fluttering around over his crib. But whenever a human face appeared over the railing of that crib, it was cold, gray eyes that glared suspiciously at the intruding visitor.

PART FOUR

Emma's Story

Emma rode the magnificent bay stallion bareback. Her long, iron black tresses streaming in the wind behind her; she raised her arms to Heaven and held on with her legs.

As they reached the crest of a grassy knoll, she spied a herd of restless mustangs. Looking about to see what might have stirred them so, she spotted a pack of great dark wolves that were circling the perimeter of the grassy plain. But closer inspection showed it was not the wolves that had them restless. It was something within the herd itself.

She directed her great mount forward to get a closer look at the disturbance. The horses were moving away from something bright in their midst. In so doing, they were opening their tightly knit defenses to the wolves, but they didn't seem to care.

Getting closer still, Emma could see a silvery white foal, trying clumsily to approach a mare, any mare to suckle, but no mare would let it near. The herd began to scatter, leaving the strange foal behind, unprotected. The surrounding pack of wolves howled in triumph and were moving in for an easy meal. The foal, beginning to realize its danger, wheeled to face the first of its attackers. Then Emma understood why the foal was shunned by the mustangs. The tiny silver nub of a horn on its forehead revealed that it was not a horse, but a unicorn. The pack closed in hungrily as the stormy eyed foal lowered its head to make its first and last stand...

"No," Emma screamed, bolting upright in her bed, tears streaming down her face from eyes already puffy.

She remembered that she had cried herself to sleep that night and had drank far too much wine. The loss of the clan matriarch, her mother, made her very heart want to stop beating. But as broken as it was, it would not stop. There was unfinished business. It had been how many weeks since they buried her mother? She couldn't recall, but she did remember her mother saying something about being willing to pay for her dreams. At such a great price. First there had been her husband, Edward only months before, and her father only months before him. That was 1953 and a great year for death, and a lousy year for an unwanted baby boy out there somewhere. The unicorn foal. She knew dreams well and understood what must be done.

"It is dangerous to offend the Sidhe," her mother had told her before.

Here was a fae child, alone in the world of humans. Who hadn't asked to be brought into such an alien world, but was called into existence by her and her mother. Her daughter, Lorry, had put the infant up for adoption. An unwed mother could not be expected to bring up such a child. Christians could not hope to comprehend the boy in their midst, in light of what they knew. But a witch would understand that human values might not come naturally for such a child. If they thought him possessed of devils because of his fae nature, they would bring down an impossible wrath upon them all, and the clan would be ultimately responsible for this. Her mother's dream would be their nightmare, and then their ending.

"I can fix this, Momma," she cried. "He's not what we expected, but I can make this work. It was a good dream. I won't let us down. As my word, so mote it be," she gave her witch's vow and bond.

***

That morning Lorry came downstairs looking perplexed at the sounds and smells of breakfast being prepared. The kitchen was spotless. It certainly hadn't been left that way last night. Johnny and the others were off trying to pull their lives back together and had left them to their own devices. Edward Junior, who insisted on being called Sonny, was spending more and more of his time running the streets with his friends. No one had seen him for days. Not that anyone was worried. He needed to learn life's lessons the hard way.

"Are you okay, Mom?" Lorry asked, sitting down at the kitchen table.

"I'm remarkable, dear," she said gaily.

It was a saying Emma's mother always used. Her daughter winced at that answer. Lorry's concern that her mother's grief might overwhelm her yet again was written plainly on her face.

"Coffee's perking, home fries and eggs are in the skillet, the sun is shining brightly, and my lovely daughter is here to share them with me." She smiled as she sat down across from her daughter and brought her coffee mug to her lips. "So tell me, dear, what sort of dreams did you have last night?"

"I don't remember," Lorry replied. "Something about horses, I think." She visibly relaxed at what was normal family breakfast conversation since before she was born.

She watched her daughter eat, thoughtfully sipping her coffee. The dream of horses was an indication to her that she had much productive work ahead of her. It felt good, knowing this. As she finished breakfast, she gathered her dishes into the sink.

Lorry grabbed a wet dishrag to wipe the table. But Emma waved her off.

"It's all right, dear," she said, waving her daughter off. "I'll take care of that.

You get yourself ready for work. I'll fix you lunch and bring it to you later."

Lorry looked at her oddly before rushing off to work. But this was Emma as always, before Lee came along and life grew dark and menacing. It was good to be back.

Her first task was to get outside and weed her garden. It was an overgrown shambles. How long had it been since she last tended it? She could set her life in order by everything she did and found within its confines. Every flower and every herb had a message to give her to make her strong and able to face life's challenges. The smell of earth grounded her. When all was satisfactory, she went back inside to prepare for the next step.

She sorted through her mother's possessions, and the grief threatened to well up in her throat, but she had work to do. The time for tears was past. First, she put on her mother's apron. There was no kind of mess in the world that she couldn't put to right when wearing it. She put her hands in the deep apron pockets, and found a folded piece of vellum in one. Opening it up, she discovered a poem of sorts, titled 'Changeling's Spell.' Her mother had given her a copy of this spell, and told her that she might have to be the one to use it as her mother and father might not be around to help her raise the child.

Momma knew a lot more than she let on at times. So now it was her place to carry on where Mother had left off. In the other pocket she found a black velvet jeweler's bag that contained a silver Celtic cross on a thick silver chain. The tiny emerald at its center gleamed merrily. It had been made for Lee originally. The baby would be too small for it, but would grow into it. It would still be useful.

I'm going to need clan help. She looked through her mother's jewelry box for her clan medallion and put it on. The real trick would be to convince them of the need to retrieve the child from the adoption agency. First, I will have to convince the agency that the child may be reclaimed by it's own family soon. This will discourage them from accepting any offers on the baby.

As it was, Johnny and his new wife were considering adopting the child, but Ruby was having misgivings with all the evil sentiment going around the family over it. She was an educated woman and claimed to be above any colloquial superstitions, but Emma knew whistling in the dark when she heard it.

She would pay a visit to St. Brigit's convent that afternoon. First, however, she would prepare a good lunch for Lorry and bring it to her at the dry cleaners.

It was a lovely August afternoon as Emma strolled to St. Brigit's. A warm, brown brick building with a red tile roof and bronze gutters that come out through stylized, concrete gargoyle rainspouts. The grounds boasted many old hardwood trees and well trimmed shrubbery. Upon her arrival, she introduced herself to the mother superior of the fine convent. She identified herself as the child's maternal grandmother and requested to see the baby.

"We don't recommend contact with the infants that are put up for adoption," said the nun. "It makes the separation that much more painful as we find them new families."

"That's the point of my being here," Emma replied. "We are reconsidering raising the boy in his own family." She wanted to be careful to say all the right things to this nun.

"That would be the ideal situation," the nun said doubtfully. "But is the birth mother ready for the responsibility to raise this child on her own?"

"Lorry's having her second thoughts," she lied. "But with the family behind her, they should have all the support they need. I have a big house, where I've raised six children, including Lorry. My husband left me a good pension fund besides the insurance that paid off the house. Lorry has a good job as a clerk at Speedy's Cleaners on North and Hudson. I think much of the decisions at the time were based on the recent deaths of my husband and my mother. The grief, having run its course, started making us all think of life anew. We need little Johnny as much as he needs us. May I see him, for just a little while?" Emma was hoping she looked as confident as she felt, and saying what the nun needed to hear to convince her.

The mother superior was warming to the idea, but no doubt the nun had some kind of misgivings that she wasn't speaking openly. It had shown itself in the way the woman kept rubbing at the silver crucifix attached to the rosary she was wearing. The nun led her down a corridor to a large, bright and airy nursery that opened into a manicured courtyard within the abbey. It was warm, with plenty of sunlight streaming in the windows. Only a couple of the cribs in the little cubicles that lined the wall actually had babies in them. The mother superior turned to speak, before allowing Emma to see the child in the cubicle they were coming to.

"You must understand, the child has been separated from its mother at birth." The nun proceeded voicing her concerns, "They don't often develop in quite the same ways a normal, healthy baby will. This one has some decidedly antisocial characteristics at times, but he seems a very happy child most of the time when left to himself," she said, with the air of one who had seen this all too often.

Emma was puzzled at this. How could he be showing antisocial traits at such a young age? These silly Christians certainly entertained some peculiar notions about life. Nonetheless, she nodded to the mother superior and stepped into the nursery cubicle to meet her new grandson. At first, the size of the infant shocked her.

This must be the wrong crib. A fair sized toddler was sitting up and laughing at something it had seen out the window in the courtyard outside. Fine blond hair and twinkling blue eyes looked very much like Lorry at about a year old. The child then became aware of his visitors and stormy gray eyes turned a suspicious gaze upon them. It was him, Emma knew. But how much time had she lost in a wine bottle? Another infant in the room wailed lustily, and the nun excused herself and left Emma with the child.

"Hello Johnny, Grandma is here to see you," she cooed.

The baby sat quietly with a tiny crease forming between his brows and glared.

"It's been too long, hasn't it?"

The child sat in the far corner of the crib and never took his eyes off her. He was rubbing his right palm, at something dark in it. Could he be hurt?

"Can Grandma look at your hand?" She asked, but the child held his arm closer to his body and made no move forward. He understands. She remembered the dream with the unicorn foal. He is the little unicorn. An idea sprung to mind of her mother's spell in her apron pocket. She pulled out the folded vellum and looked around. The nun was busy a couple cubicles away. This shouldn't be too hard.

" Let me read you a nursery rhyme," she said. "It was written by your great grandmother, just for you. 'Faery heart, burning bright. Eyes beholding deeper light. Spirit brighter than mortal men. Spirit born of faery ken. Of the unicorn, thou art the last, a magickal link to ages past. A wisdom beyond such tender years, a heart that is touched by mortal tears. Unicorns and virgins, dressed in white, seen by eyes with faery sight. Dare to withstand the power of night, O' firstborn child with second sight.'"

Little Johnny cocked his head to one side as if considering the poem. His eyes seemed to twinkle a sapphire blue and he smiled.

This was a good sign.

"Will you come see Grandma?" She pleaded, and held out her arms.

The baby, still smiling, reached out to her, a black smudge the shape of a crucifix shown in the palm of his right hand. She picked him up and held her forehead to his and hugged him.

"Grandma loves Johnny." She smiled.

Then Johnny took her cheeks in his little hands and pulled their foreheads close.

"You love it?" He asked, smiling beatifically.

Emma was shocked he could speak so. She had already reconciled that she had been in an alcoholic stupor for the better part of a year, but this child was very smart for his age. She pondered why the boy would think of himself as an "it."

"The baby is as smart as a whip," the nun said, reappearing over her shoulder.

"It doesn't usually take to people so well. Usually he just talks to himself and some imaginary friends. We get the silent treatment during diaper changing times and baths.

He's not a bad boy. Until you came, I was beginning to think he might be autistic."

"I love it," Emma declared to her grandson, suddenly understanding why he was an "it."

"He's learned speech while you talked in front of him as if he wasn't there," she said to the nun.

"We never knew he was even aware of us," the nun said defensively. "Except for that watchful eye of his, ..Oh look, his hand is black where he grabbed my crucifix when I changed him last. I never guessed it was so tarnished."

Emma licked her thumb and rubbed the mark off the baby's hand. She figured that the crucifix wasn't tarnished until the boy had touched it. Creatures of the darkside and silver don't mix well. Without loving guidance, his inclination would be that of the dark Sidhe. He was smiling and his gaze never left her eyes. More than ever, her heart tugged for the child.

"I'll come to visit him as I can, if it's alright," she said. "When his mother is ready, we'll be down to start whatever proceedings are required. Will that be okay?"

The nun looked genuinely relieved. Johnny even smiled at her when she took him back from his grandmother. Emma hated to part from him. She promised she would come back soon to visit and play with him. As the nun put the baby back in his crib, he rolled onto his back and grabbed his toes and rocked and laughed.

"Gamma love it," He chortled and rocked happily.

She had to leave quickly or never leave at all.

***

It took her another five months to convince Lorry and the rest of the family to retrieve the baby. She had to stay away from drinking in excess, which wasn't really a problem now that she had priorities. There were always spirits in the house, to be used with various home remedies. She simply had no need for them and a much greater need to help her grandson. Her daughters in the craft were adamant that the child was a cursed thing whose entire, if short lived existence, was to bring sorrow, death and destruction. They could not be swayed. Fortunately, they had husbands and lives of their own. Their favorite pastime was divining who of them would bear the next clan matriarch. They didn't agree on that either.

As the family wasn't Catholic, the baby would not be baptized as such. They would have to prove they were able to care for the child. Lorry, being the birth mother, had uncontestable rights to her son.

Interestingly enough, it was Lorry who argued privately with her, over the care and raising of the child. She feared that it was beyond her abilities to do. Emma laughed and insisted that she had an experienced, built in babysitter in her own mother. She wouldn't dream of letting anyone else raise the boy. She reminded Lorry that she had already raised a fine Johnny of her own. Against the sisters' wishes, Emma had every intention of raising this boy in the family craft. As she was undoubtedly the next wisest in line of her deceased mother, no one could overrule her. She was matriarch until the next adept was born. That might be another three generations down the line for them to wait, because the male child, soon to be in her custody, was very much an adept. He needed to be trained or risk being consumed by his own power. It was just a little scary, how much force of presence that baby boy had. She would have to be strong for the both of them. The will and the word of a witch were unbreakable.

Lorry took some time to convince, and Emma did so very gently. Lorry loved Lee very much, and she could never reconcile what he really was, with what she saw. Emma empathized, because she too, was bespelled by Lee's Otherworld charm. Had she not loved her husband Edward so much, she would have fought her own daughter for the young man's attentions. Not that she thought she had a chance, it was just how overwhelming the charm was.

***

Eventually, Emma got Lorry to go with her to visit the baby at St. Brigit's. As it was a particularly dark and stormy day, Emma worried that Lorry would equate this with her experience with Lee. There was a moment when her heart turned to ice, when they got to the baby's crib to find him looking out at the storm. The dark clouds and occasional flashes of lightning reflected in his calm eyes. When he was aware of his grandmother's presence, it was cheerful blue eyes that turned to the women and a cherubic smile.

"Gamma love it?" He asked merrily.

"Grandma loves Johnny." Emma smiled and held out her arms to him.

Just to be sure things were all right, she discreetly touched his arm with his silver amulet. There was no sign of tarnishing. Emma was silently relieved. There would be no problem introducing him to his mother.

"Johnny?" She said as the boy looked at her expectantly. "Grandma brought your mommy with her to see you."

The boy looked at Lorry and then back at her.

"Come closer, Lorry, and meet your adorable son," she insisted. "This is Mommy," she cooed to the baby and then handed him over to Lorry, who looked as if she might cry.

"You love it?" The baby took Lorry's cheeks and pulled her forehead to his and looked into her eyes.

"I love it very, very much," Lorry gushed and held him tightly.

PART FIVE

Emma's New Family

Emma circled the herd of mustangs on her great bay stallion, watching the progress of the unicorn foal in their midst. A lovely, dapple gray mare had accepted the strange, silvery white foal as her own. The unicorn was gamboling around the pasture as happy as any child at play. In the distance a long, serpentine column of smoke wound its way into the gray skies of the Otherworld. On a nearby hill a winged man in bright silver armor touch down lightly and begin removing armor and weapons. In this realm, such things were rare, but not terribly so. What was strange, was the angelic vision looked to be but a youth in the early stages of manhood. Downy, dark hair graced a noble chin, and he was dressed as a postal worker, complete with a brown leather mail pouch over one broad shoulder. The gleam of a zealot lit his blue eyes as he strode towards the herd.

Emma dug her heels in her great mount, to intercept the intruder.

"And who might you be?" She demanded.

"I am George," he said simply.

"What are your intentions for this herd?" She queried.

"For the herd, nothing," he replied. "I am here to help protect the unicorn."

"The wolves are gone," Emma observed. "What will you help protect him from?"

"From the dragon, of course," he said, glancing back to the smoke rising on that distant hill.

Emma looked too. The twisting column of smoke had taken on the form of a great, black writhing wyrm with fiercely glowing eyes.

"I think you should have kept your armor on," she said, uneasily.

"No man approaches a unicorn, dressed for battle without the unicorn's permission," George replied matter-of-factly. "I have to introduce myself first, lest he destroy me as surely as the dragon would." He walked past Emma and her mount, straight into the herd.

The gray mare was enjoying the attention of the herd stallion, and the foal was rolling in the grass alone, as the young man approached.

"George," the baby squealed delightedly and startled Emma awake in her rocking chair.

Little Johnny had been home for almost six months now. He would be two years old by the end of this month. He was playing contentedly in his playpen while Emma sat nearby, doing needlework and dozing occasionally. His ruckus had roused her, but he seemed in no present danger. As she had been trained to do, she reviewed the dream sequence in her mind, before its memory could fade. Did the foal, or the baby say 'George'? No matter, they were one in the same, the dream and the real. "As above, so below," the adage went. It would seem, that besides herself, the child would have an additional protector. She was a formidable woman, rather tall and thin, a touch of silver mixed into to her iron black hair and eyes, was the single testimony to her age being in her early fifties. Nothing seemed threatening at the moment, but she was a worthy witch, who knew things were rarely what they seemed at first glance.

"Well, young man." She stood and stretched. "It's high time that you and I load up your stroller and visit your mommy with some lunch."

A thermos of potato soup and some biscuits were the fare of the day, as she packed Johnny in his stroller for the three block trek to Speedy's Dry Cleaners, where Lorry worked.

It was a fine day for a walk. Some of the neighbors were out on their porches, calling greetings to passers by. Johnny seemed to have his favorites among them. Who'd figure any child would like grumpy old Ian MacGregor? But Johnny called him "Uncle Scotty" and would watch for him as he passed his porch to call out to him. His very favorite person, was most understandable, a heavy set negro woman, named Geraldine Smith, who had grandchildren of her own. Her warm smile and kind heart would light Johnny up, even on his worst days. He didn't have many of those, but when he did, it was hard to believe that a single glance from a two year old could make most adults do an about face and march in a different direction looking for something they'd forgot needed doing. If he didn't like them, he wouldn't speak. He watched their eyes without so much as a blink until they left. This had a spooky effect on some. There would be no winning him over.

The stray animals in the neighborhood seemed to think of themselves as his personal petting zoo. The child had no notion to be afraid of even the largest mutt. Emma tried to shoo away a large stray from approaching the baby, when it bared its fangs and growled at her.

"No, no. My Gramma," Little Johnny scolded him, and the big dog lowered its tail and head to submit while Johnny patted its head.

She knew how to charm animals, but to Johnny it came naturally. This was the sign of an adept, an almost unconscious use of spellcraft that most witches would have to work at. Her mother would have been so proud of him.

When she and her grandson arrived at the cleaners, Lorry was at her desk in front having an animated discussion with a handsome young man who was picking up some shirts.

"We've brought lunch," Emma announced, "and old Ian gave me some money to pick up his suit on the way back." She handed Lorry his ticket.

"Good. I'm famished. Mom, this is my friend Dave," Lorry said, indicating the dark haired young man with the shirts.

Johnny just smiled and stared quietly at the stranger. For once, he didn't seem to immediately like or dislike someone he had just met. Emma found this curious.

"Hello, ma'am," Dave said, dark eyes smiling. "This must be little Johnny. I've heard so much about. I'm sorry about the loss of your son-in-law."

"Son-in-law?" Asked Emma. "Oh, the boy's father. I think the summer sun has absconded with my wits today."

"Lorry was telling me about him," Dave went on. "I had a friend, who was drafted and ended up getting shot down in Korea. It must be terribly hard, raising a baby alone these days."

"We manage." Emma smiled at her daughter. "We look out for each other. Lorry is as able a woman, as you will likely ever meet."

"I'm sure she is." Dave smiled. "Lorry, I'll be by for those slacks and shirts on Thursday. Thank you for getting that stain out. It was my favorite shirt. Maybe sometime I can treat you to dinner, seeing how your mother and another young man have your lunches covered?"

"That would be nice." Lorry smiled. "Maybe we'll do that."

Emma nodded her approval and handed Lorry her thermos of soup and a bag with a couple biscuits. Little Johnny quietly watched Dave leave the store and cross the street.

"He's a 'looker,' that one," Emma commented, "and a sharp dresser too. Having a ready made family doesn't seem to put him off either. The story of Johnny's dad getting killed in Korea was a nice, simple touch. It clears a lot of 'complications.' I'll remember that one."

"It seems to be the kind of explanation that satisfies people," Lorry confided, picking up her son. "They don't pry too much after that. I have my boy, and my job, and my respect. What more could I ask for?"

"Maybe a handsome older brother for your poor, old, widowed mother?" She asked, and they both laughed.

***

Emma watched the handyman sawing the lumber to fix the porch railing. Willard was an old bachelor in the carpenter's union, who lived in an apartment over the Arrow Food Market on North Street. Everyone knew he was sweet on her, and he would offer to do repairs in exchange for home cooked meals. He had a sweet tooth and was sitting on her front porch and sharing some chocolate milk with Johnny. Johnny was almost three years old at this point, and quite the chatterbox when the mood hit him. He seemed to like the old carpenter, and Emma thought the man had as good a heart as one could expect to find in another human being. She was considering his hints at a deeper relationship as he and Johnny chatted over their chocolate.

"You've got nobody to play with?" Willard asked.

"I got big brother George," Johnny explained. "He's seventeen and works at the post office. He's teaching me how to fight dragons."

"He must be really big—" Willard chuckled in his gruff voice— "to fight dragons like that. How come I've never met him?"

"'Cause he's indaviz, innaviz, ah,.. people don't see him too good," said Johnny.

"Oh! So he's an imaginary brother George?" Willard implied.

Johnny nodded as he gulped his chocolate.

Emma smiled at the two on the porch. Johnny's favorite play area was her summer kitchen, with her big sink, pantry and herbs drying on hooks from the low ceiling. Johnny often took his meals in there, and always insisted a place be set for Brother George. If it wasn't George, then it was leaving a saucer of milk for the faeries he claimed flew in from her garden. She was certain the milk was being consumed by the stray cats in the neighborhood. It was no problem. They kept the rat and mouse population at bay and her garden flourished wonderfully. The only downside. Occasionally items disappeared from the house and then turn up in odd places. She was fairly certain that this was indeed faeries of one sort or another, as the boy could not reach some of these places.

"Pixie dust," she exclaimed. "Johnny, your faery friends are hiding things on Grandma again."

Johnny laughed and scolded his imaginary friends and then pointed to where the items in question were hidden. Once she got used to the idea that this was not a normal boy even the strangeness took on its own normal routine. With her grandson, Emma learned as much as she taught.

***

It was fast approaching Lughnasadh, the Midsummer Festival, as well as Johnny's third birthday, and the women's circle was to meet at Emma's house as she was the matriarch of the time. Johnny met his aunts. He was friendly enough, but they treated him as if he might be a poisonous reptile. Emma figured that as his guardian and primary teacher, she would allow him to sit quietly at her side during much of the talks. This would give him exposure to the clan, and they to him. Perhaps they would learn this well behaved boy was not so much an abomination as they first thought. Some notions didn't fade so easily, but she had to try.

"Mom, should this boy be here now?" Mary asked pointedly. "This has always been a women's circle. Even our husbands don't interfere."

"Like it or not," Emma replied tartly to her daughters, "he's family and he's adept. He's my grandson, and your nephew, and I will teach him properly as wisdom should be every bit his heritage as yours. It should be more so for his darker inclinations to set him straight. As you can see, he doesn't behave like a monster, and most normal three year olds would be a distraction at this point."

Johnny sat quietly watching back and forth at the ladies talking. He was content to listen to the exchange of home remedies, potions, spells, and then came the occasional gossip concerning who might be flying who's broomstick.

It was nap time for Johnny. As Emma tucked the boy in his bed in the adjacent room, the ladies brought out the gazing bowl to see what might be manifest from one plane of existence to this one. They took their time, centering themselves and gathering their concentration to a single point. Being well practiced at this, the Otherworld opened easily for them. The newest scientific fad, called 'television' would be hard put to replace what they found here. The possible exception, being yet another fad called 'soap operas.' They found themselves gazing at a sylvan setting by a wooded stream. Emma almost gasped at the white oak and the rectangular rock by the northward flowing stream. It was a place she and her mother had visited only a few years ago, but the sisters didn't know that. As they watched, a silvery armored angel with a glowing sword slashed mightily at the air to the delighted laughter of a toddler who was, likewise, slashing at a menacing looking log with a oaken switch. The child's back was to them and he was leaping in and out of the bushes.

"That's definitely angelic," said Margaret. "perhaps St. Michael?"

"But who's the babe?" Asked Evelyn.

"Not Michael, but George," said Emma. "and Mary, check on the baby, please." She had seen the angel before and knowing the nature of her grandson, she had a hunch.

"I don't hear any crying or anything," Mary replied.

"Just look in, please?" She insisted, as Mary crossed the room to peer into the boy's room.

By this time, the sisters got a better view of the toddler playing on the banks of the brook. It was Johnny who giggled and waved to them.

"The baby's gone!" Mary shouted, startling them out of their reverie. "He's not in his day bed. Search the house. He could be getting into mischief somewhere."

"I suspected as much," She said. "Maybe not to this extent, but the baby is all right. He's with his brother George."

"He's off somewhere, playing with his imaginary, brother George?" Mary queried incredulously.

"You mean he's with 'St. George' the dragon slayer in the Otherworld?" Margaret wondered aloud, staring fixedly into the bowl.

"I met him in a dream once," she recounted. "He said he was here to protect the boy from a smoky, black dragon. I didn't think a great deal about it at the time, but that was the first time I heard Johnny call George's name. I had trouble separating the dream from the real. The boy exists as a 'reality' in both realms. We 'visit' but he 'lives' there, as well as here. My guess is that part of him is still in his day bed. He is so engrossed with brother George at this point, he's not quite all there, or here. It's confusing."

The sisters actively sought to open the vision of the Otherworld in the gazing bowl. As before, it came easily. The angel was demonstrating a backhand stroke, making fierce faces while Johnny mimicked, standing on a large rectangular stone, with his switch. "I haven't noticed any toadstool rings in the yard lately," Evelyn remarked. Do you suppose he could have wandered into a faery rath? You know children like that become unreachable when they get caught up into the Otherworld for any length of time."

"Not him," Emma countered. "He's part Sidhe and can travel back and forth with no ill effects. I've suspected it for some time, but now I see it. I'll prove it to you."

"Grandma wants her boy," she called out to the vision of Johnny in the gazing bowl. "We should have some milk and cookies, and it's almost time for the Mickey Mouse Club on television."

Johnny's image promptly vanished from view, leaving the angel glancing over his shoulder at the gazers, cocking an eyebrow at them. Moments later, a sleepy looking Johnny walked out of his room towards the kitchen, rubbing at his eyes, expecting cookies and milk.

The sisters gaped as Emma got up to tend her grandson.

"How do you deal with it, Mom?" Margaret demanded. "There's nothing 'natural' about this."

"First thing, daughter mine," she snarled. "Not 'it,' him. I'll never break him of that habit of referring to himself as 'it,' as long as human monsters insist on stealing his humanity. You just can't make yourselves see a very natural boy. Can you? I see him all the time. He wants to do good. He wants to be loved. When he makes his mom and his grandmother smile, he's ten feet tall inside."

"But what will he be when he grows up?" Evelyn asked. "Will he be his father's son? Will he be like Lee?"

"He will be the man of some woman's dreams," she murmured. "He can share a world that you or I can only peek at. I have to make sure he knows the right kind of woman, or the wrong one will make him everyone's nightmare."

"He's not human," Mary stated flatly.

"He's at least half human, our half," she said. "You've seen him in his dreams. He's no monster. This is a boy who wants more than anything to be the hero of Irish myth and legend. What's more, look who is teaching him to be just that. What human boy has half of his prospects?"

"I'm sorry, Momma," Mary said contritely. "I didn't see…"

"But you did see." Emma explained, "Had we left him to others to raise, they would have no claim at all on his human side. He might well have been a monster. If not for someone wise and brave enough to do what's right, you'd have every good reason to fear him. He will fight, because it's his nature to do so. His very existence is threatened. He must fight."

"We don't really mean to threaten him," Evelyn objected.

"I don't mean you or I," she said, "though everything we do will either help or hinder him. He has a brother George to help him fight his dragons. That means his problems are bigger than a circle of bigoted, gossipy old women. Who's to say that his dragons aren't our problems too. We may need him as much as he needs us. This is the very nature of family love. Very natural. He needs a witch clan more than any living man on earth. And all of you need to be bigger than you are. Our matriarch had her dream for our future. We planned on a girl to replace our matriarch with a better one. I'm saying maybe this young wizard will be the one to help change the world's attitude about us. Let him see us at our best. We guide our men hither and thither, this one can actually do something. Shouldn't we guide him?"

"Since you put it that way," Margaret huffed. "I think we should all join our nephew in the kitchen for milk and cookies. Fig Newtons anyone?"

"That dragon is going to have a real fight on it's scaly talons," Emma murmured.

PART SIX

What Johnny Sees, Johnny Gets

The scream awoke her with a jolt, shook her down to her very soul and made every hair stand on end as if they would never relax again. Emma threw on her robe and ran to her grandson's room. Johnny was sitting bolt upright in bed staring wildly about, but somehow didn't seem to be aware of her as she came in. The street lights shining through the window cast strange reflections on his eyes as though they were lit from within. She resisted the urge to grab him and hold him close and watched him a moment longer to see if she might discern what had upset him so.

Johnny looked about the room as if he were looking for somebody or something and couldn't find it. The look on his face was not so much terror as a dreadful loneliness that seemed to pervade the room. Great shuddering sobs wracked his diminutive frame. Her heart threatened to burst for him. His gaze passed right over her and he showed no sign of recognizing her as even being in the room with him. It was dark but the lace curtains allowed plenty of light in from the street, and Johnny had never shown any sign of fear of the dark. In fact, he seemed to have no trouble at all negotiating her dark basement when he wanted to play hide and seek. He could see like a cat. He was either still dreaming or blind. He had contracted scarlet fever some months before and they feared they might lose him then as his heart rate soared and he became prone to nosebleeds when he got excited. But he got over it and snapped back to his old self like a charm. Was this a relapse?

"Johnny, Grandma's here," she murmured close to his ear.

He looked like he might jump out of his own skin, but his eyes went from that terrible sadness to bright hope in the same heartbeat as he recognized her next to him.

"You still love it, Grandma?" He asked as she sat on the bedside and pulled him close to her.

"How could you think your grandma doesn't love you anymore?" She chided her grandson gently.

"Everybody went away and left me, " he sobbed and hugged her in a death grip.

"It was only a bad dream, sweetie," she consoled her heartbroken boy. "In the morning you'll see us all at the breakfast table and we'll all talk about your dream and you'll feel much better and see we all love you very much."

She laid him back on his pillow and stretched out beside him for a while until his breathing calmed and he was sound asleep again. With his mother's recent marriage to David and Willard's proposal of marriage to herself, perhaps the boy was feeling a bit left out in their affections. Gods knew that only a four years ago he had been evicted from his mother's womb and put up for adoption as an unwanted child. He seemed not to take anyone's love for granted as though he expected to be sent away again at any time. His aunts would have highly approved such a move at one time, but were beginning to warm up to him a little. He could be such a charmer when he wanted to.

***

Emma contemplated the morning sun shining over the grape arbor outside her kitchen window as she finished up the morning's dishes. Dave and Lorry had bustled off to their respective jobs and Willard had a remodeling job he had taken on from his landlord. Willard lived a block away and Dave was renting one of the unused upstairs rooms, the beginnings of a new family were meeting around the dinner table once again.

Little Johnny was playing quietly in her garden where he loved to be in the morning. His appetite was voracious for such a little guy. At breakfast he wolfed down no less than four helpings of pancakes and home fries. He hadn't seemed to want to talk about last night's dream, and that was puzzling. Perhaps he was just shy with Dave and Willard around, but it was good to have a family life for the lad. Gods knew they would fill his head with garbage of how big boys don't cry and had no idea how important it was for him to try to fit in. Even if it was only a mythic American male value, Johnny would die trying to live up to it before he let out so much as a peep. She would have to talk to them later and help him balance his values to a healthier degree. The image of him staring about blindly in his room, believing he was all alone in the world haunted her most of that day.

Johnny was entertaining himself in front of the television set with the usual early evening fair of Mickey Mouse, Davy Crocket and assorted cartoons. With the exception of the sounds of Donald Duck throwing a tantrum coming from the living room, one would never know there was a four year old boy in the house. He was enrapt when cartoons or his favorite heroes were on the set.

Dave and Lorry came in shortly after five and Lorry gave her son a kiss and patted his head before coming into the kitchen to help with dinner. There was something on their minds they wanted to discuss with her. So tangible, it hung in the air about them.

"Work went well today?" Emma coached them as she lay sliced potatoes in the baking pan for tonight's dinner.

Lorry and Dave looked to each other before responding.

"Dave has a line on a good factory job as a machinist, Mom," Lorry replied.

"It sounds like a well paying job with a future. I'm glad to hear things are beginning to work out better for you than that bartender's job. What are your plans now?" She asked.

"Well, with this job I'll make enough where Lorry won't have to work at the dry cleaners any more and it pays well in worker's benefits and retirement. We can get our own house by this time next year." Dave was positively beaming with pride.

"So much good news doesn't come without a little bad mixed in," she said, looking up from her scalloped potato dish. "You want to share the rest of the news or will I have to pry it out of you both over dinner?" She smiled her wicked smile at her daughter.

"The job is with Rohr Aircraft Company, and the bad news is that we'll have to relocate to Riverside, California." Dave continued, "The good news is that I have a sister out there that we can stay with until we can get our own place."

Emma stopped cold in her tracks and looked at her daughter.

"And what of Johnny?" She asked, cocking an eyebrow.

"Mom, we wanted to ask you if you would take care of him for us," Lorry pleaded. "It's only until we can get a place and get settled in, and then we will send for him. It's such an important move for Dave and me. Could you please?"

Relief washed over her like a cool shower until the realization hit her.

"He knows," she murmured aloud.

"Who knows what, Mom?" Lorry asked. "You are the very first person we told, I swear. Who knows?"

"Johnny knows." Emma sat down feeling light headed all of a sudden. "He doesn't understand, but he knows you're going to leave him. He dreamt about this very thing last night. I laid with him myself when he awoke crying."

"It's just a coincidence, Mom," Lorry said. "Don't think too much on it. Would you care for him until we can send for him?"

"Of course, I will," she said, pulling herself together. "I wouldn't have it any other way without a fight. We're going to have to talk with him about this so it doesn't hit him so hard later, you know."

"What if we have a little party to celebrate," Lorry suggested. "Just the five of us. You, Willard, Dave, Johnny and me and we include him in all the celebrating and explain it to him then."

"I'll go now and get some soda, ice cream and treats for after dinner," Dave volunteered as he got up from the table and headed out the back door.

"Get some balloons too," Lorry called to him.

But it wasn't going to be quite so easy. Not for her, and not for Johnny. She'd have to comfort him through it all and make it so he didn't feel deserted again. Still, she was glad she would have her grandson for a while longer. She had so much to teach him about who he was and what he could be. She didn't want to think about the time she would have to part with him when Lorry and Dave settled in their new home. California was so far away. It might as well have been on the other side of the moon as the other side of the country.

Dinner that night was quiet with suppressed excitement. Dave had met Willard at the Arrow Market as he was picking up groceries and balloons for the party and explained the evening's events to him. Lorry had to keep warning Johnny to save some room in his bottomless pit of a stomach for a big surprise after the dinner dishes were put away.

Johnny helped his mother put up balloons in the living room. Willard lifted him up to the ceiling and Johnny stuck the taped side of the balloon to the stamped tin. It was a family affair and the boy seemed to glory in the moment. Emma and Willard danced to The Penguins' hit single 'I Only Have Eyes For You', playing on Lorry's record player in the living room while Lorry and Dave talked with Johnny over some ice cream in the kitchen.

Willard, who had once tried his hand as a Golden Gloves boxer in his younger days had the rough exterior and the facial features of a bulldog, however friendly, and the muscle mass to show he was still a formidable specimen of a man. But for all these rough hewn features, it was tenderness, gentleness and an adoring love that radiated from him as they danced. Emma decided to herself that she would have to marry this man as no other could be expected to help her make the home that Johnny would so desperately need. These two men, both old and very young looked at her with a need that only a goddess could fill, and she was feeling very much up to the task.

"What was that on your mind, Willard?" She whispered in his ear as they danced.

"I was wondering what it would take to convince you to marry me, Emma," he said, never wavering from her eyes.

"Are you prepared for a ready made family?" She looked hard into his own.

Willard sighed and looked toward the kitchen where Johnny was getting the news he would dread most.

"The boy needs a good man as much as you do, Emma," he said. "I could do no less by him than by you. I'm thinking of taking on some more work besides, so I can be a man again and provide for a family. I think this is the best thing that could happen to me. Would you, Emma? Would you marry a man like me?"

"Do you love it, Willard?" She put her forehead to his and squeezed him tightly.

"I love it, Emma," Willard replied, squeezing her gently as a doll he feared he might break.

"Let's raise a family together, Willard dear," she said as she kissed him squarely on the lips.

"That's a 'yes'?" He queried.

"Of course, it is. You big, strong, wonderful man of mine." Emma hugged him.

Lorry, Dave and Johnny came walking together back into the living room. Johnny was putting on a brave face, but a telltale sob made his little body shudder and gave away his broken heart. She stooped to hug her grandson as Willard knelt nearby.

"You understand—" she urged her grandson — "that this is all really good news for everybody?"

"Yes, Gramma," Johnny sobbed and dried his eyes on his sleeve. "But I'm still gonna miss Mommy and Dave."

"Well, you always have Grandma. Now don't you?" She asked. "And you know what else you will need while Mommy's away?"

"More ice cream?" He asked, looking confused.

"No, silly." She squeezed him close. "You're going to need a Grandpa to help us have a real family."

Johnny's eyes lit up with wonder. He reached over and grabbed Willard by the face and pulled their foreheads to touch.

"Will you be my grampa, Willard?" He asked earnestly. "'Cause I don't have one and Brother George likes you too."

Willard choked for a moment and clearly had trouble finding his voice as his eyes brimmed with tears.

"You guys told me big boys don't cry," Johnny questioned the emotion he saw on their faces.

"Sometimes, even the biggest guys have to cry," Willard whispered gruffly. "It's what makes us into good men. I would be so happy to be your grandpa, Johnny. You and George are such good boys."

Emma hugged them both as Lorry and Dave joined them on the floor together. This just might be just a little easier than I thought.

PART SEVEN

The Not-So-Big Wedding

For such small wedding plans it was a very hectic day, and it didn't help matters with a four year old bundle of restless energy running about yelling "Stop it, stop it, stop it" at the faeries he insisted were hiding things on the adults so that they could enjoy the ensuing circus of frantic activity.

"Johnny, maybe you could help Grandma by taking your faery friends out to the garden until we all get dressed." Emma shooed him out the back door. "And don't get your nice new clothes all dirty. You want to look nice for Grandma's wedding."

Willard had made a friend of Pastor Gibson at the Lutheran church at the edge of town where he had taken on a carpentry job repairing the bell tower that had recently been struck by lightning. Since money was nowhere near plenteous and he so much wanted to give Emma a church wedding, the pastor had agreed to do a small ceremony in the church nave in front of the altar. There would only be seven people in attendance besides the good pastor, so a simple honorarium to cover the filing fees and license would be sufficient.

Dave had agreed to be Willard's best man and Lorry was Emma's maid of honor. Old Ian and Geraldine put on their Sunday best and came as witnesses. It was nice to have Geraldine present to keep a kind hand on Johnny, who had never been in a church before. Willard looked uncomfortable in the only suit he owned, as though it might have been lacking a decent pair of bib overalls to complete a proper ensemble. Emma had curled her long, black tresses and wore her nicest floral print cotton dress with a wreath of flowers from her own garden in her hair. Willard had insisted on buying her a bouquet to hold at the altar. Old Ian stood gaunt and stoic in his finest blazer and kilt dwarfed next to Geraldine's massive frame, bright blue cotton dress and summer hat. Johnny stood quietly with Geraldine's gentle hands on his shoulders and gawked at all the stained glass and carvings in the huge nave.

Dozens of unlit candles lined the nave on brazen stands. On the altar, only two candles were lit as there was no one else in the church. The pastor had pulled a fine linen cotta over his suit and a heavily embroidered green silk stole draped over his shoulders as he thumbed through his missal for the appropriate ceremony. Emma looked over her shoulder again at her grandson. Johnny was beginning to fidget and staring wildly about the church.

"Friends!" Johnny exclaimed, raising his arms and smiling beatifically.

"Yes," Geraldine agreed with a slight tear in her eye. "We're all friends here."

Pastor Gibson was squinting at his book through his spectacles when all the candles in the nave lit simultaneously, as by an unseen hand.

"That's so much better," he said as he found his place, and then looked around with a start.

"Automatic candles," Geraldine remarked. "What will they come up with next?"

Everyone had stopped and were staring quietly around them as though seeing the church for the very first time. But Johnny had his hands over his mouth and was smiling with his eyes at something only he could see to either side of the altar.

"Remarkable that no one told me about the new candles," breathed the pastor, and he began the ceremony.

Indeed it was remarkable that Emma, who had misgivings of being in this church as a Christian pretender that she dared not even voice to Willard, felt exhilarated and welcomed within its hallowed walls. She was not blind to her grandson's nature, nor did she deceive herself as to what he was, but she could well discern that he was not a bringer of doom and gloom to her family. The love she immersed him in always came back in blessings. She was doing the right thing and the fickle forces of nature approved.

The not-so-big wedding went off like a dream out of a story book. The simple ceremony, the lights and the ambience of the place made the whole event seem on a grander scale and better attended than if it had taken place in England's Westminster Abbey amongst Europe's reigning royalty. Her mother would be so proud of her and the boy. Gods how she missed her so. Then Willard leaned forward and kissed her. Of those in attendance, he seemed the least fazed of the magickal happenings and probably the most enchanted as he never took his eyes off her. There was only slightly less wonder when the lights dimmed as they made their way out of the church to leave for Niagara Falls for the weekend.

They left Pastor Gibson pondering the mystery of the 'automatic candles' that seemed to have no reason to remain lit. Johnny would stay home and spend some quality time with his mother before Lorry and Dave would be leaving for California. Emma suspected the little, half-blood, adept wizard in their midst had caught them all in the spell, but it was such a blessed spell as was ever woven.

PART EIGHT

Schooling, and Then School

Tall pointed crowns on broad brimmed hats and dark cowled cloaks shadowed features to anonymity, while eyes hidden in darkened depths scrutinized her mercilessly. Emma felt uncomfortable and vulnerable. Was she being foolish in her decisions? She looked deep into her own heart. This was not the easiest choice but it was the right one. The wise one.

"Yes," she replied to her shadowy inquisitors. "I, as matriarch of our clan, will deviate from our tradition to raise this boy as an adept witch of the blood. As my word, so mote it be."

"It is well," replied a sibilant trio of voices. "That you have considered your actions long and hard as you should. This is no light thing as such males are rare among our kind and he needs be well taught to keep destruction off our heads as persecution has all but destroyed our kind in this world. When once we counseled kings, the Burning Times have caused us to hide our wisdom away in the shadows while the world of men grew in the knowledge of destructive sciences and their souls shriveled in ignorance. Teach him well, Emma. He must be as much warrior as wizard if he is to survive. When the time is right, we will send him a Sidhe mentor, but you must find him a warrior of no small courage to foster him in warcraft beyond your means. Such a lad can be our boon or bane. Be wise, Emma Iron Locks. Be wise for more than yourself, matriarch."

"Help me," Emma pleaded the trio. "I am no adept as our last matriarch. I am but a lowly kitchen witch compared to my mother. I have no great gift with which to guide our clan by. If I rely on only what meager gifts I have, I will fail them all. I need to be bigger than myself to do these things. Bless me to the task, I pray thee."

"You are very wise in that you speak truly," the trio responded in unison. "And the love that moves you is a gift above all gifts to reign with. But as you wish, so mote it be."

The cloaked arm of the center witch reached upwards and the silvery blade of an athame was extended to touch Emma's forehead. As the cold blade made contact an icicle of cold searing pain shot into her head. She saw stars.

"Blessed be, Emma Silver Lock," the trio gave their benediction and Emma could remember no more.

***

Willard and Johnny sat at breakfast with mouths agape when Emma entered the kitchen. Their eyes fastened to her forehead, or more specifically her forelock. Her reflection in the window over the sink revealed a startling streak of silver in her iron black tresses in the top and center of her forehead. It had not been there when she went to bed last night.

"Did you do something to your hair?" Willard asked, clearly puzzled.

"It looks... special," said Johnny with a note of wonder in his voice.

Emma poured herself a cup of coffee from the pot that Willard had prepared on the stove and sat down tiredly with her amazed men folk.

"It would appear the poets were correct about life being but a dream within a dream," she remarked cryptically on the topic.

Her head was buzzing strangely and the coffee seemed to help her find her wits again. She had much to ponder over her grandson, who had just turned five years old and would be starting at public school in a few weeks. He was growing fast and smart as a whip, but he had to learn there were some things one didn't mention around outsiders and she wasn't sure how she would break it to him. If he learned those lessons the hard way, Danu only knew what it might bring of his darker nature.

***

Emma had allowed herself another day to consider her course of action and belted on her long knife under her apron and had a canvas shopping bag tucked under her arm. Johnny had been equipped with an army surplus day pack he wore on his back. Together they walked to Cobb's Hill Park where she would begin teaching him wood lore. There were a few acres of woods there where particularly potent varieties of flora could be found for her pantry. It was a bit of a hike for the little fellow, but he never seemed to tire of anything his heart was in and was certainly eager to be with her.

"You can help Grandma gather some supplies for the summer kitchen," she said. "Won't that be nice?"

"Will you show me how to pick sassafras?" Johnny asked excitedly.

"Especially sassafras," she said while tousling his hair. "We'll need some white oak acorns, some may apples, some sulfur shelves, lemon balm and what other goodies we might find there too."

"Are we going to the woods," Johnny puzzled. "or are we going shopping?"

"Why both, of course," she replied.

It was a beautiful day strolling around the meandering trails in the woods. Johnny quickly learned to fill his bag with the plumper white oak acorns as opposed to the red oak variety that were narrower and had more bitterness to be removed before they could be eaten by humans. He was eager to know where root beer came from and was checking hollow trees for crocks of brew and faery treasure as Emma plucked a nearby branch and sat down on a log and called her grandson to sit with her as she explained.

"The strength of a tree may be found in its roots," she said. "For any of these trees to grow strong and tall, they must have equally strong and deep roots growing beneath them."

"But if they are underground, how will we know where to dig for root beer?" Johnny asked.

"You must first learn how to recognize the tree itself," she confided. "There's a story that goes with the sassafras trees to help you remember how to recognize them. It is a medicine tree and the number three is a potent number for medicines and magick. If you look at this oak tree here, you'll see that on its branches, all the leaves have this same wavy look to them. All the sugar maples have the same shaped leaves, but look at the branch in my hand. Can you tell me what is different about it?"

Johnny looked carefully at the branch. He didn't seem to be catching on as he looked and looked and then his face brightened.

"It's got different leaves on it," he said proudly.

"That's right, boyo," she congratulated him. "It has three different shaped leaves on the very same branch. This one is shaped like a football. Your Grandpa loves to watch that about this time of year. And this one is shaped like a mitten, and we'll soon be wearing those again as the weather gets colder and this one looks like a ghost about to jump up and yell 'BOO!'"

Johnny jumped back startled and then laughed delightedly at the joke.

"What we have to do now is find a patch of young skinny trees with leaves like these. All three kinds on one branch, remember. And then we dig up a couple where there are too many to grow healthy, so there will always be more when we want some."

Johnny couldn't wait. He scampered about examining each tree in detail. It didn't take him long to find a patch of young sassafras.

"Are these it?" He asked excitedly. "Can we dig 'em up?"

"Let's see," she replied, taking her long knife out to scrape a bit into the bark where Johnny could sniff it.

"What does it smell like?" She asked her grandson.

"Mmmmm, root beer," Johnny replied.

"We clear off the debris around this sapling," she instructed while moving leaves and sticks away with her foot. "And we dig here."

Johnny dug away with Emma's garden trowel that she had put in his day pack, and then started digging in with his hands like a dog. When enough of the root system had been bared, she started tipping the tree this way and that to loosen it up more before she started pulling it up, roots and all. Johnny braced himself and pulled up yet another sapling all by himself and brought it to her by the log they had been sitting on where Emma used its surface like a cutting board and used her long knife to trim the roots into manageable sections that she dropped into her canvas shopping bag. Johnny stuck his face in the sack and inhaled the heady root beer fragrance. It appeared to have an intoxicating effect on him, so she carried it herself.

The boy was in love with the woods. He had to climb into every hollow tree to meet its faeries. Walk every fallen log and chatter at every squirrel. He seemed to have a talent for imitating any sounds he heard and loved the reactions he got from the creatures he mimicked. Emma picked a few more plants for her sack. Reading the corner of the woods, she called her grandson nearer.

Up ahead the trail made a sharp curve to the right towards the city reservoir and to the left several houses had backyards that backed right up into the woods. Johnny had already pointed out a large silvery sphere resting on a marble table in the backyard of the first house and wanted to make straight for it when Emma placed a firm hand on his shoulder.

"It's somebody else's property, son," she explained. "You just can't go charging into their yard uninvited, and some you want to be careful in even when you are invited." She scanned the surrounding woods when her eyes found who they were searching for.

"Blessed be, Emma," a small dark haired woman in a black dress with a dark blue apron carrying a small basket called her from the wooded trail to her right.

"Good morning, Vy," she returned, purposely avoiding giving her blessing. "Gathering a few things too, I see," she said, nodding at the basket.

In spite of her small size, the woman advanced quickly up the trail towards them and had eyes for only Johnny as she spoke to her.

"This must be the grandson I've heard so much about," Elvyra spoke aloud as she steadily scrutinized the boy. "He looks like the spitting image of your Lorry, but the resemblance ends there. His aura is certainly Sidhe if ever I saw one. What a prize you are, boy. What's his name?"

"Johnny, after his uncle," Emma supplied. "Johnny, this is Elvyra. She lives in that house over there."

Johnny glanced back at the silvery sphere he wanted to check out earlier and to the woman who was studying him and recoiled into Emma's arms where he never took his eyes off Elvyra until she was forced to look elsewhere. The effect it had on the witch was tangible.

"The fae boy, and now some changes to you too, I see," Vy observed in a flat tone, pointing to Emma's silver forelock. "You'll want to hang onto that one, Emma. It won't do to let him wander off, you know." She gave them a smile that didn't encompass her eyes and carried her basket back to her house.

"Johnny, I want you to remember this woman and this house," she instructed her grandson. "And I want you to never let her get her hands on you. Om biggun tu?"

"Tiggum, Grandma," he replied readily in Irish. "I understand. She makes me feel bad. But why?"

"She's a witch, that one," Emma said. "A very powerful witch, who doesn't care much who gets hurt to get her even more power."

"Are all witches bad, Grandma?" Johnny asked as Emma did a double take at her grandson.

"Not usually," she replied as she led him away from the area. "We're like everybody else. Some of us are nice people and some of us are not so nice, but all of us are people with secrets."

"Are you a witch too, Grandma?" Johnny asked.

"Yes, and my mother and her mother, and your aunts and even you," she pointed out.

"Me too?" He asked, wide eyed. "and Grandpa?"

"No, not Grandpa, I'm afraid," Emma rejoined. "Not many men ever become witches or wizards, son. You are the only one I know. Most people are afraid of things they don't understand, and when they're afraid they will do terrible things."

"Will Grandpa be afraid of us, Grandma?" Johnny asked.

"Not if he knows how much we really love him first," she said. "He needs to know that above all else. Someone once said that perfect love casts away fear. Now someone like Elvyra... well, she'd rather people be afraid, and maybe it's a good thing they are. But you and me, we're going to love them first and show them we aren't bad folks at all. Aren't we?"

Johnny nodded eagerly. Emma hugged him close.

"You see how much I love you?" She asked, as she put her forehead to his.

"Grandma,—" Johnny's eyes got big as saucers—" I hear you," he exclaimed.

"You hear me, but do you understand I love you?" Emma coaxed him.

"No. I mean, yes. I mean I hear you like I hear Brother George and the pixies in the garden. You talk like us now." He pointed to his forehead.

PART NINE

Peck's Bad Boy

Willard searched the house from top to bottom in a frantic effort to find his union pin. He had an election to attend at the Carpenters Union Hall and he didn't want to show up without it proudly displayed. Occasionally some pocket change would turn up missing or cuff links, but they would always turn up eventually. He didn't like to think that Emma or Johnny would actually steal from him, but he was a strange boy to say the very least and he always knew where to look for missing cuff links and other missing items. Perhaps it was time to ask the boy. He was going to be late if he didn't hurry and he didn't have time for any more nonsense.

Johnny was dashing about in a play area that he had fixed for the boy in the far back section of the yard. He had cut down the tall weeds and rearranged some of the junk and some planks to build a fort. He also had some saw horses set up where he could work on a few projects of his own as the need arose. There he found the lad, charging with his sword drawn, up a plank over his fortress wall. He didn't slow as he reached the top, but sailed into space over the fort, whirling, parrying and slicing at some invisible foe and then resumed an upright position as he touched down lightly on the other side of the enclosure. Willard's heart was in his throat as the boy ran around the play fort to take yet another run at the plank.

"Hold it right there, boyo," he called out, as Johnny skidded to a stop. "Holey moley, but you're going to give an old man a heart attack leaping about with that sharp stick like that."

"It's not sharp, Grandpa," Johnny replied holding his sword out for inspection. "You sanded it down all nice and smooth, 'member?"

"That's right, I did," he said, admiring his work. "But I would have made it out of rubber if I knew you were going to carry on with it quite like this. If you get hurt jumping about like that, your Grandma will never forgive me for making this stuff for you, and I won't be happy either with a broken down grandson to play with."

"I'll be more careful, Grandpa," Johnny promised contritely.

"Good boy," he said. "Now, can you tell your Grandpa what you might have done with his union pin?"

"What's a union pin?" Johnny asked.

"It's a little round brass pin with some letters and numbers on it, about the size of a quarter," he said, while holding his fingers in the approximate size. "Now, your old Grandpa's in a hurry, so let's not pretend you didn't take it and just tell me where you put it, okay?"

"Grandpa, I never saw your union pin," Johnny whined, tears beginning to form in his eyes. "I wouldn't take none of your things. Grandma says that's stealing, and stealing is a bad thing. I keep telling those pixies to stop it, but they think it's a game."

"Oh, for crying out loud," he said in exasperation. "Don't be upset, son. I'm not mad at you. Just in a hurry to make an important meeting. Could you please just tell me where to find my pin?"

"I'll ask," Johnny sobbed, and walked towards his grandmother's garden. "You guys have done it this time," he scolded the garden. "My Grandpa's upset and thinks I took his stuff. Now you give it back and stop this game. It's no fun anymore. Stop it or I won't play with you any more."

Willard watched impatiently as the boy finished his tirade at the garden. Whatever it took to get the pin back, he'd just have to endure. He was going to have to speak to Emma about this before it got too far out of hand. It was about time the boy out grew this nonsense talking with pecks. He watched as Johnny seemed to become intent with something in the garden as a sly look crossed his features, and then a look of enlightenment.

"I know where they put it, Grandpa," Johnny announced excitedly. "Follow me."

"Of course, you do," he responded in sarcasm.

But Johnny was already dashing for the back door. Willard followed him inside. Johnny was standing at the door of Willard's bedroom looking about wildly and then focused on the bed and dropped to the floor, peering underneath.

"It's under there," he said, pointing. "They've been hiding stuff way back in the middle under there."

The bed barely cleared the floor by four inches, and Willard could not imagine how the boy could reach so far under such a large bed frame. He figured the boy must have tossed the pin underneath or it had rolled and he couldn't reach it. Willard grunted and hunkered down for a look under the bed. In the dim light and the dust bunnies he could see the gleam of something metallic towards the center of the bed. There was no way his thickly corded arms were going to make that reach in so confined a space, so he opted to just move the massive bed aside to retrieve his union pin.

Muscles bunching in his powerful shoulders and neck, he heaved the large bed aside to reveal the cache. There on the floor, amidst the dust bunnies were several neat stacks of silver coins and bus tokens with his union pin balanced neatly on top. There was absolutely no way the boy could have gotten under there. Much more so, he couldn't make such a neat stack of coins among all that dust.

"Pecks," Willard exclaimed in realization. "Great jumping jack rabbits, pecks did this. Son, you are the original 'Peck's bad boy.'"

"I'm not a bad boy, Grandpa," Johnny whined. "I told you where they hid it. I was being a good boy, honest. Witches' honor." Johnny held two fingers under his eyes and peered over them.

"That's right, me boyo," he said, laughing aloud. "You ratted on them pesky pecks and saved your Grandpa's stuff. You're Grandpa's good boy, but the pecks' bad boy." He lifted his startled grandson to his shoulder like a conquering hero. "You said something about a witch's what?"

"I believe he swore on his witches' honor," Emma said while entering the room to investigate the ruckus.

"Pecks, witches and what else goes on here?" Willard set his grandson down gently. "Emma, can we talk more about this when I come back from the union hall?"

"I've been looking forward to having just such a talk, my dearest," she replied as she kissed him and handed him his hat.

"You know something," he addressed his new wife and grandson. "You could just about knock me down with a feather right now. But I feel like a stupid lump for being surprised at all. It was right in front of my eyes the whole time. Am I the luckiest Joe in the union hall or what?" He smiled and tipped his hat at a rakish angle and sauntered off before they could answer.

PART TEN

Double, Double, Another For Trouble

To Emma's relief, Johnny got through his first few weeks at school without any major scrapes. Between his meeting Elvyra and their talks with Willard, which went better than expected, Johnny was learning to be discreet about his unusual heritage. He even seemed to like school and his teacher thought him to be an absolute joy in class. He was so attentive for such a young boy. Already he had mastered his ABC's and could count to a hundred. After that he had a tendency to count 200, 300, 400 and so on. Still, it wasn't bad and he was learning his runes at home as well. The boy was a sponge just looking for more knowledge to soak up. While Emma was building him up a library of select books on history, geography, the sciences, some classic literature and some ancient tomes on arcane wisdom, Willard was building the shelves for them all to go on.

Willard adjusted surprisingly well to the idea of the witch clan and Johnny's fae nature. His mother had related a good many tales of such things from the old country to him as a boy, and he never forgot them. It seemed that his family had more than a midwife or two and the odd kitchen witch and he confessed he had often wondered at why he felt so at home with Emma and her strange grandson. Emma smiled to herself. Willard was not the only one who was feeling extraordinarily lucky about their new life partner. Willard, like herself, would rather treat a problem with a home remedy before tossing good money at some uppity doctor, and he knew more than a few of these. He held no allusions of being a witch himself, but he was very supportive of his new wife, if not downright proud of her.

She sighed with contentment. Life was turning around nicely for her.

***

Halloween was only a week away. Aside from Johnny getting severely offended and downright belligerent with the Christian kids at school for depicting Halloween witches as green faced hags, the fall days were cool and pleasant. Emma was busy making him a cape and mask so that he could trick-or-treat dressed as the swashbuckling Zorro. She had a long talk with him about how people of different families celebrated holidays in different ways. This year she would take him out trick-or-treating like the other kids in his school, but she reminded him that this was not the clan's way of celebrating Halloween.

Johnny was practically bouncing off the walls with excitement. Emma couldn't imagine what the effect would be like after he had consumed all those sweets. As the sun was beginning to set and the street lights came on, she escorted her little highwayman down the street for an evening of mooching sweets. Even beneath his broad brimmed black hat and mask, his face lit up with fascination at all the jack-o-lanterns, ghosts and ghouls on display on every porch and yard. Old Ian was his usual frugal and grumpy self as he appeared in his doorway dispensing apples to the little devils and hobgoblins on his porch. Emma waited back by the street with the other parents as Johnny went forward to demand his treat. Ian failed to recognize him and Johnny wouldn't dream of leaving without thanking him.

"Thanks, Uncle Scotty," he exclaimed, beaming through his mask.

"Wait a minute," Ian said in a shocked tone as recognition crossed his gaunt old face. "I know who you are. You're that masked highwayman they call Zorro. Aren't you? No doubt you are out this very night, to take from the rich and give to the poor. Well, I won't let you carve a 'Z' on my old carcass, so I'll just give you this shiny nickel to add to your loot. Now be off with you, masked man. I have no more to give." In spite of the theatrics, old Ian smiled and winked at the diminutive bandit leaving his porch.

At Geraldine's house they found the elderly black woman was not at home, but out escorting her older grandchildren in their rounds of the neighborhood. Her daughter was at home and having a party for the younger siblings and passing out treats as Johnny came up to the door. Emma hung back on the sidewalk as Essie took Johnny into the house to use the bathroom and show him to the other kids. It was full dark now and older trick-or-treaters were beginning to make their appearance on the street. No doubt some soaped windows and toilet paper strewn trees would be the outcome of the tricks for treats tonight. Then a devil masked boy in a hooded sweatshirt spooked a youngster and made a grab for his candy bag. The youngster took off just in time to keep his treats.

Thinking the hijinx was over, she almost missed him. He was so quiet just standing there at the corner clutching his bag of candy, but the lad in the devil mask had spotted his next victim. For some reason, Johnny just stood there, sans his mask and hat as the larger boy pushed him down and took his bag of candy.

"You unhand my grandson right this minute," she scolded as she charged up the walk at the fleeing miscreant. "Johnny, are you alright, honey?"

"Grandma?" Called a familiar voice from the yard behind her.

She whirled to respond, and there was Johnny, still in his hat and mask and still clutching his bag of treasure. She spun again. There on the sidewalk was his identical twin with that familiar face in full view.

"I'm okay, Grandma," Johnny in the mask spoke behind her. "Is something wrong?"

"I don't know, sweetie," she stuttered, looking back and forth between them. Johnny's double got up from the sidewalk with a haunted expression in his eyes as the masked Johnny came forward to see. They both stood there, neither taking their eyes off the other. The only difference being that one was fully costumed and the other had only a makeshift cape draped over a sweater and blue jeans. Masked Johnny set down his bag and plunged both hands into it and brought out two fistfuls of candy, which he deposited into the arms of his double. A big smile crossed the face of the haunted boy that never seemed to reach his eyes and he ran away into the darkness with his treasure. Masked Johnny returned with his bag and hugged her.

"Who was that boy?" She asked her grandson.

"Apple Banger," Johnny said uncertainly. "He says he's a duck made out of wood."

"I didn't hear either of you say anything, sweetie," she coaxed him. "How did he tell you this strange thing?"

"You weren't listening, Grandma," he admonished, pointing to his forehead. As she was bending over him he reached up and pulled her forehead to his and Emma had the shock of her life. Since her eyes could not focus so close to his face, all she could see was a wooden mallard decoy, used by a duck hunter, sitting serenely on a quiet marsh pond. The vision was as clear as if she was looking from shore on an overcast autumn day.

"He's a 'decoy,'" Emma said aloud, breaking the contact. "He's here to protect you."

"Apple Banger." Johnny nodded sagely.

"I think 'doppelganger' is the word you're looking for," Emma corrected.

"That sounds right," he said. "You listen real good, Grandma."

"And sometimes, wise old grandmothers—" she said smiling, tapping her temple with her index finger— "learn marvelous things from their grandchildren." She pictured herself getting a big hug from her grandson and Johnny immediately threw his arms around her and squeezed tightly.

"You talk good pixie too," he said.

So this was the crones' gift to her. That thought made her smile.

PART ELEVEN

The Lioness and the Unicorn

Another year has passed since her daughter had moved to California with her new husband to start work at an aircraft company. The latest news Emma received was that Lorry was pregnant with a new baby. It was rough starting out in a new state. They were sharing a house with Dave's sister and her family. It had been decided that Johnny would be sent for when they purchased a house of their own and had gotten settled in. After all, it was the American dream. Johnny was content to be with her and she with him as it was her face he had grown up seeing the most of. He missed his mother, but he loved her all the more fiercely, and that was fine with her.

With Lorry and Dave in California, and family spread over New York, Pennsylvania and Ohio, the U.S. Mail was a regular part of Emma and Johnny's life. Lorry made it a special point to send pictures and hand print a letter just for Johnny to practice reading and the little guy made certain to include his own hand printed letter in with his Grandma's reply. Mary, her eldest, was becoming the focal point for the sisters who had relocated in the Cleveland area, but on those special holidays everyone made it a habit to return home at least to visit for a weekend. Evelyn had a promising ten year old daughter named Leona Mae, that she was considering fostering to her for the summer vacation for training in the family craft. Emma broke the news to five year old Johnny, who was excited to have a new playmate for the summer.

By the end of June, just before the July 4th weekend, Evelyn, her husband Ralph, and an imperious little blond bombshell made an impact on her front porch. With Evelyn being one of the more outspoken and adventurous of Emma's girls, she expected there might be a few issues that would have to be settled with her granddaughter. It started when Leona Mae demanded that Johnny give up his downstairs bedroom for the guest room upstairs. He knew full well that a guest room was meant for people who wouldn't be staying and was trying to figure why he was suddenly being replaced and cast out by his elder cousin.

"I need this room so that I can be near Grandma as she trains me this summer," she commanded her younger cousin.

"But Grandma trains me too," he objected, nearly in tears.

"Don't be silly," Leona insisted. "You're nothing but a devil-boy, without any parents who want you, while I am a witch of the blood. Now move your things upstairs."

Emma was listening from the kitchen table as the children were attempting to establish their dominance in the next room, when Johnny bolted like a blur for the garden outside. It was time to set the rules straight.

"Evelyn, if I might have a ladies meeting with you and Leona in the front room for a moment, please?" She halted her daughter in mid sentence.

Evelyn complied and followed her mother to the front room, pulling Leona along with her on the way. Evelyn and Leona sat down on the couch while Emma remained standing to address them.

"Is there a problem, Mom?" Evelyn asked, glancing between Leona and her.

"It depends on what everyone wants to make of it," she replied. "I'll be more than happy to train my lovely granddaughter this summer, but it will be necessary for some things to be understood first. First being: Johnny lives here. This is his home and you are his guest, Leona. Om biggun tu?"

"What?" Leona asked perplexed.

"It's Gaelic and means 'Do you understand?'" Evelyn coached her daughter.

"Then why didn't she just say so?" Leona complained.

"I did," Emma interjected. "You are here to learn, and I will teach you a good deal more than you might expect. I'll expect an open mind, and you will supply that or you will return home with your mother and not waste anymore of my time."

"Yes, Grandma," Leona replied contritely. "I just thought it would be better if I was close to you for the summer, for training and all."

"Your bedroom is directly over mine," she said. "That's just perfect for our purposes here, and Johnny may be younger than you, but he's already a couple years ahead of you in training."

"You're training him as a witch?" Leona was incredulous. "He can't be a witch, he's just a—"

Emma's eyes became hard as flint as she glared at her granddaughter.

"Devil boy?" She finished for her dumb stricken grandchild. "Any good witch of the blood would know it is a dangerous thing for any mortal to offend the Sidhe. Except maybe you. In times past, human settlers displaced them off the land and now the most foolish witch in the world wants to displace one right out of his own bedroom. You certainly aren't thinking about living long enough to become good at any of this, are you?"

"Mom, you don't think he'd—" Evelyn broke in wide eyed.

"I think that proper etiquette is necessary for all concerned," Emma finished. "Cousins must behave as cousins should. We are family here and should treat each other as esteemed family members. My house will be respected. I set my own rules here, and you will follow them and be blessed. Om biggun tu?"

"Tiggum," Evelyn coached her daughter. "It means you understand. Nee Higgen, means you don't understand."

"Tiggum, Grandma," Leona said. "Knee higgin sounds funny." She chuckled.

"Yes." Emma smiled. "It does at that. Now, young lady, for your first and most important lesson as a witch, and you will be careful not to use this word in front of any of the uninitiated, is to go out to the garden and make things right with the Sidhe child you hurt, and have him teach you the Threefold Law. Then by supper tonight, you will tell me why it was so important for you to learn this law today. Now go."

Leona cocked her head to one side as she puzzled the instructions and then walked through the house to the back door, deep in thought.

"She is a fine and strong-willed lass," she remarked to her daughter. "A lioness. I'm sure she will do the family proud."

"I was sure you would think so," Evelyn said. "Which is why I so much wanted you to foster her for a few summers. You don't think there will be a problem with her and the boy, do you?"

"Johnny has a good and strong heart beating in that little chest," she said smiling. "He can be very forgiving. But there's more at stake than just him to consider, Evelyn."

"How's that, Mom?"

"Didn't you ever pay attention when your grandmother told you the family tales of where we come from?" She asked.

"Well, sure. But how does that figure in all this?" Evelyn puzzled.

"The thing in our family blood that produces witches the caliber of your grandmother comes from the Sidhe. You and your sisters treat Johnny like a devil for his mixed blood, but it is the same mixed blood that stirs you all. With him, a bit more so. No males have ever been a part of our heritage, but then, no males have ever turned up with the gift. This little boy has more of it than I've seen in any of you and maybe even more than your grandmother. It was her dream to have the perfect witch come out of our line to change the world for the better."

"I've heard her say as much, Mom," Evelyn responded. "But it was a mistake. She wanted a new matriarch and what we got was a little boy and a lot of death. It cost her, her life, and the lives of your husbands. The Sidhe didn't honor our pact."

"They gave us a Sidhe child," Emma disagreed. "The father broke faith by nearly killing your sister and by that he almost killed his own son. A Sidhe in modern America was a bit too much. Something had to give and it was his darker nature. We saved our family out of this tragedy, and even the Sidhe could not fault that. But what of the child we asked for? When you invoke their names, when you use their talents, and when you denigrate their blood, what do you honestly expect from them?"

"The Threefold Law," Evelyn murmured. "Everything we do or say, be it bad or good, will return upon our own heads, threefold. I've heard it a thousand times, and it never dawned on me. I am personally responsible for my own bad luck and my own blessings. I wanted to talk to you about Ralph, when we have a moment privately. But now I understand exactly what the problem was. I can fix this all by myself, because I did this."

Emma looked askance at her babbling daughter, wondering what problems she was going to fix and how. Evelyn was ecstatic in the midst of her personal epiphany, when she stopped babbling suddenly and looked up.

"Momma," she asked. "Did you do something new to your hair?"

Emma fell down beside her daughter, laughing herself to tears and held the younger woman tightly.

PART TWELVE

A Bigger World Begins in a Tiny Garden

Leona walked from the summer kitchen at the rear of the house, out into her grandmother's backyard. What would she say to her little cousin? She was a little taken aback by what she found here. It looked like a country garden, but it was in the middle of a growing, industrialized city. Not as big as Cleveland, but it was big. The yard was bounded on the western side by a tall hedge, interspersed with morning glories, their lavender and white trumpets still glistening with dew. Towards the far end there was a plum tree, an open hedge that led to a smaller back lot, a small apple tree, a larger pear tree, a brick fireplace for cookouts and a grape arbor that extended from the pear tree along the eastern fence towards the front yard. To her immediate left was a waist high, white picket fence with an arching trellis at its northern gate, where the smell of fragrant herbs intermingled in a way that imprinted itself on her memory. She would never forget this place as long as she lived. There, sobbing on a wooden bench, was her cousin.

He looked up at her when she entered the garden, never bothering to wipe the tears off his face. There was a look in those watery blue eyes that seemed to wonder what depths of outrage he might suffer from her now. Suddenly he didn't look so much like a devil boy. Maybe she was the monster and not him. He wouldn't speak, but kept staring as if he was waiting for the inevitable end. She found it hard to look long into those eyes and she sat down beside him on the bench. Dragonflies buzzed around the chamomile as she chose her words carefully.

"I'm sorry, Johnny," she said as she placed an arm around his shoulders. "I was being mean. It's been a long ride and I felt awful, and now I feel worse for being so rotten to my little cousin. I said some bad things that weren't true and I hurt your feelings. Would you forget I said them and let's start over and be friends?"

"Can I stay in my room?" He asked with a shuddering sob.

"Of course, you can," she said. "It's your house. You live here and I'm just visiting. I should have asked you where I could stay."

"We fixed you a room upstairs in the front," he said, pointing up to the second story. "I helped Grandma fix it up special so that a girl would like it. I picked out the quilt and Grandma made the doilies and the curtains just for you."

"You guys did that for me?" She asked, genuinely surprised.

Little Johnny nodded.

She reached over and gave him a big hug and bussed him on his forehead. A strong, satisfying sense of belonging washed over her, causing her to sit back down on the bench and just look out on the garden and sigh.

Johnny sighed too.

The two of them sat there for a moment taking in the morning freshness from the garden.

"So Grandma's been teaching you the craft?" She asked.

"Oh, yes," Johnny said eagerly. "I learned my runes. How to get groceries and medicine in the woods. What witches to stay away from. I can write a little bit and read letters from my mommy. I know most of these plants and how to pick them. I help Grandma with the canning."

"Do you know something called the Threefold Law?" She asked.

"Oh, yes," he said, nodding like his head might come loose.

"Could you teach it to me?" She asked.

"You want me to help you learn?" He asked, wide eyed.

"We're cousins. Look at us," she said. "My mom always said I look like your mommy when she was my age. We look like each other. We're family and witches of the blood."

"Witches of the blood," Johnny agreed, looking furtively around to see if anyone might overhear them. "I'll help you. Witches' honor," he said, holding his two fingers beneath his eyes and peering over them.

"I'm afraid you'll have to tell me what that means too," she said.

Johnny was all too eager to finally be able to share the wonder of his Grandma's teachings with someone nearer his own age, though Leona was fully twice as old.

They spent the morning with Johnny showing her all his favorite parts of the backyard and ate sweet pears as they sat in his back lot play area on a seesaw they made with a plank and a saw horse. He told her about Grandpa Willard's experience with the pixies hiding his things, and she laughed as he mimicked his gruff voice so well, but got tongue tangled when he tried to say "pesky pecks."

"You guys really have faeries here?" She asked. She had always dreamed of meeting real faeries but never dared speak of it aloud lest she be treated like a silly little girl. She hated that.

"Yep," Johnny said, nodding enthusiastically. "We even had 'lepperkawns' once but Grandma said she'd rather have cockroaches and we made 'em go away."

"I've never seen a real faery before," she confessed. "My teacher says there are no such things. They are mythical creatures from the old days when people didn't know any better."

"People weren't so stupid in the old days," Johnny insisted. "Grandma's from the old days, and Great Grandma older still and nobody knows as much about magick as they do."

She couldn't argue that point. She had heard much from her aunts about her great Grandma Ella's legendary prowess at healing and conjuring. The uninitiated couldn't be expected to be aware of these things; therefore their assumptions about the world were flawed, she reasoned to herself. Still, she had never seen a real live faery before and the idea struck her that if Johnny was half Sidhe, then he was half faery himself and her dream was coming true by her just being here with him. Her cousin was a special boy and she had all summer long to enjoy in Grandma's magickal household.

"Would you like to meet some pixies?" Johnny asked.

"Are you kidding me?" She asked incredulous. "I always dreamed I would meet real faeries one day. I would love to."

"Grandma says that dreams are important," he said solemnly. "We gotta get up before Grandpa, if I'm gonna be able to show you some pixies in Grandma's garden."

Shortly after lunch, Leona kissed her parents goodbye as they packed up to go visit some relatives in Philadelphia for the Fourth of July celebration. She was officially on her own with her Grandma for the summer and could cease speaking in hushed tones about the craft where her father might overhear. Grandpa Willard understood and respected the craft, so it was okay to speak with him in earshot. She wasn't sure what to think about her new grandfather, but this singular point raised him up a couple notches in her esteem.

At the supper table, she excitedly shared what she learned about the Threefold Law, and about a witch's honor being in their unbroken will and word. Johnny beamed proudly as Grandma looked back and forth between the cousins.

"My Lioness and my Unicorn," Emma declared. "Neither of you have let me down and I'm so proud of the both of you."

Leona could swear that Johnny grew another couple inches sitting right there at the table. She was feeling a bit larger herself. After dinner they all helped with the dishes and Johnny lugged out the garbage to the cans in the shed. She went to bed exhausted that night between the long road trip from Cleveland and the day spent in the backyard with her cousin.

In her dreams, there was a little faery prince who was introducing her to all the members of his court and a dark presence coming through the backyard hedge as she jolted awake, being shaken by her little cousin. It was still dark out and the street lights were shining through her curtains, and she could clearly make out Johnny dressed in his housecoat and slippers. He held his finger up to his lips as he handed her robe and slippers to her.

"We should go out to the garden now," he said in a hush. "It will be time to cross soon."

Leona thought it was entirely too early to be out of bed, but she had asked to see faeries. The thought energized her to get dressed quietly and sneaking out the back into the garden.

A large full moon was sinking in the west, and the sun hadn't yet begun to peek over the eastern horizon. It was an eerie light in the backyard garden, hidden away from the street lights of the city in its hedged and tree shadowed depths. The summer's fireflies were still winking occasionally in the bushes beneath the apple tree and along the garden.

Johnny indicated she should have a seat on the bench and stood in the midst of the garden, tilted his head back and held his arms out from his sides. The fireflies began to light on him as if called. She wondered what he might have that attracted them so. They only stayed on him for a moment or so before they spiraled up and away from him as the morning sun drew closer to peeking over the horizon. The twilight sky took on a different aspect of lighting, being neither day, nor night but something in between when new arrivals came to replace the fireflies.

From various points around the backyard and the trees the hum of dragonfly wings whirled before she could spot them. When they came into view in the curious ambience of twilight, they were about twice the size of the dragonflies that had flitted in the garden yesterday. Rainbow hued wings and multicolored iridescent bodies about two and a half inches long began gathering in the garden around her and her cousin.

"Here we are," he was still speaking in hushed tones. "This is my cousin, Leona Mae. She is a witch too."

Upon closer scrutiny, the largish dragonflies were not insects at all, but tiny little human shaped pixies with iridescent silk pajamas and eyes like bright fire opals. They buzzed at Johnny, while some of them lit on his shoulders and head. Others came to investigate Leona and touch her silky blond hair as if they were considering it for fabric.

A snow white dove landed on the trellis and before her eyes it took the form of an angel dressed in shining armor about eighteen inches high.

"You must be the faery prince," Leona observed aloud.

"He's no prince." Johnny giggled. "That's my big brother George."

"Somehow, he doesn't look so big," she said.

"They do when they want to," Johnny replied.

The garden was brightening more as the morning sun made its climb to peek over the horizon, but a darkness was forming in the hedges to the back of the yard. A dark robed woman walked out from under the apple tree towards the garden. The angelic looking man drew a silvery broad-sword from his scabbard and turned to face the oncoming specter.

"Put your weapon away, shining one," the woman commanded. "I have no wish to hurt anyone this morning. What I do wish is to get a look at those who would dare crossover into my realm."

"Auntie Vyra," Johnny admonished, his brows forming creases as his eyes flashed like cold gray steel. "This is my Grandma's yard and not your realm. We didn't invite you here."

At this, the angelic man spread his wings and leaned forward as if to spring at the dark robed woman.

Leona was feeling less in wonder and more than a little threatened.

"I'm leaving, I'm leaving," the woman assured. "I see that among your other talents, you are a little gate master as well. If your matriarch is wise, she will keep a close eye on you two or you might just... disappear." As if to make a point, the woman vanished from view.

The sun resumed its climb, as though the whole world had been holding its breath and as the first rays hit the dew sprinkled garden, Leona looked about to find herself and Johnny all alone. A pair of morning doves cooed in the pear tree.

"You called that woman Auntie Who?" Leona asked.

"Elvyra," Johnny replied as though it were all normal to him. "She's not really our auntie. I was being polite. Grandma likes that and she hates it." He giggled mischievously.

"She sounds dangerous," she said.

"Grandma says never let her get her hands on you," he said, sitting next to her. "Don't worry, George and everybody likes you. We'll protect you from that wicked ol' witch."

Leona sat on the bench and looked around in awe. Would she now wake up in a strange bed to find she had been dreaming?

PART THIRTEEN

Witch Blade

Emma arose and wound her way to the kitchen to find Willard had arisen at the crack of dawn and made the coffee. That in itself was not unusual. Nor was it strange that Johnny was not in his room but out in her garden, probably communing with the faeries. What was unusual was that Leona was out there with him so early in the morning after such a long day yesterday. The lass was never known to be a morning person. She peered out the back window and found the cousins were quietly sitting on the bench in her garden having an animated discussion of gods knew what. She grabbed a skillet and some leftover boiled potatoes from the fridge, then dropped a dollop of bacon grease in the skillet as it heated. She took her long knife with her as she walked out to the garden for some fresh chives to go with breakfast.

"My, you two are certainly up early today," she said to the children as she sliced off a sprig of chives.

"I wanted Leona to meet the pixies," Johnny volunteered.

"And did you get to meet any pixies, Leona?" She asked.

"Grandma," Leona asked. "Did you ever have a dream while you were awake, or while you were asleep and thought you were awake?"

"I know exactly what you mean, sweetie." She smiled at the children. "But somehow, I'm pretty sure you didn't dream what you thought you were dreaming."

"Elvyra is real?" Leona asked.

Emma stood and looked over her shoulder.

"Elvyra was here?" She asked.

"Don't worry, Grandma," Johnny boasted using his cowboy voice. "Me and George sent that varmint packin'."

"Speak respectfully of your elders, Son," she admonished. "Did she say what she was doing here?"

"She said she wanted to get a good look at the two of us who crossed over into her realm," Leona said. "Like she owned your backyard or something, and Johnny and George made her leave like he said."

"I've got breakfast going into the skillet," Emma replied nervously. "You two need to come in and get washed and we'll talk some more about this when your Grandpa leaves for work. I don't want him fretting over something he can do nothing about."

***

She didn't like serving the children strong beverages, but Leona had been up since well before dawn. Her granddaughter looked as if she needed the stimulating effects of a cup of black tea with some milk. Johnny had the energy of any three children but she couldn't let him feel left out. She put more milk than tea in his cup and they all had tea with some toast and jam.

"Did we do anything wrong out there this morning, Grandma?" Leona asked, looking askance at her little cousin.

Johnny was licking jam from his fingers and trying hard not to be messy.

"Not that I can think of, sweetie," Emma replied. "I remember my mother could crossover. Elvyra lives in a crossover place, and I knew Johnny could crossover. I didn't know he could take anybody with him though. You and Grandma have to try that little trick of yours sometime, Son."

"Wanna go see the faeries, Grandma?" He asked, looking like he would go right now.

"Not quite yet, honey," she calmed him. "But we'll try it real soon. I want to know what Elvyra's so all fired possessive about there to call it her realm. Is that the word she used?"

"Yes, ma'am," Leona said. "And she called Johnny a little gate master and said if you weren't careful we just might disappear, and then she disappeared. What kind of witch is she, Grandma?"

"The worst kind, sweetie," she said. "The kind that doesn't care about anything or anyone but what they can get for themselves. Sooner or later the Threefold Law catches up with them no matter how long they think they can stop it from happening."

"So when it all comes back on her, it's going to be really, really bad." Leona surmised.

"That's right, dear," she said. "You might not know all the spells and have quite the power, but you're turning into a brighter witch than her already."

Her granddaughter blushed at the compliment.

"I'm helping her, Grandma," Johnny said proudly, looking up from his teacup.

"That you are, boyo," she said. "You make sure she learns how to stay safe too. Don't the two of you crossover without your Grandma in tow. Eventually, we are going to have to take a little hike to the woods to pick up a few necessities and pay that wily witch a little visit."

"Are you gonna thrash her, Grandma?" Johnny asked with a little too much enthusiasm.

"I certainly hope not," she replied, appalled at the idea. "Listen well, youngsters: It is a serious thing when witches war among themselves. As you can see, the world is not particularly friendly with us as they don't understand our ways. If we don't look out for each other, we are in grave danger. Elvyra has said some things, that on the surface would appear to be threatening. She is a very powerful adept and it would be foolish of me to go charging after her in offense, when perhaps no offense was actually given."

"But she said—" Leona started.

"I know what she said, dear," she interrupted her granddaughter with a finger raised. "But with many people, words can mean many things. Perhaps she was warning of something she had foreseen through scrying, or maybe she has something not so nice in mind. But we should not persecute her simply because we want to believe the worst in her or we are as bad as the folks who hate and fear witches, and we bring the worst aspects of the Threefold Law upon our own heads."

"I hadn't thought of that," Leona said contritely.

"Ooooh, bad thing," Johnny agreed with a solemn shake of his head.

***

For once, Emma arose before Willard would stir. Today she would meet Johnny's fae friends. She got dressed, gathered some salt, a small china bowl, a fruit jar with some cream, her witch's long knife belted under her apron and went to awaken Johnny who was already dressed and sitting quietly on the side of his bed waiting for her. They went out through the back door of the summer kitchen into the garden. Emma took her box of salt and spoke her prayers and invocations to the four quarters and tossed a dash of salt into each to cleanse the area of any unwanted influences. Figuring her grandson's proclivity for faery folk, she poured a generous splash of sweet cream into the china bowl on a central stone in the middle of her garden and then used her knife to scratch runes of blessing and protection on the posts of her fence.

As she carved, yet another piece of the brittle iron blade chipped off the home made athame. Her father had made it for her many years ago when she was but a little older than Leona. He heated and hammered the twelve inch, double edged blade out of an old worn out file. He carved the handle from a piece of white oak and burned her name into it with a magnifying glass in the sunlight and made the sheath out of a scrap piece of cowhide. It was a homely old thing, but she treasured it for the memory of her father who was so accepting of her mother's foreign ways as a Celtic witch woman. She was thinking she had best retire the old relic to a chest and get herself a proper athame, but it would be like leaving an old friend behind.

The sun was nearing the horizon and the twilight time beginning. In the old days past, it was known that the between times and between places were the best used for certain magickal operations because then the veil was thinnest between the Otherworld and this one. She nodded to Johnny that he could begin his procedure.

He stood towards the middle of the garden and leaned back his head with his eyes closed and held out his arms from his sides as he turned himself counter clockwise. Fireflies that had been winking intermittently in the hedges near the back of the yard came forward and swarmed over him and lit him up like a Christmas tree. For only a moment, they stayed with him before they spiraled up and away as the ambient light of the garden took on a golden hue.

Her head buzzed with bright images that flashed in her mind in a myriad of impressions. There was a feeling of welcoming, of bright joy and the simple pleasure of lapping sweet cream. Looking over at the bowl, several winged faeries hovered around the china bowl dipping their faces to the cream inside. Gratitude and sweetness touched her mind from several directions at once. It was almost dizzying the way the fair folk communicated. She could sense their traits in common with her grandson. She sat back down on the bench to catch her breath and watch the display of aerial acrobatics as the creatures played with her and Johnny. He was thrilled to introduce his grandma to his fae friends and they seemed genuinely touched she came to visit and brought such a wonderful gift with her. It was a timeless party in her honor and she only lacked a crown and scepter to complete the honors.

She looked down at her long knife laying beside her on the bench. Two pixies were trying to lift it as a couple others came forth to help. For a moment, Emma wanted to call out to them not to take her precious knife, but that was selfish. Humans rarely got to see what she was seeing even now, or experience the bright spirits of the fae as she did. It seemed the least she could do to let them have the broken old knife. A solemn look crossed Johnny's face and he came forward to comfort her as though he knew what it meant to her.

"They want to fix it for you, Grandma," he said, hugging her. "They say you are a mighty grandma. They will bring it back when they fix it, and it will be better than ever."

"Bless them," she said softly. "Bless them all."

It seemed as though a whole day had past, but the sun rose on schedule and Willard came out to find her and Johnny sitting together on the bench in the garden.

"I thought I'd find you two out here," he said. "I took the liberty of making coffee and French toast if either of you would be interested. Leona is still fast asleep. I didn't have the heart to wake her."

"Let her rest, dear," she said. "She's probably dreaming about faeries."

"There's been a lot of those kinds of dreams lately, I noticed." Willard chuckled.

***

Emma felt naked without her long knife belted underneath her apron. Besides being a ceremonial implement, it was her trusted tool. She had been tying back some of her climbing roses to the posts on the front porch and kept finding herself reaching for the knife that was not there when she needed to cut some twine. Maybe she could get another few years of good use from it after the faeries fixed it. All the old stories suggested that when it came to repairs, the fair folk were not to be surpassed and when they did such a thing, some unusual blessing or curse might be included in the making. Maybe they'll make me a knife that will never grow dull or break. That would be nice of them. Even her father would have been honored that the spirits of the earth would bless his handcrafted blade. He always said having witches in the family was lucky for his tribe. Willard's attitude about the craft reminded her a bit of her father. She smiled.

She stood high on the step ladder, just above the eaves of the front porch. She was going to have to get down to find a knife to cut off a sucker vine that was growing over the gutter and not producing any blooms. She was about to call it quits when a bright silvery gleam caught her eye from the gutter next to the rainspout. Peering over the edge, she found the gleaming came from a silver pommel on the end of a polished wooden handle to something sticking out of the rainspout. Reaching up and over the eaves into the gutter, she extracted her knife and sheath out of the rainspout. It was breathtaking. If it weren't for the concentric ovals in the opalescent grain of the rich golden hued wooden handle, and her name burned in rich umber hues into the oaken haft, she would not have recognized her own knife. The old cowhide scabbard looked polished and new with Celtic knot work designs laced round about the entire length. She drew the blade forth. It had been completely reforged and polished to a high sheen. A silver crosspiece guard had been added and the old basic diamond cross section was now noticeably wider with a central blood groove on either side. Engraved carefully down the groove was the runic equivalent for "Witch Blayd".

It seemed a fair analogy for a witch's athame. It was so wonderfully done that she hesitated to use it for such a mundane task as cutting a piece of twine or pruning an unproductive creeper, but then tools were only valuable when they were used. She uttered a word of thanks to the fair folk and applied the blade to the thorny vine only to find that as soon as the blade came into contact, the severed vine fell away. Razor sharp hardly described the steel in her hands. She wiped the blade on her apron and replaced it in its sheath.

"No more pruning roses for you, old friend," she muttered. "You're obviously intended now for greater things."

PART FOURTEEN

The House Only Half in This World

Emma ran for her life through the deep forest gloom. The branches and thorns caught at her face and her clothing and hindered her progress. Her skirt and petticoats clung to her legs like warm wet blankets further impeding her ability to gather any more speed to escape the nightmarish creature that stalked her. A familiar weight slapped against her thigh as she ran for all she was worth. Up ahead a clearing appeared and she took hope that she might make better speed after she left the confines of the forest. Bursting out from the trees and underbrush into the clean light of the full moon she skidded to a halt. The ground dropped away into a yawning precipice.

There was no where left to go.

Her heart hammered its exertion in her breast and the sweet metallic taste of adrenalin coated her mouth as she drew her long knife and turned to face the horror that was hot on her heels through those haunted woods. It was not her old knife in her hand, but something new and yet familiar. The moonlight gleamed along the length of its rune carved blade like a living thing and extended itself into the gaping maw that crashed through the brush to occupy her clearing. It never made it another step closer as the nightmare was consumed in moonbeams at the forest edge. She looked with wonder at the deadly thing of beauty in her hand. On its warm wooden haft a familiar name confronted her, burned there years ago. It said...

"Emma." Willard shook her gently. "Are you alright, babe? You're having a bad dream or something. I got some coffee perking and the kids will be up soon."

"I'm okay," she said groggily and stretched. "It was a doozey of a dream, but it came out alright in the end. That's what matters."

Getting dressed to head out for the kitchen, she stopped to admire her long knife. It was hard to believe that it was not just a dream. The old chipped and scarred blade was now a thing of exquisite beauty. The forces of the Sidhe, she had so feared offending, were proving her most valuable allies. It was because of Johnny. Had she left the little fellow to fend for himself at the convent... she shuddered to think of the wave upon wave of misery that would afflict her and her family, and quite possibly more than that.

Blessings as big as this didn't come frivolously. There was an underlying reason. Mother Nature always provided a bumper crop, the year before a long drought or a bad storm. Danu took care of her own and nothing was left to chance. Counting one's blessings usually meant marshalling their forces. The sound of Leona scuffing on her shoes overhead broke her out of her reverie. There was breakfast to be made and budding young witches to train. She belted her knife under her apron and availed herself of Willard's coffee.

***

The forest was warm and cheery in the beams of sunlight that broke through the ancient oaks and assorted hardwood canopies. The children didn't wander very far from her side as Johnny had already warned Leona that Elvyra lived near these woods. Emma spotted a section of rotting logs, hoping to gather sulfur shelves. The kids were walking the logs pretending they were bridges high up in the trees as she searched the lower sides for mushroom growths.

Suddenly, Elvyra appeared with her basket over her arm.

'The old hen is out with her fledglings today, I see," Elvyra said smugly.

"They are learning well to hunt for themselves," she boasted. "I have my granddaughter to train as well."

"We've met," Elvyra responded shortly.

"So I've heard," she replied, looking askance at the woman. "Sometimes, innocent things people say and do get taken for threats." She drew her long knife from under her apron slicing the orange and yellow banded mushroom shelf off the log into her sack.

"Where did you get that...thing?" Elvyra gaped in horror at the runic blade, backing away.

"It's a gift from some old family friends," she remarked casually, wiping the blade on her apron and sheathing it. "No self respecting witch should be without one."

"You should be careful with that weapon," Elvyra remarked.

"You know, something," she replied testily. "That makes the third time in recent history that you've left instructions that I should be careful about my children and now my tools. If I were the suspicious type, I might construe all this as some sort of vague threat from a sister in the craft." She tucked her hands in her apron meaningfully and gazed steadily at the retreating witch.

"I just know that a wise woman like yourself would never tempt the Threefold Law by working or wishing any ill on a single soul," she said. "So, tell me, sister, what are you trying to say? Are you suggesting that you may possess information that me or mine just might be in some kind of danger?"

"It's possible," Elvyra blurted in obvious agitation. "When you delve into powers that you have little knowledge or control over, awful things have been known to happen."

"I'll be sure to keep that in mind," she replied evenly.

Elvyra bustled away in the direction of her house. The children had frozen in mid-step on the log and watched the transaction quietly.

"You two can stop holding your breath now." She smiled at them. "I think we should resume our lessons for today. Have you ever seen a house that wasn't really there before?"

"Wow!" Johnny exclaimed.

"What?" Said Leona.

"Follow me, kids," she said. "I need to show you something to fore-stall a little of the wrong kind of adventuring."

She led them to the back section of the woods where Elvyra's backyard intersected with the woods. The other woman was not in sight and likely preparing her herbs in her kitchen.

"The stone table you see here is used as an altar when she wants to perform ceremonies to get help from eldritch powers," she pointed out. "The shiny glass ball is called a witch ball and has been used for centuries to keep certain types of spirits from hanging around and for catching certain kinds of witches."

"What kind is that?" Leona asked.

"The curious kind," she replied, looking at her grandson. "Now I want you to take a really good look at this house. The color, the shape, the shingles... everything. Can you remember this?"

"That's easy, Grandma," Leona said. "It's not like any other house around here. And the color is so dark."

"Well, I never want you to go too near this house," Emma insisted. "Now follow me and we'll go down the trail and out into the street that goes around the front."

They walked past a fenced tennis court and a small garage and Emma treaded a path between two such garages to the street. The private road circled back on itself to an access road that connected with the main avenue. There were five houses located within this small circle near the woods. Three were white colonials, a fourth was a yellowish chalet style structure and the fifth, nearer to the tennis court was a yellow brick house with shuttered windows. Nowhere on this street was any house that remotely fit the description of the two story, dark shingled, gingerbread style of Elvyra's house.

"It's not here," Leona said, looking about and trying to see if it might be hiding behind the smaller brick structure somehow.

"It's gone," said Johnny, shrugging his shoulders.

"Let's go back into the woods," Emma instructed.

Back between the two garages and on the forest trail they hiked back past the tennis courts to find the dark shingled gingerbread right where they left it.

"How can that be, Grandma?" Leona asked, perplexed.

"Elvyra lives in a rift," she explained. "It's a place where two worlds meet. The front half of her house doesn't exist in our world, while the back yard opens up into our woods."

"How does she do that?" Leona asked.

"Part of it has to do with power channels called ley lines," she supplied. "And part of it has something to do with maintaining some kind of power to hold open an unstable rift that gives her a permanent foothold in both worlds. This hill is a very powerful energy spot, which is why the plants and herbs are so potent from this area. If my house could back up to two worlds, I would pick this spot for my backyard too. Probably for the same reasons."

"There's two worlds, right here?" Leona asked.

"Probably more than that, sweetie," she replied. "When Johnny showed you to the faeries, you weren't in this world anymore, but the Otherworld where the faeries went to live after men drove them out of the land."

"But we were still in your garden," Leona objected.

"Sometimes the Otherworld is a mirror image of this world," she tried to explain. "Things can be the same in both worlds, while some things are very different. Did you notice how much prettier the garden looked when you saw the faeries?"

"It was like out of a storybook," Leona reminisced.

"Well, the other garden probably never needs to be weeded because there are no weeds in that world. There could be hundreds of worlds. Your great grandmother could open doors to different worlds too. That's where Johnny's dad came from."

"Do you know my daddy, Grandma?" Johnny asked.

"I knew your dad, son," she said. "I'll tell you more about him as you get bigger and wiser. Meanwhile you've got Grandma and Grandpa and Leona and your mom and all kinds of family to love you and take care of you."

A slight pang of guilt shot through her for bringing up the boy's father in front of him like that. He had asked about the discrepancy only a couple times before. He knew something was missing from his life and he was trying to identify it. But it was important that she had plenty of time to establish a loving relationship before she had to share his darker side with him. He had some serious choices to make in his life, and she wanted him to make the right ones. That was true with everybody, but then everybody didn't have the potential for good and evil that Johnny had.

"But what I want from you kids," she said, raising her index finger. "is to avoid doing any crossovers when Grandma is not around. There's plenty that Elvyra hasn't said that worries me more than anything she said. Until we get this all sorted out, if you feel you must visit the faeries that badly, then I have to go with you.

"I still don't feel good about her, Grandma," Johnny said, indicating the house-that-wasn't-there.

"I don't feel right about any of this, son," she said. "Brother George or no, I want to be with you anywhere you go. I don't want to lose any of you to anything. Om biggun tu?" "Tiggum," the children replied in unison and gave her a hug.

PART FIFTEEN

Family History Never Tasted So Good

Leona helped sort out the day's pickings from Emma's sack in the summer kitchen. First, everything was washed under cool running water with a scrub brush to get off any residual dirt in the big, deep sink and then sorted to dry into separate baskets and hooks from the low ceiling. As her grandmother instructed, she took items already dry, from occupied hooks and baskets and transferred them to glass topped jars and canisters in Emma's windowed pantry shelves along the west wall of the summer kitchen. It was about time to begin preparing dinner so Emma brought out some potatoes and some of the sulfur shelves to the kitchen with her. Leona helped by peeling potatoes while she watched her grandmother cut the fungus shelves into small pieces and drop them into a saucepan of boiling water with a little crushed garlic, a bullion cube and some corn-starch to make a thick gravy. Acorn flour was used to make biscuits and added to a meatloaf mixed heavily with mushrooms, bell peppers, onions, eggs and herbs from the garden. Leona made notes on how many wild ingredients were used in the meal into her Book of Shadows.

"You really do use the woods like a grocery store," she remarked.

"In the old days, if folks suspected you of being a witch," Emma explained, "they wouldn't sell you groceries because they feared that God or the church would hate them for helping a devil worshipper."

"That's silly," she said. "We've got no devils in our religion, and if we did, who would be crazy enough to worship one?"

"Well, chances are that no one would let you live long enough to explain that little fact to them." Emma drained the hot water from the potatoes and pulled a large bowl from the cupboard to mash them in. "They would only believe you were lying to deceive them and steal their righteous souls anyway. So the first step would be to try and starve you out of their community."

"I get it," she supplied. "So we'd go and get our food from the woods so we wouldn't starve, right?"

"That's right," Emma said. "But that wouldn't be the end of it. When everyone was poor and hungry and we failed to starve to death, it was assumed that we were using our dark arts to conjure our food, and stealing away fat little babies to eat."

"That's awful," she said, shocked. "That's like that Hansel and Gretel story where the witch puts them in the oven."

"Exactly," her grandmother said, adding milk and a lump of butter to the potatoes as she mashed them. "The early church, after it got a foothold in the land, spread all kinds of evil stories about us so that people would obey them and not return to the old ways. Where once having a witch around to counsel the king and deliver the babies and heal the sick was a good thing, now everything that happened that was bad was because God was angry at the witch in their midst. So many of us were forced to go into hiding, and we hid in the wilderness where superstitious people feared to go, or we hid in the cities and never let on who or what we were."

"So that's why we're not permitted to talk about this stuff to outsiders," she surmised aloud.

"And it's also why you're learning herbs, medicines and wild foods as part of your craft," the older woman added. "Because if and when it should ever happen again, you will not starve or get sick because no one will care for you. Danu takes care of her own."

"The Danu of the Tuatha De Danaans?" Leona brightened.

"It means 'the people of Danu' in the Old Language," she said. "There's even a river named after her in Europe."

"Would that be the blue Danube?" She asked. "Like in the waltz?"

"One and the same." Emma covered the mashed potatoes and grabbed her pot holders for the meatloaf. "Before our ancestors fled the Romans to the British Isles, we lived throughout most of Central Europe. In some places, the Old Ways are still practiced today by people the Roman Empire never got around to completely ruling."

"So there are more of us than just us?" Leona asked.

"And where once we shared our wisdom with the kings of the earth," Emma said, covering the meatloaf. "We survive now by keeping our secrets to ourselves."

"That's sad," she said. "I learned in school how some people are starving in some places in the world. We could help them better than the Christians."

"Well, even so," her grandmother said. "That would depend upon how much of their land is blighted. Sometimes even the wild food and medicine is affected in a drought."

Willard came into the kitchen carrying a brown paper sack like a prize. Known for his sweet tooth, he often brought home a treat for after dinner.

"Save a little room," he said cheerfully. "I brought some ice cream for dessert." He opened the fridge and pushed the quart container into the icebox.

"We can all have homemade root beer floats," Emma said.

With Johnny's help, Leona set the table for dinner. They spread out the tablecloth and set the bowls heaped with mashed potatoes and acorn biscuits beside the vegetable and mushroom laced meatloaf and the sulfur shelf gravy on top of it. The place settings were added and Willard said a brief word of thanks, then everybody dug in.

"This tastes like white meat chicken," Leona remarked at the piece of sulfur shelf dangling from her fork and popping it into her mouth.

"Not surprising," said Willard. "My brothers and I used to call that stuff 'chicken-o-the-woods' when my mom used to send us out to find it."

"Your mom was a witch?" She asked wide eyed.

"Not likely." Willard shook his head. "My folks were good Christian folk and we were very poor. Back during the Great Depression there wasn't a lot of money and few jobs. When you got enough for a little bit of meat on the table, you stretched it as far as you could, like this meatloaf here. My mom used to stretch hers with a lot of bread, but your grandma uses acorns with vegetables and mushrooms. You almost don't know she didn't use much meat at all."

"I like it like this," she said.

"It's yummy," Johnny agreed.

"Being poor never tasted so good." Willard laughed gruffly.

"We're poor?" Johnny asked.

"No, silly," Leona chided affectionately. "If you were poor, you wouldn't have all this neat stuff and a nice house and the TV and all."

"Oh," said Johnny, still looking like he didn't understand.

With dinner finished and the dishes washed and put away, Johnny took the garbage out to the shed. Her grandmother and Willard pulled out a glass gallon jug of sassafras brew from the fridge and shook it up until it made a fine pinkish froth on top. Leona brought over the soda mugs and helped pour each of them a tall mug of the brew. It was further sweetened with a scoop of the vanilla ice cream that Willard brought home and they retired to the living room to watch "The Honeymooners" together on the television. Johnny insisted that she help him spoon a little of his into a shallow china bowl and setting it out in the garden before relaxing with the family. An extraordinary amount of fireflies lit up the backyard. All in all, it was the end of a perfect summer day.

PART SIXTEEN

The Itch

Emma drifted invisibly through the night time wood like a specter. The moonlight searched through the trees to the forest floor below, allowing her to recognize the trails and landmarks. Some teenaged boys had decided to camp overnight in one of the many hollows where their campfire would be hidden from any authority figures who might object to their private party in the park. There were many stories that parents would tell to keep their children from this wood at night and the truth of the matter was far more to be feared than the fiction. The boys were sharing some of these stories around their campfire.

"...and his blood stained jacket was all they ever found," a tall boy in slicked back hair and a leather jacket finished his tale of terror for his comrades.

"You've watched too many Lon Chaney movies," said a pimple faced lad with false bravado.

"I'm turning in," said another.

"You think I made that up?" The tall boy said. "You need to learn to read the papers more often."

The boys had built a couple wooden lean-tos from all the dead branches and poles available on the woodland floor. Their campfire provided most of the light as the warm summer night required no real heating. Each had brought blankets and a pack with some sandwiches and bottled soda to drink. It was just to be an overnighter to impress their other friends with their bravery.

The sound of something heavy snapped a large dry branch over the ridge of the hollow and the boys looked at each other with wide questioning eyes.

"Tim? Mikey? Is that youse?" The pimple faced boy called out. "C'mon guys, quit clownin'."

The groan and crack of splitting wood preceded the large dead tree that came crashing down the slope of the hollow. A deep throated canine howl reverberated through the campsite as the boys tore out of their makeshift bed gear in a hysterical dash for the opposite slope. A large section of log landed and crushed one of the lean-tos. Blankets and packs lay scattered as two creatures that vaguely resembled the Egyptian god, Anubis, with a hangover tramped into the vacated clearing and howled after the long fled boys.

Not fearing discovery in her spectral form, Emma followed the boys' progress through the woods and passed near where Elvyra's home intersected with the forest. Drifting closer through the trees, the clearing in the woman's backyard nemeton was bathed in silvery moonlight. The dark witch was laughing hysterically at the events she saw unfolding in her gazing bowl. Her laughter cut off suddenly as Elvyra's eyes grew wide and she looked about in near panic.

"Who's there? What do you want?" She insisted, her head snapping back and forth searching for something she couldn't see, but perceived. She tossed the liquid out of her bowl into the woods beyond and hurried back into her house, looking over her shoulder.

The forest fell silent again to the normal night sounds of crickets and owls. The jackal headed monstrosities were no where to be seen. Emma frowned, perplexed. What was that witch up to?

***

The next morning, during the breakfast dream discussions, Leona voiced a barely remembered dream of large barking dogs, but no more than that. Johnny spoke of a dream where he scared some big kids into wetting their pants by pretending he was a big, mean dog. Though he and Leona giggled over that oration, given her grandson's connection with the Otherworld, Emma didn't like the inferences this dream gave her. Was Elvyra manipulating the boy's darker fae nature through his dreams to create wraiths to keep trespassers out? Somewhere there was a connection between Johnny's ability to crossover and Elvyra's unusual home, as well as the woman's vague threats towards the children. She had to discover what it might be before it became more than just a warning. But worrying herself to a standstill was not constructive time spent. It was a rainy summer day and she had to occupy the children with something productive. Like itching.

The children were playing out of the rain on the front porch, and she brought them each some paper and a sharpened pencil. On Johnny's she drew a face and a crude body as he couldn't write or spell very well.

"Now here's a game you can play almost anywhere," she said. "that will improve your abilities as a witch. We call it 'The Itch.' First you imagine you feel an itch, like on the left side of your nose. Leona, you will write that down on your notepad, and Johnny, you will make an X on the left side of the nose on your picture. When you can feel it on yourself, you will then imagine that same itch on the other person. You will not scratch your own itch but promise yourself that you will not feel relieved until the other person scratches the itch on the left side of their nose. When they do that, you may show them your paper so they know how good you are and check off your example as done. Johnny, you will draw a circle around the X's you have been successful with. Got that?"

For the first half hour, Emma sat with the children as they tried to make each other itch and scratch. It was worth the entertainment just to see them making faces as they tried harder to concentrate on sending an itch.

"Kids," she said, "straining the muscles in your faces will do absolutely nothing to help you. It is not a muscle thing, it's a mind thing. Relax your face and your body. The only thing you should feel is the itch, and then you pretend it is not on you at all, but on them. It is not even your itch. It is their itch and they need to scratch it. You could probably just close your eyes and take a nap, but then you'll miss it when they scratch it, and that's the fun part."

Johnny sat there pensively as Leona reached up and scratched behind her right ear. Like a jack-in-a-box, he jumped up and shown Leona his X on the right ear of his picture and drew a circle around it.

"No fair," whined Leona. "I was busy thinking of an itch somewhere else."

"Where was that?" Johnny asked, scratching his left knee.

"Right there!" Leona jumped at him, showing her notepad triumphantly.

It was off to a good start, and Emma thought she might get some laundry started and a little cleaning done in the house. The cousins were battling with itches and each trying to out do the other.

At lunchtime she called the children inside. They came in giggling merrily as they went to wash up. When they sat down at the kitchen table, both of them appeared as if they had both broken out in hives on every square inch of uncovered skin.

"Okay," she said. "We'll call it quits with the Itch for today before the both of you scratch your skin clean off."

"It was fun, Grandma," Johnny protested.

"But how will it help us to be better witches?" Leona asked.

"Well, anything you can feel, you can transmit to someone else," she said. "Did you ever feel it when someone was looking at you?"

The children nodded thoughtfully.

"For one, you can be sensitive to other people's scrutiny," she added. "That's a helpful thing sometimes. Or let's say a big mean dog is barking at you and you feel afraid. What would happen if you took that feeling and sent it back to him?"

"He would run away instead of me running away and getting bit," Leona said, smiling.

"I could make him run away and pee hisself." Johnny giggled.

"As well as you two witchlings do those Itches," Emma agreed. "I'll bet you could frighten away just about anything. But suppose you wanted to make friends with the big dog?"

"I'd make him feel like he wanted a pat on the head or a scratch behind his ears," Leona said.

"It sounds like something you'll have to make a point of trying someday," Emma told them. "But never promise them anything you won't or can't give them."

"The will, the word, and the Threefold Law works in all this too?" Leona asked.

"Indeed it does," she said. "As it does in everything else. It's called a 'universal truth' because it is always true, no matter who does it, and not just witches. When you learn them, you'll understand more about how the world works and why and how you can affect changes in a positive way. The more of these you know, the better a witch you'll be."

"You must know a lot of these, Grandma," Leona observed.

"That's why your mother sent you here for the summer," she pointed out. "She's hoping you'll learn most of them."

"Did you learn the Itch when you were little too?" Johnny asked.

Emma stood there thoughtfully and the children burst out laughing.

"I was just thinking what a silly question that was," she said smiling.

"I was going to ask if you were any good at it," Leona said, giggling uncontrollably. "but it was just too silly."

Johnny shrieked and fell off his chair laughing.

PART SEVENTEEN

Dreams Amok

Emma harvested mandrakes by the light of the full moon in her backyard garden. The pixies provided additional lighting with their luminescence. Leona and Johnny were dancing a merry jig in the yard past the garden gate. It occurred to her that she had never planted mandrakes in her garden, nor could she ever expect them to grow there if she did. Was she dreaming? With this knowledge, she looked back to the children with new eyes and a will to determine what the dream's symbology might mean.

In the shadows of the far end of the backyard a cavernous maw opened up.

"Johnny," it called.

Displaying his curious fae nature, her grandson cocked his head to one side contemplating the new cave entrance and began walking towards it. Where he could see like a cat in the pitch blackness, Leona was ambiguous about walking into the dark entrance.

"Johnny, come back." The girl called.

"I told you not to let them out of your sight," Elvyra said, her hysterical laugh reverberating painfully in her head and filling the yard.

"Don't go in there," she yelled, an ominous chill filled her.

Only Leona heard her and the girl dashed after her wandering cousin to try to stop him from disappearing down the dark tunnel.

Emma dropped her mandrakes and charged out of the garden after the disappearing children. Johnny was already out of sight down the tunnel. She had managed to lay one hand on Leona's shoulder as she called out to her cousin. Even for so close, her voice seemed to be coming from another room.

"Johnny, come back," Leona's voice carried from her bedroom upstairs.

Emma rolled out of bed and donned her slippers and housecoat. Willard was already in his robe and moving towards the door.

"I'll check on Johnny," he said, and headed towards the boy's room.

Emma took a hard left and up the stairs just as Leona stumbled out of her blankets onto the floor and scrambled to her feet and ran towards the hall, only to bounce off the wall in the dark and fall sprawling and crying to the floor rubbing her head.

"It's okay. It's okay, sweetie." Emma sat on the floor beside the girl and held her trembling body close. "It was all just a bad dream," she assured her hysterical granddaughter.

"It was so awful," Leona said through her sobs. "Johnny and I were playing and we saw this lovely fairy cake, and when I went to get some a huge metal bar came down and held me so I couldn't breathe. Like a really big mousetrap. And when I looked for Johnny, he was stuck in one too. Only his mousetrap had him by the neck and his eyes looked really awful and he started to fade away."

"We're all okay, dear," she confirmed. "In fact, it's early in the morning. Let's all go downstairs and get some breakfast. Maybe some tea and toast. Doesn't that sound nice?"

Leona nodded and Emma helped the girl find her slippers and housecoat to go downstairs. Getting Leona seated at the kitchen table while the teapot was heating, she then went to check on Willard and Johnny.

"Is he okay, Willard?" She asked.

"He was awake when I found him," Willard replied, holding his grandson close and rocking him gently. "He couldn't seem to talk and his eyes... I never seen his eyes get like that."

"What about them?" Emma asked, sidling closer to them both.

"They were black," Willard said. "Like looking down a deep well."

"They don't look bruised or anything," she muttered to herself while examining her grandson's tired and tear stained face.

"Not bruised," Willard insisted. "His eyes had no blue, no whites, only a deep, deep blackness." He shuddered.

"This sounds like a dream all of us are better to wake from," she concluded. "Leona's in the kitchen waiting for tea and toast. Let's all join her."

"I'll make the coffee," Willard volunteered.

Johnny looked exhausted, as if he had crawled back from the pits of hell. Emma could only wonder at what his young eyes might have seen this night. She helped him into his slippers and robe and relief only came when she saw his tired smile light his face when he saw his cousin at the kitchen table. Some black tea with milk and sugar along with some toast and bramble berry jam were the medicines called for this morning. The invigorating brew and the sweet preserves did much to bolster the children from their lethargy and night terrors. As the sun rose with the new morning, the household was beginning to resume some normalcy. But some issues were demanding to be resolved, and she wasn't sure of how that was going to happen.

It was a warm Saturday morning and promising to be a beautiful summer day. Willard thought a daytrip to Sea Breeze would be the best thing to clear a child's mind of the dark dreams that plagued them all. He would let them ride on all the amusement park's attractions and play in the penny arcade to their heart's desires. Down the block they could catch a bus that would drop them off at the front gate of the park and then bring them back home later. Emma had elected to stay home and take care of some chores and ponder the situation while Willard and the children enjoyed some quality time together.

Opening all the windows and putting a sprig of rosemary in each pillowcase and a sachet of fragrant herbs on each windowsill sweetened the disposition of the house as she cleaned rooms and made beds. A pinch of salt, flicked off the end of her witch blade along with a whispered prayer at the four corners of her property set her boundaries for protection. Only then did she relax and take tea under the pear tree and considered all the omens.

Elvyra figured heavily into all these dreams and portents. Whether she was warning of a threat, or the actual threat herself was as yet to be determined. Johnny, by his non-human traits, was a key figure in this threat. Crossing over into the Otherworld was where it would all begin... or end. Was it his abduction, or the darkness that might bring about that posed the real threat? Leona was undoubtedly tied into this, though probably as a result of her relationship to her fae cousin and her affinity for faeries. The bottom line that all the Fates drew was that she as Matriarch would be held responsible for whatever came of this and was forearmed as much as forewarned. If she only knew why this was happening, as opposed to what was happening, she would have a better idea of how to prepare to deal with it. Perhaps her mother's gazing bowl could provide her with some answers.

She found the plain wooden bowl her mother used in a cupboard in her summer kitchen. She took the bowl, a cup of water and a bottle of brandy with her to the living room and set them on the coffee table in front of her favorite chair and pulled the curtains closed to dim the light in the room. Sitting, she relaxed and took a few good breaths and expelled them to center herself, allowing the questions on her mind to come to the fore as she poured water into the gazing bowl. When the water settled and calmed she added a single drop of the brandy. Instantly, the surface changed as the liquor mixed with the water of its own accord.

Instead of the water growing brighter in the bowl as when they had cast so often into the faery world of Gwynydd, it clouded and became dark as ink. This was not the faery Otherworld, nor was it this one. It dawned on her, as the dark and twisted shapes stretched forth in the gazing bowl that this might be Annwn (An-noon), a hellish plane of damned souls and foul spirits. She fought to keep an open mind as she looked deeper into the bowl to find the source of the disturbance to her household. A twisted dark forest of moving phantasmal shapes beckoned her. A black trail tunneled through the agonized trees deeper into the haunted forest to end finally at a cliff before a yawning chasm. A twisted obsidian tower stood at its edge as though it had been, and would be there, for all time. As she scrutinized the inky facing of the tower, a woman's reflection appeared on the time polished surface. It was definitely not her own. The red haired, green eyed vision of her mother with a white forelock spoke as clearly as if in the next room.

"Go back," the woman shouted. "Only evil awaits you here!"

Stunned as if she had just touched an electrified fence, Emma fell back in her chair and kicked the bowl over onto the floor. Looking down, she was relieved to see only water on her hardwood floor and not ink. She missed her mother's presence mightily. Had that desire influenced the vision to appear or was someone or something playing dirty in order to better hurt her? She grabbed an old towel and cleaned up her mess. She put the bowl and brandy away, but not before pouring herself a small libation of the brandy to calm her nerves. But now she had more questions than when she began searching. She sat and meditated a moment or so with her drink and got up to prepare dinner for the family when they would return from their daytrip.

***

Emma pulled some muffins mixed with pieces of sweet pear from the oven to add to her fare of breaded pork chops, au gratin potatoes and string beans from her garden when Johnny came bursting in to the kitchen wearing a cowboy hat and shoving a huge calico kitty stuffed toy in her face.

"Grandma," he yammered excitedly, struggling to hold up his prize. "I won this for you."

"That's a pretty big kitty to come from such a little boy," she exclaimed, accepting his prize. "How did you win this?"

"I shot a bumble bee," he declared proudly. "And then I shot a whole bunch of ducks too."

" Eagle eyed Johnny the Kid—" Willard announced coming in— "the toughest sharp shooter east of the Genesee River."

"That's me," Johnny said in his cowboy voice, swaggering and tucking his thumbs into the waistband of his dungarees.

"Grandpa taught him how to shoot a BB rifle at the shooting gallery," Leona said while unloading armloads of kewpie dolls and assorted booty. "and Johnny shot all the ducks for prizes. Then the man told him if he could hit the bumble bee, he could have any toy he wanted. He gave Johnny three tries and he got it in two, so he picked out the big kitty for you."

"Well, I hope all my wild west heroes have saved some room for supper," Emma said.

"Grandpa said no more treats after two o'clock and the man at the shootin' gallery said I couldn't win no more prizes today," Johnny explained. "So I'm hungry enough to eat myself a bar," he said in his cowboy voice.

"Maybe just a little bear for me, Grandma," Leona said, giggling at her cousin's antics.

"I was beginning to wonder what those tin ducks might taste like all afternoon," Willard said, snatching his grandson's cowboy hat off his head. "Git yourself washed up there, Cowpoke, and set down for some good grub. I'll race ya to wash off at the horse trough."

Johnny dashed to beat his grandfather to the bathroom sink.

"All afternoon." Leona sat down at the table and rolled her eyes at her grandmother. "I felt like I was living with a midget Hop-along Cassidy and a full sized Gabby Hayes. I don't know how you cope with them, Grandma."

"Tarnation iffen I kin figure that one out myself, ma'am," she said, mocking her grandson and tucking her thumbs in her apron strings. "I just runs the chuck wagon and they just runs the doggies." She and Leona fell to laughing as the sharply contrasted men folk arrived fresh from the proverbial horse trough wondering what they had missed.

Dinner went over well as Willard and the children were all in high spirits from the day's activities. After the kitchen was cleaned up and everybody had a snack of milk and muffins, Willard and the children went to bed exhausted while Emma sat out on her bench in the garden and wondered into the night. Why would her mother appear to tell her that anything at all, awaited her in Annwn? What would any such thing have to do with Johnny? His ancestry is of this plane of Abred and of Gwynydd. What could possibly even suspect his existence in that dark and twisted world? Will her answers be found in the black tower on the edge of the abyss? How did Elvyra fit into this? There were no easy answers.

PART EIGHTEEN

An Ancient Enemy

Friday night, it was horrific mouse traps. Saturday night, it was an obsidian prison on a tall cliff. Last night it was Elvyra's ghost coming to each of them and telling them to stay away.

It was Monday morning and as Willard had left early for work and she decided enough was enough. Everyone had dark circles under their eyes, including herself, she noted as she washed her face and looked in the bathroom mirror. Children were resilient creatures, but nobody could take this kind of anguish every night and not be worn down by it. She would pack some things for a day trip and she and the children would pay Elvyra a visit at her home.

No more vague threats or warnings. It was high time for specifics. She belted her witch blade under her apron and called to the children on the front porch to come and pack their gear for a day trip.

Leona helped her by wrapping three fried egg sandwiches on fresh baked bread in waxed paper. A few leftover muffins were added to the lunch menu and Johnny brought in a couple sweet pears for each of them from the backyard. To this Emma added two bottles of Willard's stash of soda pop and included a folding camp knife with a bottle opener in Leona's day pack. The children would share one. Lunch packed, she locked up the house and they set out for Cobb's Hill Park. She had her canvas handled shopping bag folded flat and tucked in her apron strings, but didn't really think she'd be picking up much today.

A few puffy clouds wafted overhead. There was not enough overcast to make her worry about any real chance of rain. A slight breeze sighed in the trees, but otherwise not the sound of another living creature could be heard in the woods today.

"Shhh!" She stopped along the trail trying to listen for the bustling traffic through the city outside the park. There was none to be heard. These woods were strange at even the best of times, but something certainly wasn't right today. Without hesitating, she headed straight for Elvyra's back door to the woods.

When they arrived at the trail behind her house, Elvyra's gathering basket was setting on the marble table in her backyard. It appeared to have been laying there for sometime as the greens inside were withered from sitting out too long. If nothing else, Elvyra was fastidious. Emma was worried.

Johnny and Leona wanted to explore their way up the side yard to the front of the house that was not visible from the street, but she forestalled them from wandering about and had them accompany her to the back door where she rapped loudly. There was no sound anywhere to be heard. Not even a breeze to rustle in the leaves.

She looked through the glass on the back door, taking in an airy kitchen with pots and pans hanging from hooks and herbs drying in tied bundles. In the living room beyond, a large fireplace mantle of fieldstone dominated the room with several iron pothooks and a cauldron hanging from one, but no fire in the hearth. Still getting no answer, she tried the door latch to find it unlocked and hesitated just a moment before opening the door and searching inside.

"Elvyra?" She called. "Are you home? It's Emma. We've got to talk."

She looked around for clues while the children stood huddled by the kitchen door as if ready to bolt at the first sign of the dark witch. The kitchen was spacious, with plenty of counter space. A single blue china teacup on a matching saucer with a little cold tea in the bottom was the only indication that anyone had even been here recently. She continued moving on through a large open arch to the living room area. She paused at the hearth. Nothing but cold ash. Any embers had burned away many hours ago. The big surprise came when she moved for the doors that went to rooms in the front of the house. Both were closed and nailed shut with planks, metal straps fastened across the doorframe and bits of twine and ribbons with runes printed on them stretched across to bar entrance. It was obvious that Elvyra had not passed through these doors and hadn't done so in years. Whatever secret these doors held, Emma would let them keep their secrets for now. The basket outside suggested that Elvyra had returned from gathering in the woods, but not into this portion of the house. This left the options that she had either moved through the yard to the front or had returned to the woods without her basket. Trying the walkway to the front was her first choice.

Returning outside, she had to remind the children to restrain their natural curiosity to dash for the front of the house they had never seen. As much as it intrigued them all, there was no telling what they might find there in a world not their own. The sky was growing steadily more overcast and darker, though the day hadn't yet reached the noon hour. About halfway through the yard to the front, she stopped and withdrew her witch blade and scratched a crow's foot shaped rune into the paving stone.

"What's that for?" Leona asked. "A rune for protection?"

"Always a safe bet," she replied. "It will also mark that we have been this way as well as the direction we are traveling."

"We're just walking to the front of the house, Grandma," Leona pointed out.

"A part of the house that does not exist in our world, little witch," she said. "And is not subject to the rules we know. Anything can happen, and probably will."

"I'm wishing that we didn't have to come here," Johnny said.

"Me too, Son," she agreed. "But nothing is going to leave us alone until we face it and sort it out."

"I was afraid that was what it was going to take," Leona confessed.

Arriving at the boundary of the backyard, they came upon a six foot high, arched wooden gate with runic figures carved along its posts and trellis. Some were familiar, while others were completely foreign to Emma. The ones she recognized had no message of impending danger in them, and since there was no repeat of the sealing of the inside doors, it seemed safe enough to pass. The latch worked without any problems and they passed to the front of the house. The structure was consistent with the back of the building and complete with a front porch and gabled roof. The windows were glassed and had lace curtains much like her own, but the house was dark within and nothing beyond the curtains could be seen from the outside. The front lawn extended another forty feet to a low trimmed hedge bordering a dirt road showing no signs of any recent use. Beyond the road, on the other side was the dark, twisted woods they had seen in their dreams. Johnny stood silently on the front lawn and gazed long at the haunted forest across the road as if his fae sight could penetrate its gloom.

"You stay put in this yard, young man," she admonished him. "We don't want you disappearing on us while we try to find Elvyra."

She grasped the front door handle but the latch seemed to be frozen in place. Try as she might, it couldn't be turned or jiggled. Moving to investigate the front windows, she and Leona looked up. Elvyra stood in the window, looking past them with an expression of pale horror frozen on her face.

"We'll get you out of there, dear," Emma promised her. "Don't you worry. Stand back now."

Emma unfolded her canvas shopping bag and held it flat across the glass of the window and drew her knife and smashed its pommel hard into the center of the sack on the pane. The glass panel gave a resounding bong but would not shatter. Looking at the light play across the runes on her blade, she decided to try another tack and pointed the blade at the glass.

"I need you to cut for me now," she muttered, and pushed the gleaming blade into the glass as if it were made of wax. Drawing the blade slowly in a large oval, the big piece of glass clattered to the porch but did not break. Only then did Elvyra's voice reach her ears.

"I warned you not to take your eyes off that boy, you fool," Elvyra shouted. "He's gone now and we are surely doomed."

As one, Emma and Leona turned to look where Johnny had been standing in the front yard. He was gone. Across the road she could make out his tiny form walking into an opening in the thick growth and disappearing into the darkness.

Leona was nearly hysterical over the loss of her cousin as Emma helped Elvyra out of the front window of the house.

"Take it easy, sweetie," she said to her granddaughter. "It's not as if we didn't have plenty of warning that this might happen. First, we'll arm ourselves with information, and then we'll get him back."

Elvyra looked as if she might suffer a fit of apoplexy, but Emma fixed her with a stern eye and addressed her in a low growl.

"Before you open your insulting trap, sister," she warned through gritted teeth. "You will address me as though I just might possess the intelligence that befits a witch and a matriarch. You will not only tell me what I want to know, but as best as you are able, you will tell me why. The children and I have been suffering from vague threats and ominous warnings for weeks now with no indication of what it is we need to be watching for. Your nonsense has disrupted my house to no avail and in rescuing your haughty bustle from this side show funhouse of yours, I have lost my grandson to your nameless threat. If you thought you were in danger before, it's doubled now. The good news is that I won't lock you in your house, and the bad news is that I won't lock you in your house." She shook her hand with the witch blade in Elvyra's direction for emphasis as she spoke.

"Please, put that thing away," Elvyra said, recoiling is as though from a living serpent. "It's not necessary. I too wish to stop the madness before it brings destruction upon us all. I will answer all the questions I am able. But please put the Sidhe blade away."

"For someone who has your affinity for rifts and crossovers," Emma puzzled. "I would have assumed you would have a strong fae connection. Perhaps even as strong as Johnny's."

"It's true," Elvyra said. "But there are fae and then there are fae."

"Quit being so cryptic," she warned. "I'm fast running out of patience."

"Johnny's father was Sidhe," Elvyra explained. "Though of a darker nature than most, he was still a Sidhe of the ancient Tuatha De Danaans. My father was Formorian of the ancient Corca-Oidce. Before the coming of mankind, these races were mortal enemies. The Formor, also called Fir Bolgs were driven out by the Tuatha De Danaan, and they in turn were driven out by the Milesians, or humans. My dual nature allows me as a child of both worlds access to the gateways that is denied to the full bloods by ancient decree."

"That decree wasn't so strong when Johnny's father was made to crossover," she observed.

"There are times and circumstances where being in the right place at the right time," Elvyra explained. "a single individual can crossover from their plane of existence to this one. That is how my father crossed also and why part of this house is inaccessible. He left a hole in place, and yet another fearsome creature of the People of Darkness, called Behir awaits to grow strong enough to make the crossing in those locked rooms."

"Will it be able to get out through the window I cut?" Emma asked with a start.

"No," Elvyra said. "I was sealing Behir into a single room from the front when the Vough locked me inside because I wouldn't help."

"Behir is the beast you spoke of," Emma concluded. "But who is this Vough?"

"The Vough is my great grandmother," Elvyra admitted. "She is a mad woman with a hatred for the Sidhe folk and humankind that transcends the ages. She can't call the black lightning to make Behir stronger. She has been awaiting the day when I could. But I understood her madness and made it a point to never learn. Your Sidhe child will give her exactly what she wants, because by his very nature the black lightning will be attracted to him here. All three planes, of Gwynydd, the Sidhe plane, Abred, the Earthly plane and Annwn, this dark plane are adjacent on this hill. Your grandson represents Abred and Gwynydd here and if the Vough gets her hands on him she'll have the perfect key to send murder and mayhem into the other planes. Who will then have cause to drive the Fir Bolg deeper still. No one will benefit from this madness. Only grief will come of it."

"Where might she be likely to take him to work this evil?" She asked.

"Dun Cruachan is the most likely spot." Elvyra pointed out beyond the dark twisted woods. "A tower built on the edge of a chasm said to be bottomless."

"A black, obsidian tower?" Emma asked.

"Why, yes," Elvyra said in surprise. "Have you seen it?"

"In my dreams," she said. "I've seen a lot in dreams. Like the creatures you turned loose on some teenaged boys out there one night. How can I trust you?"

"Don't be silly, woman," Elvyra huffed. "I love that forest every bit as much as you do and for the very same reasons. I don't want it to become like this place. I'm half human too, you know. I belong as much there as here, and I happen to like there much better. Those boys would have been in danger of far worse harm than the simple wraiths I sent to discourage them had they stayed in those woods for the night. The hill opens easily to Gwynydd during the day, but Annwn reigns in the night. It is not a safe place then."

"That's what I thought," she said. "I needed to hear it from you and you've vanquished more of my doubts than I expected with it. Welcome, sister. Let's see if we can stop this sinister thing."

"Easier said than done, sister," Elvyra said pointing over the dark wood.

The overcast was growing considerably thicker, and a jagged streak of black could be seen like an afterimage in the eye, descending from the sky to the west to some unknown landmark that Emma could only guess.

"I take it that this is the way to the black tower?" She asked, nodding in the direction she had seen the lightning.

"It will take a few days to reach it on foot from here," Elvyra nodded solemnly. "For every time the black lightning strikes the tower, Behir grows larger and stronger trapped in that room. Eventually, he will be strong enough to burst out on his own."

"Then we need to be after my grandson," Emma surmised. "Before he can reach the tower."

"You'll need provisions for the journey," Elvyra said. "The Vough will use every means to get him there well before you. He has no faery friends here. Piskies are not pixies and he may not understand the difference. A couple stout staves for the hard journey are best picked of the oaks of Abred in my backyard as opposed to the twisted, sickly things of this world. Some additional food from my pantry will see you a lot farther as you can trust nothing here. But I must stay here to redouble the spells to keep Behir locked behind these doors. You don't want him sneaking up behind you on the trail."

Taking the advice, Emma and Leona pushed through the gate to the backyard and cut a pair of oak staves from the saplings in the forest. Leona stripped the bark off the walking sticks with the folding camp knife while Emma stocked Leona's daypack and her canvas shopping bag with a box of kitchen matches, some acorn breads, dried fruits and nuts from Elvyra's pantry. A pair of skin water bags was given them to take on the journey. One was filled with a heady sassafras tonic as a fortifier, and the other was filled with pure water from the park reservoir.

It was a little past noon when Emma and Leona said their good byes and crossed the road to the dark trail through the twisted woods. She could only wonder what would happen should they find Johnny too late.

PART NINETEEN

The Haunted Woods

Crossing the road into a field, a little over a hundred feet wide that bordered the haunted forest, the dark, twisted trees loomed ahead and were still not recognizable as any species that Emma had hitherto encountered. Leona stayed close at her side as she contemplated the arthritic limbs bearing dark, waxy, almost holly-like leaves that reached in every direction in frozen agonized silence. She was almost relieved that the yawning maw of the trail entrance was wide enough not to have to come into close contact with the unhealthy looking trees. It was disturbing that in looking into the forest gloom that specters of baleful blue, gruesome green and sickly salmon could be barely discerned in places between the twisted boles throughout the woods. Holding her staff in a white knuckled grip, Emma pushed on into the darkened woods with her granddaughter.

Eyes adjusting to the woodland twilight, she scanned the details of a path wide enough for three men to walk abreast plunging deep into the woods ahead. Growing on the rocks and tree trunks, several varieties of phosphorescent lichen and fungi accounted for the pale spectral shapes seen through the trees. Mushrooms, toadstools and puffballs the size of hassocks thrived in the decay found in the forest loam. Looking about, Emma found a large stick and drew her witch blade to sharpen one end and placed it on a rock with it pointing into the forest ahead. Then she scratched the horizontal, V-shaped rune Kano into the top of the rock in a way so the V pointed to the trail entrance.

"Are you working a spell?" Leona asked.

"In the strictest manner of speaking, yes," she replied. "This is a spell of orientation. The sharpened stick leans against the rock and points in the direction we are heading, as opposed to any of the side trails we'll see. Kano, being the rune of Opening, tells me the entrance is that way." She pointed in the direction they came as the field or the road were no longer visible to them.

"So, all spells aren't magick?" Leona asked, looking a little more comfortable in the normalcy of being taught her skills.

"Almost no spells are really magick, dear," she said. "Anything people don't understand, to them, is magick. The way a light bulb lights a room. How a radio or television make sound and pictures from so far away. It's all magick and none of it is. When you understand why something works and make it do so, to some, it is magick, but to you, it is merely another craft. In a strange place, how would you keep from getting lost?"

"Maybe do like Hansel and Gretel did and leave a trail of breadcrumbs?" Leona guessed.

"Ah, but that didn't work," she said. "Birds ate the breadcrumbs and they got lost anyway. They also wasted valuable food, and we might have to be here a while. Johnny remembers landmarks by names he gives faeries of that area. This stone he might call 'Frumpy,' and he knows that several yards to Frumpy's right is the trail entrance. But neither of us knows the spirits of this land, nor can we trust they will help us in any way. So, I'm relying on an Indian trick my father taught me by marking my trail in subtle ways like setting up sticks and stones to point my directions and leave me clues should I have to pass this way again. You can tell that this sharpened stick didn't break off and just happen to fall there. The rune was my own personal touch and if Johnny comes by this way, he'll know what it means too."

"Now I understand what my mom meant when she said you make your own luck," Leona said. "I thought it was in a potion or something."

"That too." She winked. "Now, let's get moving and every few hundred feet or so, we'll mark our trail."

Emma coped with the panic that threatened to well up in her by keeping her mind focused on the steps she could make towards progress, instead of the things she had no control over. When she had done all she was capable of, she rested in the thought that she had done her level best and that more could not be expected. She didn't fear for Johnny's immediate safety because madwoman, though the Vough may be, she had a use for the Sidhe boy and needed him alive. This gave her time to close the distance and find a means to rescue her grandson. She didn't give in to fear. Like the Itch, in her mind it was the Vough who needed to be afraid for her safety. Very much.

The day grew steadily darker and Emma began looking for a shelter to spend the night. A rocky outcropping of slate and shale below a ridge they had crossed appeared to be their best bet for the night. On a large, flat slab of slate along the trail she scratched Eolh, the crow's foot shaped rune of Protection so that it faced her resting place. Her and Leona then gathered all the dry wood and kindling they could find, into a pile next to the rock overhang they occupied for the night. Being in a wooded hollow, it would be out of the wind. Not that there was any.

Using the kitchen matches, she built a campfire at the entrance to their stone shelter and together they ate fried egg sandwiches and washed them down with a few swallows of water from the skin bag. They huddled together, with their backs to the rock face and listened to the crackle of the fire and the night sounds in the forest beyond.

"I keep thinking of Johnny," Leona said. "Out in these spooky woods all alone and afraid."

"I know what you mean, sweetie," she said. "If it will help you rest any easier, he is probably neither of those things."

"How so?" Leona asked.

"For one," she explained. "Whatever coaxed him into these woods is with him, to get him where they're going. The Vough wants him alive. For two, Johnny is not afraid of things he doesn't understand. He's much too curious. If he saw a real, fire breathing dragon, he would be too fascinated to run away. The last thought through his silly little head would probably be something like: I wonder what he does to make the fire come out like that?"

"He spent a whole afternoon watching ants carrying a dead bee to their hole," Leona interjected. "He knew they weren't going to get that big thing down that little hole, so he watched while they took it apart and carried it down, piece by piece."

"And no doubt," Emma said. "He was satisfied at the end of all that, that he knew how they done it. I would always tell him: 'Curiosity killed the cat.' And he would reply: 'Satisfaction brought him back,' with that mischievous smile of his. He will miss us as much as we miss him. But he is probably safer from danger than we are right now. We should try to get some sleep so we can go after him at first light."

Part way through what was only a fitful sleep, Emma was startled by the sounds of rocks sliding down the slope she was camped on, and the sounds of clawed feet scrabbling for a purchase on the loose talus. Quickly she tossed a few dry sticks in the dying fire and watched as the light flared back up fully. Several sets of red eyes winked at her out of the inky blackness. A dark form made a little progress up the slope to her and came within the lighted boundaries of her campfire and she could see what she was dealing with.

"Rats!" She shouted, rousing Leona from her sleep.

They were rats the size of beagles. They tried throwing stones at the large crawling rodents, but it would only be a short time before they would be too tired. She needed to find a way to discourage them. A means to make attaining this cliff the least attractive idea in their greedy little minds.

"Are you scared?" She asked Leona.

"Yes," Leona admitted, tossing a saucer sized piece of slate at a rat.

"Good. Don't waste that feeling," she said. "Send it out to them."

"I'll try, Grandma," Leona said, sobbing.

"Don't try. Just do it." Emma tossed a couple firebrands down on the rocky slope, and touched an ember to the back of Leona's hand.

"Ow!" Leona whined. "What's that for?"

"Remember, if you can feel it, you can send it. Send them the pain from that too," she said. "Fire, smoke and pain are things they understand and fear."

The forward progress of the rats trying to climb up to them was halted. It was easier for them to sit in their overhang, behind the fire and send fear and burning pain to anything they became aware of scrabbling through the loose talus slope. Within the hour, the rats had left for easier victuals elsewhere. Anywhere else.

Morning came, cold and gray, with a little bit of fog. A few more sticks in the fire warmed them, and a quick breakfast of an acorn muffin apiece and a couple swallows of the invigorating sassafras brew got them on their way.

PART TWENTY

The Dark March

"Lost, lost" came the pitiful crying.

Johnny tried peering through the hedge, but he just couldn't see what was making that sound. He walked to the opening where the walkway met the road in front of the house, hoping to spot the creature that needed help. Glancing back at his grandmother and cousin, they were busy trying to get into the front of Elvyra's house, so he took it upon himself to just peek around the hedge to see if there was something he might do to help some little person in need. He wouldn't go very far.

About thirty feet down the road along the hedge, a shaggy little creature was limping away from him and across the road, whimpering its lament of being lost. It looked like it might be injured as well. Perceiving that the entity was certainly not human, and probably some fae creature he had not met as yet, he tried calling out to it in the manner of the pixies he knew.

Picturing himself and his grandmother holding and nurturing the shaggy individual he projected the scene at its back as he followed it across the road and through the field towards the twisted woods. He was about to enter the wooded trail when it occurred to him that his grandmother might not approve if he strayed too far out of sight.

He turned to call out to her, but in so doing, he discovered he couldn't see the house, the road or the hedge. He couldn't have gone so far. He hadn't walked very long. Just across the road a little. Where could the house have gone? The house was a strange one. Existing here, but not there. It wasn't a thing that could be trusted, so he tried reaching out from his heart to find his grandma and his cousin, but he couldn't feel their familiar lights coming from anywhere near. It was as if they were nowhere in this world, and he didn't like that prospect at all. Feeling about for someone or something familiar, he could feel the faintest touch of a kindred soul. It seemed a far ways off, on the other side of the haunted forest he now faced.

Looking into the darkness of the forest trail, he could make out pale ghostly lights between the trees. This intrigued him, and seeing the little shaggy creature ahead of him on the trail, he just had to go in and get a better look. The shellycoat looked like a shaggy haired teddy bear, or roughly about the same size. It's dark eyes gazed up at him through matted hair and a mirthless, toothy grin cut across its hirsute face.

"Are you alright?" He beamed at the critter.

"I'm doing better than you are," it wickedly shined back at him.

"I only wanted to help," he insisted.

"And that was your undoing," it projected sinister thoughts at him. "Someone is here for you, wicked child."

"I'm not a bad boy," Johnny glowered. "Where's my grandma?"

"You have no more grandma," a woman's voice chimed in. "She will have no more to do with such an evil brat."

"My grandma wouldn't leave me," he shouted in panic. "She loves me. She wouldn't do that. I'm her boy."

"Then where is she now?" The Vough came forward into his view.

She was a tall and gaunt figure of a woman, with wild, pale blond hair that ran down her back. She wore a long green dress with wide sleeves. Her features were elongated with long spidery fingers ending with nails that more resembled talons. In those hands she carried a polished wooden scepter with an orange glowing orb at the end.

"You were a bad boy, leaving the yard like that," she scolded. "Your grandmother cannot be troubled watching the both of you if you're going to be traipsing off like that, so she left you to me."

"I just wanted to help the little furry guy," Johnny whined, tears flowing freely now. "I wasn't trying to be bad. I want my grandma."

"It's too late now, wretched Sidhe child," the Vough said. "You'll have to stay with me at my place until your grandmother has time to come for you."

"She'll come to your house for me?" He asked hopefully.

"If she wants you and something doesn't eat you first, you filthy thing," she spat back viciously. "But I can't imagine who would want such a devil boy."

Johnny was stunned and shocked to his heart. The images and the slurs struck home with a familiarity he couldn't deny. Perhaps his mischief had gone too far this time. Grandma was always defending him from others who thought he was damned. He berated himself for not being more helpful to her and being more obedient. Even though eventually he would be left to himself, he didn't want that to happen so soon. He had only himself to blame, because there was no one else. Now maybe Leona could have his room next to Grandma's. Maybe if he was good, he could come back and they would let him stay in the guest room. That wouldn't be so bad. He would follow this hateful woman and be the best he could be until his grandma came for him. He wanted to cry, but he knew that would just annoy them even more, so he held in his tears and put on his brave face.

The shellycoat scampered ahead of them up the trail. There was no trace of a limp or any injury. It was beginning to dawn on him that the belligerent little creep had purposely fooled him to get him into trouble. The idea of kicking it and giving it a real limp crossed his mind and gave him a moment's pleasure. He didn't want to do anything that might forestall his grandmother coming to get him soon, so he satisfied himself by beaming that image to the shellycoat. It turned and bared rows of needle sharp teeth at him. Johnny grinned back and focused his feelings of forlorn upon the creature who had caused them. The shellycoat howled and tore off the trail into the woods and kept running.

"Now what has come over that stupid peck?" The Vough wondered aloud. "No matter. We've got a ways to go and no time to waste, you foul thing. Keep up with me now, or no telling what may snatch you off the trail here. This world isn't exactly friendly to Sidhe kind, you know."

He didn't know, but then neither was the other world he knew. They had run his kind out of it at sword point centuries ago. He had a few human friends but he understood the human capacity for love was limited and should never be pushed. He dare not push it at all here. He shined a plea for Brother George or some of his pixie friends but it was like shouting in an empty room. There was no one to hear his call. He was alone here, without the benefit of his grandma. Maybe this woman would like him a little better if she got to know him and he was a good boy. He didn't like her much, but she was all he had, so he would try harder.

***

The Vough led him through the depths of that strange wood all that day and into the night. Not being human, she didn't tire. Being only half human, Johnny was just a little tired. His human half rested in its dreams, while his Sidhe half probed the darkness and touched and examined the myriad life forms he sensed watching their progress. The orange glow of the sceptered orb cast little light in the nighttime forest, but then his fae eyes needed little light to see, and he had other senses that extended out to satisfy his incessant curiosity. He made it a point not to fall more than a step or two, at most, behind the Vough.

There were winged creatures flitting about, that loosely resembled pixies, but these kind had none of their light. Where pixies tended to be playful, and sometimes to the extreme, these beings were cruel and enjoyed tormenting any hapless creature they found. They had a rat cornered in the hollow bole of a tree and were taking turns piercing the rodent with long thorns. It would turn to try to dig itself farther into the tree and one by one the piskies would dive down and place yet another thorn in its tattered hide. Such were the number of thorns piercing it, that if human daysight was all that Johnny had, the rat would have looked like a porcupine with inverted quills. The animal was weakening noticeably from blood loss and insects drawn to its scent made the poor beast all the more miserable. Was his proximity to the Vough all that kept himself from becoming the object of piskie malice? He drew closer as she cleared away the largest spider web he had ever seen for them to pass down the trail.

Johnny was very hungry and as snappish as the Vough could be, he thought it best not to nag her verbally about his needs. Instead he chose to superimpose his feelings of hunger upon the woman herself. This worked well as she decided to stop their trek long enough to draw her obsidian knife from her belt and cut a portion off a giant puffball. It looked as unappetizing as a rising lump of bread dough, but the insides were dry and not gooey as he expected. She sat down on a stone and offered him some, but he settled for the fried egg sandwich he had in his daypack and a piece of sweet pear. Removing it from its waxed paper wrapping, he folded the wrap as his grandmother had taught him and placed it back in his pack. Eating his lunch so much reminded him of home, he could not help his tears from falling, but he made no sound to draw unwanted attention. He had a bottle of his grandpa's soda in the pack, but no bottle opener. There were still some nuts, muffins and another pear. He rationed these for later.

Having satisfied her hunger, the Vough rose from her seat and tirelessly continued their trek down the forest trail to her home as the gray light of day broke through the dark forest canopy. Johnny followed close behind.

The trail came to a wide chasm that had a sluggish waterfall that spanned a couple hundred yards at the north end. A sluggish river dribbled water over a hundred foot precipice into a black pool below that emptied into a series of streams that flowed southward through a marshy valley that was a little over a half mile wide at this point. The trail continued in a ramp down into the marsh and crossed the numerous streams by a series of log footbridges.

As they picked their way across the footbridges to the small, grassy hillocks in midstream, he was fascinated by the variety of plants he saw there. A tall plant topped with a flower that looked like an wide, open, green clamshell lined with thorns had just snapped shut on some kind of bird that had gotten too close. He decided he would not let his curiosity get the best of him this time and followed the Vough, who was dragging the hem of her long dress through all the filth of the swamp.

At the top of the chasm on the other side, the mad fae turned and waved her scepter over the valley below and chanted gutturally. When she was satisfied that she had said enough, she continued leading them through another section of dark woods that gradually led to higher, broken ground interspersed with evergreens. He was curious about what it all meant, but was afraid to ask. The strong feel of impending rain was in the air. His grandmother would be along to get him eventually, and he would be waiting and on his best behavior.

PART TWENTY ONE

Gregory The Peck

In Abred, their own plane of existence, it would be a warm, sunny summer's day. Even if it were a rainy day, the bright rays of the sun would find a way to pierce fluffy, bright clouds and dazzle the wet landscape. Here, in Annwn, the morning started cool, foggy and gray, only to become a little less misty and lighter as the day went on. It was still a warm summer day, but overcast and humid beneath the threatening skies. Even the ugly tree canopies were a break from the monotonous monochrome sky. Occasionally, something dark or dun colored and winged would flit amongst the branches and cry out, but Emma was certain they weren't birds.

Marking their trail with pointing sticks, stacked stones and runes for clarification, Emma led the procession making good progress that morning. They had stopped to eat a sweet pear from their packed stores and drink a little water when the raucous, panicked cries of the unknown winged creatures ahead on the trail. Bringing their light meal to a quick end, they repacked their supplies and moved cautiously up the trail to investigate the disturbance. The trail curved sharply to the right to avoid a tight cluster of strange trees, and rounding the bend, they came upon something wholly unexpected.

A spider web blocked the trail ahead. It stretched about twenty-five feet across the trail to trees on either side, and fifteen feet up into the branches. The squawking and chirruping came from what appeared to be winged pixies in a variety of earth toned hues instead of the brighter, iridescent species of the other planes. The largest of these were only slightly larger of size and wingspan than the average sparrow. A few of these were caught in the web. To Emma's horror, the more the poor creatures struggled, the more entangled they became. Those who had not become entangled, flitted about excitedly chattering at the captives and among themselves. The agitation reached its peak when an extremely efficient looking arachnid, about eighteen inches across scampered nimbly over the web and cut loose one of the captives and carried it back to her funnel shaped hole near the base of the left most tree.

If she wanted to help them, now was the time to try and free some of the creatures from that web. Regardless, she would have to remove it from the trail to pass. As she approached the struggling forms in the sticky strands, the free flying creatures buzzed her angrily and pulled at her hair. Leona did what she could by swinging her staff at them to ward them off.

"I'm only trying to free your friends," Emma snarled. "You ungrateful imps."

"Piskies are not pixies, sister." Elvyra's voice seemed to surround them. "I've been trying to keep track of your progress in my bowl as time allows. These are not the friendly creatures of Gwynydd, but She-who-waits will stay in her nest until you pass as you are not a part of her natural diet."

"Thanks, for the timely tip, sister," she replied. I'll do what I can here and be on my way."

She drew her witch blade from under her apron to cut the strands. From the moment the gray twilight struck the blade and glinted its warning, the remaining piskies shot through the trees for cover and squawked their protests from a safe distance. She tried gingerly to cut the remaining piskies free of the web, before attempting to cut the trap loose to clear the path. All were horrified of the approaching blade, and some even tried to bite and claw her as she set them free. The last of these was either unconscious in a dead faint or simply resigned to its fate. She couldn't tell which, but she cut it loose without any resistance and began cutting the connecting strands to clear the trail as it stood calmly at her feet and cleaned its wings. Moving back up the trail a few yards, she scratched the crow's foot rune of Protection upside down on a boulder, so that the stem pointed upwards. Moving an equal distance to the other side of the formerly blocked trail she carved the same symbol in a fallen log.

"Why did you make it like that, Grandma?" Leona asked, taking an interest.

"In reading runes for divination," she explained, "when inverted they have the opposite meaning. Where Eolh, right side up would designate 'protection' in some form, being reversed implies 'the need for protection' to those who might read it."

"So, it's a warning that this spot might not be safe," Leona surmised.

"Exactly, sweetie," she replied. "Although, I'm not sure which is really worse, the giant spider or the piskies. Still, the ward will keep us from unpleasant surprises."

"This one doesn't seem to want to leave," Leona said, pointing to the remaining pisky that made it a point to flit to the nearest branches along their way and not join his noisome clan at a safe distance from the intruding humans.

"It seemed like his friends didn't want them freed from the web," Emma replied, thoughtfully. "I have no idea how intelligent they may or may not be or what their intentions might be. Our faeries are perplexing enough at the best of times, and I understand them best by watching Johnny. I wonder if they had seen him pass this way, and how he got around that web."

Her forehead was buzzing like the day her forelock turned white and she sat down on a log with her granddaughter to rest a moment. Was it a result of the pisky bites? She examined her hands for wounds. Nothing she found there was deeper than a minor abrasion at the most. She sparingly poured a little water on her scratches and shared a drink of the sassafras brew with Leona. Looking down on the log beside her, she was surprised by the lone pisky standing there, looking up at her hungrily, but making no move towards her or the skin bag that held his attention. Its nostrils flared for the scent of the sassafras coming from the cap.

"Where are my manners?" She said. "Would you like a drink of this?" She hefted the bag of brew.

He cocked its head, like she had seen her grandson do on so many occasions as he considered something and nodded his head with enthusiasm and wiped his mouth as if he might be salivating. She uncapped the bag and poured a tiny libation in the cap and set it down on the log in front of him. He bowed his head reverently to her and then plunged his face into the cap and drained it. A shiver of excitement spread throughout his tiny body and extended to his sparrow like wings. Originally, she wasn't sure if they were furred creatures or clothed in odd furs as she cut them loose of all the webbing. The rest had fluttered in her face much too aggressively to make out much detail, but this one beside her gave her pause to examine him in detail. He was about four inches tall, with brown hair and black eyes, dressed in a grayish brown fur tunic that came to his knees. It appeared to be the skin of some sort of mouse. The tunic was belted with a length of tough, dried grass with a two inch, black thorn tucked through the left side along with a tiny pouch.

He was looking at her oddly, head tilting from side to side as her mind buzzed annoyingly. Forcibly relaxing herself from the tension she got from the buzzing, an image of her grandson as though he was being watched from up in the trees filled her mind. He was following a tall, gaunt woman in a long sleeved, green dress that trailed behind her on the forest floor. In her hand, she carried a stick about the size and shape of a baseball bat with an orange glowing orb imbedded in the wood at its top end. It was this she had used to clear away the web from the trail. Looking at the hard packed path, she could spot the small scuffs worn by Johnny's shoes in places, but not a trace of the tall woman.

"Are you alright, Grandma?" Leona asked timidly.

"Oh, yes, dear," she said, breaking out of her reverie. "I was communing with our new friend here. We'll have to make up a name for him so as not to offend him. Got any ideas?"

"I was just thinking of the time Johnny was mocking Grandpa's 'pesky pecks,'" Leona said, "and thinking how funny it would be to hear Johnny try to say 'pesky piskies' and was wondering if Gregory Peck had any fae blood in his family. My mom thinks he's the handsomest actor in Hollywood. How about Gregory the Peck?"

"Well, he's a handsome little fellow," she said. "And you haven't lost your sense of humor. Let's try some names."

Emma concentrated on an image of Johnny and spoke his name three times slowly. The pisky nodded. She pointed to Leona, also picturing her and spoke her name likewise, and the creature gave a little bow to her granddaughter. Tapping herself and trying to visualize herself with the new silver lock, she spoke her own name thrice and received a courtier's bow. Lastly, she pictured the noble creature and spoke his new name three times and he lit on her shoulder and smiled.

"I think we've got the names established," she said, without looking at her granddaughter. "Here's the test. I want you to gently call his name."

"Gregory?" Leona asked.

To which the pisky craned to see past Emma to her grandchild as if enquiring of what she might want. Leona offered a sliver of sweet pear from the core she still carried, which was accepted with relish.

"I believe that Gregory the Peck, and your pear core are fully acceptable to our new friend," she announced. "Now, let's hope he can help us in our quest to find Johnny. Time is wasting and we need to make some distance today."

The trail had took a downward turn into a small, sharply cut valley. Emma considered the path that cut across the wetlands at the bottom where pairs of logs, covered in rough planking spanned the small streams of slow moving water and oozing mud to small grassy hillocks to be followed by yet another footbridge across the next creek. Gregory stayed perched on her right shoulder where he could shine his advice to her should she need it. Leona walked single file behind her as the trail got narrower through the boggy lowlands of Annwn.

Far to their right was a wide rock ledge that stretched over two hundred yards at the narrow head of the valley with water falling about a hundred feet to a deep black pool about a half mile from the path they were using. Water spilled over its edge sparingly, but the cut of the valley attested to the fact that this would not be a good place to be caught during a heavy rain. The log bridges and the plant life looked like they had been undisturbed for at least a couple years, but nothing here looked much older than that. Emma wasn't sure of what the duration of wet and dry cycles was in a place like this, but she was aware that this was the dry cycle and had been so for a moderately long time. The constant overcast of the skies added to her anxiety of being in such a spot as she could not tell when they might decide it was time for a cloudburst. Patterns. Wizardry was about watching and recognizing the patterns in nature, her mother would say.

"When are we going to stop, Grandma?" Leona complained. "I'm hungry."

"We'll stop and take a break when we get out of this swamp, dear," she said. "I don't want to spend any more time down here than I have to."

Emma wondered what the medicinal qualities of some of these plants might be. The plants she could recognize, Venus flytraps, jack-in-the-pulpits and pitcher plants the size of garbage cans suggested that what life was here, was robust if nothing else. Carnivorous plants would not grow to such size on mosquitoes and flies alone. All the more reason to move along quickly.

The first sign of trouble came with a plunk in the stream near the bridge they were crossing, followed by another and yet another. It could have been frogs jumping from the banks into the water, but a golf ball sized raindrop soaked her hair in the next instant and Emma's worst fears were realized. A jet black bolt of otherworldly lightning struck a twisted oak at the waterfall's edge, shattering its branches like glass and the rain came in earnest.

"Let's hustle that bustle, little lady," she shouted over the din to her granddaughter. "It's about to get very deep, very fast."

They both broke into a sprint across the rapidly swelling streams of mire and water. Gregory took up a position in the top of Leona's daypack as the torrential downpour severely limited his flying ability. They were still a quarter mile from where the trail would rise and ramp its way up the canyon wall on the far side of the valley. The falls had assumed a more generous flow than before. Even so, they had to pick their way across the broken, swampy terrain. The last footbridge had swayed sickeningly just before the current swept it way. Leona narrowly missed being swept away with it by leaping the rest of the way and Emma snatching her by her pack straps and hauling her ashore. On the far side of the hillock they occupied, a similar bridge over a ten foot wide stream loosened and was threatening to vacate the tree stump it was resting on in midstream. The hillock was too narrow, wet and slick to get a running leap so Emma thought she might put their walking sticks to good use. Both of them had at least six foot lengths of supple oak to work with.

"Have you ever seen something called 'pole vaulting'?" She asked.

"Yes, we tried it in school once, over a small bar," Leona said, squinting through the rain at the swelling stream. "But I couldn't get very high when I tried it."

"We don't need to go very high," Emma shouted. "We need to hold our sticks tight at the top, stuff them into the center of that stump, and kick both feet up in front to land on the far side of that stream. Can you do that?"

Leona hesitated only a minute before she nodded and Emma set her grip high on her staff, and told her to squeeze hard and kick off fast. Leona's jitters gave her the spring she needed to clear to the far shore, where the water was now about ankle deep. With Gregory hanging onto her collar in a death grip, Emma sprang with a passion and kicked up her heels in a most unladylike fashion to clear the torrent as the rest of the foot bridge washed away. They ran through the cattails and brush to where the trail began to climb.

Once they reached higher ground, it became slower going as the hard packed clay floor and loose rocks, along with the heavy rain made visibility poor and the footing slick and treacherous. The last thing they wanted was to take a tumble off the trail into the raging torrent below. Cautiously they picked their way along the switchback, digging in hard with their walking sticks and shortening their strides up the slippery trail.

Since they were already soaked to the skin, once the trail headed back into the forest, they made use of the downpour to rinse all the mud and debris off their clothes, shoes and skin. It was a warm and humid day to start with so the cool shower didn't feel all too bad. The forest canopy kept the worst of the rain off them as they hiked the trail at a slower pace, in search of a good resting area. She made certain to mark her trail in the usual manner.

The terrain ran steadily upward and became more broken and rocky as it went westward. At least, it would have been westward back in her own plane of existence. The fungi favoring the northernmost parts of the tree trunks to be out of the sunlight was her only indicator of direction since she had entered the woods. More and more evergreens were making an appearance among the variety of trees now. These and some good sized boulders to back up against would make excellent shelter. The rain was more a steady drizzle now. The two large slabs of sandstone were going to be her best effort at finding shelter before nightfall.

Using the witch blade to cut notches in the higher end of the stones, she placed Leona's staff across the open end like a curtain rod. Then she cut long boughs from the lower branches of the evergreens and cut notches in the thicker end and hooked these over Leona's staff, laying them at a slant for the rain to drip off the branches behind their stone shelter. Leona gathered the loose pine needles to cushion the floor of their shelter and gathered all the dry sticks she could find and piled them just inside. Placing her own staff just behind Leona's, Emma hung their outer clothes across the entrance to their shelter and built a small fire on a flat slab of rock in front of their temporary home. The heat would help dry their clothes and keep most animals away. Some nuts, sweet pears, and two acorn muffins were the fare of the day, topped with a warm bottle of Willard's soda. Gregory shared their meal and a capful of soda with them and sat near the fire all night as piskies, like most fae creatures, don't need much sleep. The ladies, however, slept as deeply and as soundly as they ever had.

"Don't just lay there, you two," Ella Mae scolded them gently. "We have to work out some way to get our boy back from the Vough."

Emma sat bolt upright the instant she heard her mother's voice.

Leona sat up groggily and complained.

"But I was just getting comfortable," Leona whined. "And I was so tired."

"It won't matter anyway, silly girl," Ella Mae said cheerfully. "You're still asleep. You'll be just fine in the morning. That peck of yours would fight a bear to protect you."

Emma stared at the apparition of her mother, sitting in the pine needles with her knees drawn up, her green eyes twinkling merrily in the firelight that streamed in between their drying clothes.

Gregory tossed another dry stick on the fire and looked over his shoulder at her, nodding once and resumed his vigil.

"Mom, how do I know that this is really you and not some nasty enchantment?" Emma asked as Leona plainly was struggling to gather her wits.

"It's simple, dear," Ella replied. "You don't. Even I'm not sure of everything I've seen in this place. I can't believe I'm seeing all of you here now. Especially when I watched you from the gazing bowl and told you not to come here." Ella waved a stern finger at her daughter.

It was Emma's turn to be stunned now. She had discussed none of what she saw that day with anyone. Could something be tapping her memories to befuddle her?

"Great grandma," Leona broke the momentary silence. "I was at your funeral when I was only five. Are you a ghost?"

"I remember seeing you there, when you came up to say good bye, dear," Ella Mae said. "But all of us are ghosts, sweetheart. Yours is as trapped in your body as my body is trapped in that box they buried it in, but I don't live in it anymore. We are, all of us, immortal creatures. We live forever, just not in the same way. We grow. We change over time."

"Are you happier now?" Leona asked.

"About this?" Ella said incredulously. "Oh, no. My great grandson is in the clutches of a ruthlessly mad fae woman, and my daughter and great granddaughter are risking their lives to get him back. If you don't get him away from her before she can unleash her madness, our clannadh won't survive another year. If you can get him away, but she turns him dark, our family will be cursed beyond imagining. Which is not a happy thought either. I'd have to say I've seen better days than this one, dearie."

"What can we do, Mom?" Emma asked. "It sounds like we're damned if we do and damned if we don't."

"What did you have in mind when you came here?" Her mother asked. "How are you prepared for this?"

"This and a heart full of magick my grandson gave me." She patted her sheathed athame.

"Let me sort this out a minute," Ella said. "You are about to charge the very gates of hell with a rusty old knife your father made for you?"

Emma drew the blade for her mother to see. The wonder that registered in her mother's eyes gave her hope that she just might be equipped to do this.

"Well, it is, but it isn't the same blade at all," Ella remarked wonderingly.

"Johnny's fae friends reforged it as a gift for me," she explained. "It seems to cut just about anything now."

"And more than that, I'll wager," her mother said. "But still, it will not serve you in an absence of wits. You will need a strategy to win."

"I only know he'll be in a dark tower, on the edge of a cliff to the west of here," she said. "I also know she'll keep him alive as long as she has a use for him, and she wants him to draw the black lightning to her tower to transform something called Behir to do her dirty work for her. Elvyra is doing her best to keep it penned up in a locked room in her house. If we can breach the tower, stop the Vough and rescue Johnny before he can be made to call the lightning, and get him back home across the flood, I have a reasonable chance of raising him as a respectable witch."

"There's an epic sized 'if,'" Ella said. "for a pint sized witchling. And then there's this matter of all the 'we' in this assessment. Leona, how do you feel about all of this?"

"I'm afraid of what might happen," Leona admitted. "We've been through so much already. He's my cousin, and I love him. He tries so hard to be a good boy, and he listens to everything Grandma tells him. If we can save him, I think he'll be a very fine witch. If we can't, I'm not sure I want to leave without making the Vough pay dearly for this. We'll never be safe. I'll do my best. I know he would do as much for us if he could, and he would try even if he couldn't."

"It's settled, then," Ella Mae concluded. "I would suggest we divide and conquer."

"How so?" Emma asked.

"Send Leona inside to influence Johnny, if she can," Ella Mae said. "And you try to draw the Vough away and stop her any way you can. I would suggest a spell of binding, but this is her world, and not ours. But she must be stopped. Dividing her from our grandson is the only way to conquer her." With this, Ella faded into shadow and dreamless sleep ensued for Emma and Leona.

PART TWENTY TWO

The Black Tower

It was late in the evening when they arrived at the Vough's home in Dun Cruachan.

The black tower was a place of wonders that rivaled Grandma's summer kitchen. He had no interest for what might have been bubbling in the cauldron in the hearth, but the myriad of astrolabes, bottles, vials, crocks and beakers that sparked, flamed, sputtered, bubbled, boiled and smoked of their own accord was almost torture for him not to investigate. He was determined not to do anything to get himself in further trouble with his grandmother. The Vough had gotten them into the structure by touching the orb on her scepter to a raised plate next to the door. She had put her scepter away in a drawer under some shelves and was busy fiddling with a series of levers on the far wall.

In the center of the room a series of iron bars descended from the unseen apex of the tower to make a circle within a circle of silvery glyphs embedded in the polished ebon stone floor. With the exception of a twenty inch gap, the bars were about five inches apart and enclosed a ten foot cell that contained a cot, a commode chair like the one he had seen stored away in his grandmother's attic, and a bench. It looked like a circular jail cell without a door, or even a place to put one.

"That will be *your* room until *your* grandmother comes for *you*, foul fae," snapped the Vough.

It may have lacked for privacy, but it gave him an unrestricted view of all the fascinating happenings within the eldritch tower and he couldn't possibly miss seeing his grandmother when she came. It suited him just fine. In spite of the Vough's waspish invectives, with a tired sigh, Johnny went in and took off his daypack and laid it on the bench and tried out the cot for comfort. Indeed, he had been up for two days and the rest was welcomed. He never even got his shoes off before he fell asleep. The sound of three iron bars clanking into place were not enough to raise any suspicions in him and he slept soundly.

***

His sleep was almost dreamless. Dreamless, because there was nothing to hear or see. Almost, because he was still there and aware there was nothing to hear or see. He reached out of himself, into the darkness to find someone. Anyone. In the distance, just beyond his reach, was a vaguely familiar presence that wished him well. Try as he might, he couldn't get any closer to it or identify it. A coldness met him that permeated his bones. He sat in the darkness alone and wondered when someone would come for him. He was trapped there. To move only a few feet in any direction, he met with a cold black wall that he couldn't perceive anything beyond.

He remembered another time, so far away, when a spiteful elder, male cousin had locked him in Grandma's basement and shut out the lights. Even in the darkness, he could make out the rough hewn stone walls, the furnace that had been converted from coal to oil and the rough, old, wooden bin the coal used to be delivered to. He knew where everyone was in the house, and who was in the house. Even though they were hidden from his eyes, his soul could reach out and embrace their essences. He could even perceive the tiny lights of the spiders and the mice that shared the basement with him. He was never really alone, and had no reason to be afraid in the darkness there. Help, should he need it, was always near.

He awoke. At least it seemed like he was awake. The difference being only that his human half was cognizant and there in the dark place were the three pieces of furniture of his circular cell. He could not see the iron bars or beyond them as all was blackness from that point outward. He could see around his area well enough, but had no idea of where the light came from. His first feeling was that he was cheated of the opportunity to watch events unfold in that remarkable tower his cell occupied. His second feeling was anxiety that he would not be able to see his grandmother when she came for him. He could not feel her anywhere. Could she find him in this dark place? He reached out of himself to find out who might be near and was met with a rushing coldness that circled his living space. Trying to touch the formless wall that encircled him, his fingers met with a cold, so severe that it burned to the touch. He jerked back his hands and sat on the bench and considered his plight.

For lack of anything else he could do, he emptied out his daypack and laid out his belongings on the bench. He counted two whole and one half eaten sweet pears from Grandma's backyard. Two fruit muffins that she had made for them the day Grandpa taught him how to shoot at Sea Breeze, and a warm bottle of grape Nehi Soda. There were a few odd twigs that turned out to be bits of sassafras roots. The smell of these gave him warm memories of home. There was also a four inch long, rectangular shaped piece of red sandstone that he had scratched some runes on with a small nail, and the nail that he had used to make them.

He tried to slip the point of the nail up under the cap of the soda bottle, but it was too thick around. Perhaps if he flattened the nail, he could make it into a bottle opener of some sort. He placed the bottle near the wall-that-wasn't-there to chill while he looked about for something to play blacksmith with. His piece of sandstone and the stone floor appeared to be his best bet for a hammer and anvil. The stone was nearly flat on five sides, He had found it at the beach where the water and sand had smoothed the rocks to all sorts of interesting shapes. This one looked sort of like a four inch tall obelisk with the corners all rounded. Originally, the idea was to carve runes into its sides to make a knick-knack for Grandma's shelves. Now, it would be his smithy hammer as he held it in his little fist and pounded away, flattening the point of the nail on the stone floor.

It didn't look like much of a bottle opener, but he was able to slip it under more of the bottle cap. Working it back and forth loosened the cap a little, but it still wouldn't come off. Tapping his stone on the nail head while the point was set underneath the cap favored him with a satisfying 'pop,' and the sweet grape soda was his to enjoy. He promised himself that he would reward himself with a sip every once in a while if he was good, and set the bottle aside under his cot with the cap set back on top.

His nail looked like a pixie-sized spade. What kind of buried treasure would a pixie dig for? Turning it around in his fingers, he thought if he hammered it farther up the shaft, it would look like a pixie-sized broadsword. One never knew when some pixie-sized hero might drop by and have need of a good sword. His mind and his hands were occupied and it allowed him to pass the time. He hammered away on his little project and left about a half inch of the nail at the head untouched for the hilt. Using the rounded top of his stone, he flattened the tiny sword's edges until they were almost a real blade, but it was still too dull. He worked the edges against his stone like he had seen his grandfather do to sharpen a knife until a satisfactory edge was obtained. Later, he laid on the cot, playing with his tiny sword until he fell asleep. He could not even dream of anyplace outside of the cell. He was alone, and every time he called, he was answered by the numbing black cold.

PART TWENTY THREE

A Wise Women's Council of War

Emma awoke early and sat with Gregory by the fire. The rain was more intermittent now, with the occasional jet black streak of lightning to the west of them. The frequency of the strikes and the proximity suggested that the Vough already had Johnny and was using him somehow to call down the energy to empower Behir. Elvyra would have her hands full as the monster became more powerful. Spelled or not, sooner or later it would breach those doors and begin its rampage into the connecting planes at Cobb's Hill.

Divide and conquer, her mother had said. Send Leona in to soothe Johnny or try to influence him in some way while she drew out the Vough. To what? How do you reason with a mad fae woman? A trial by combat? There had been no reasoning with Lee when his darker nature overwhelmed him. The ancient Sidhe had driven out the Formor, and the early Celts displaced the Sidhe. The Vough hated humans and Sidhe, but mostly Sidhe, as she had managed to produce hybrid humans in her family too. It's not as though she would have to drive out an entire race of Formorians. Just one, and maybe her demon.

The monster, Behir, was the Vough's weapon of vengeance. Disarm her, and maybe she could be reasoned with, though the idea of tackling a creature of unknown size and shape was not a task she relished. But in her dreams, she had already done just that. She would have to make herself a gazing bowl to contact Elvyra.

Drawing her witch blade, she scooped a shallow depression in the opposite end of the slab of stone their fire was built on. She let this fill with rainwater as she carved runes around the bowl to focus her intentions. Her first was Gyfu, the rune of Partnership. She needed partners in this venture. The next was Lagu, the water rune, the feminine element and she needed sisters in the craft. Thirdly came Tyr, the rune of the Spirit Warrior as this would be a war council. Fourth would be Os, the Messenger rune. The knowledge that communication would bring was needed. Lastly, she carved Peorth, the rune of the Initiate. This was a witch-to-witch call. From last night's experience, this was the perfect place to make such contacts as needed. She would leave her record etched in stone.

Leona had awakened and crawled out of the pine needles and was brushing herself off by the fire and getting all the night's debris out of her hair.

"Grandma, I had the strangest dream," her granddaughter said. "We were talking with..."

"Your great grandmother," she interjected. "I know, dear. This is one of the many reasons I ask you about your dreams every morning. It is one of many vehicles a witch will use as it opens us up to greater possibilities. Sit with me, little witch. It's high time you learned the fine art of the gazing bowl. We have a witch-to-witch call to make, sweetie."

Leona pulled up a stone and sat across from her and she gave the girl some last minute instructions.

"I need you to join me in contacting Elvyra. I'll do all the talking and you just join me in the gazing. Relax your eyes and let them rest on the surface of the water in this bowl. Straighten up your spine a bit, dear. Don't slouch. Take a couple slow, deep breaths in through your nose and out slowly through your mouth. Use your tummy to draw in the breath and to help push out the breath. All you need to have on your mind is that we are calling Elvyra, and remember what she looks like. Nothing more than that."

The rain had stopped for a time and the water in the bowl smoothed to a glassy mirror. In moments, Elvyra's nervous image appeared in the bowl.

"Oh, thank the powers-that-be," Elvyra said, relief showing on her face. "You're still alive. Behir is growing larger and stronger by the minute. Your grandson is being used to call the lightning and she is channeling the power to Behir. I don't know if I can hold him in there much longer. Something has got to give."

"That's my reason for calling, sister," Emma replied. "I want you to remove the warding off the doors to the front of your house, and concentrate on keeping the back ones sealed. If something has to give, let it release him back into this world and not the others. Also, I need to know if there is any way we can access the black tower when we get there."

"The tower door has a plate that is sensitive to power objects," Elvyra said. "It is an ancient design that only an initiate can gain entrance to. When I've visited there as a child, I scribed the rune of Opening with my wand on the plate to go in. You might try the same. But, you realize, that when Behir escapes, he will return to the tower to attack you and then seek to receive new commands from his mistress. If she returns here with him, I will not be able to stop them from crossing over."

"Let us worry about that, my friend," she replied. "The valley is flooded between us and we have a plan."

"The flood will only slow him a little, my sister," Elvyra said. "I only wish your Sidhe blade was a bit bigger. My blessings to you all."

Her image faded in the bowl and the rain began to sprinkle again.

"What did she mean by that?" Leona asked. "Just how big is that thing in her house?"

"There's no telling at this point," she said. "For every bolt that Johnny calls he'll get bigger and stronger. On its own, it wouldn't be much more of a threat than a single bear or a mountain lion. Dangerous enough, to be sure, but what the Vough wants is something huge and powerful that can move back and forth among the planes and create great havoc and murder there. It will kill many and then slip away into another plane before any can find or identify him and do it again and again. Very many will die and those who can manage the craft may be incited to war in order to try and isolate themselves for protection. If the Corca-Oidce, the Children of Darkness, become emboldened by Behir's rampages, this could escalate to unheard of destruction in all the planes. We must stop him here, or there may never be another chance to catch him at his weakest."

"What do you want me to do, Grandma?" Leona asked as a look of grim determination replaced the apprehension on her face.

"Divide and conquer, my mother said," she replied. "We split up. We try to get you in to Johnny, and see if we can get a little Hansel and Gretel scenario going, while I try to take away the Vough's best weapon. But I think I'll add yet another strategy to this campaign... the Trojan Horse." She looked meaningfully across the fire at Gregory, who smiled and gave a warrior's salute with his trusty thorn in hand.

Having had their breakfast, they dressed in reasonably clean and dry clothes, broke camp and trekked westward up the trail towards the Vough's tower. Emma had taken off her mother's clan medallion and wound its chain tightly around the top of Leona's staff, fastened it in place and inscribed the Rune of Opening in its top. It was still daylight when they broke out from under the forest canopy to a clearing on the panoramic cliffside. Off to their immediate left was the eldritch black tower. As if to punctuate the introduction, a bolt of jagged ebon lightning struck a series of rods at the tower's pointed peak. Behir would benefit from that strike.

Leona bravely set off for the door of the tower as Emma watched from the shelter of the trees. Her granddaughter had traced the rune, Kano, just as she had been instructed and the door opened to her. Relieved that this part of the plan had been accomplished, she raced back down the forest trail to set a trap for Behir. The longer it took him to get there, the more time she had to prepare every kind of obstruction she could craft. For something this dire, every little bit might help.

PART TWENTY FOUR

The Trojan Horse Gambit

Determined that she would do her level best to help rescue her little cousin, Leona put on a brave face and considered what she might say as she used the tip of her staff to mark the Rune of Opening on the door plate. The walls before her looked as though they were made of polished obsidian blocks and she could see her own reflection standing there with her staff in hand. The door opened soundlessly before her.

A little surprised that it was so easy to gain entrance, she stepped inside and gawked at the large circular room. Her first sight was a series of black iron bars that came down in a ten foot circle from the upper recesses to the middle of the room in front of her. Johnny was sitting on a bench within sipping a half empty bottle of grape Nehi Soda. Something didn't look right about his eyes. They were so dark.

"Johnny," she called to him. "Are you okay, Cousin?"

But he showed no sign of having heard her as he replaced the cap on his soda and placed the bottle under his cot. Noting the strange silvery glyphs encircling his cell, she assumed it was enchanted somehow. There also didn't appear to be any kind of door to this cell. It was a series of long bars that were spaced about five inches apart the whole way around running from the floor to the unseen ceiling.

It occurred to her that she had forgotten something. She had not seen the Vough. Looking around the room, she examined tables full of bottles and beakers, shelves full of books and scrolls in an unknown script, a fireplace with a cauldron hanging on a pothook, and a panel of levers with strange markings above them. The closest lever had a glyph marked above it that resembled a cage. That had to be the release mechanism to free her cousin.

She pulled the lever all the way down and a panel opened in the wall to her right with yet another lever inside. The cell remained the same, except that Johnny looked so forlorn in there. As if in answer a cold rush entered the room from above and the cell darkened considerably. The glyphs on the floor turned jet black until they blended in with the ebon stone tiles. The tower had taken another hit and Behir would be getting stronger. She had to get her cousin out of that cell.

Reaching into the wall panel, she tried to pull the release lever, but it wouldn't budge. She tugged at it with both hands and bracing her feet against the wall and the lever started to move. From somewhere in the panel recesses a black leather strap encircled her wrists and cinched itself tight. A strong cord popped out of a wall seam and tightened, pulling her hands over her head and lifting her off of her feet by nearly a foot.

Across the room, a bookcase slid aside and a tall, pale blond woman in a long and filthy green dress stepped out from behind it.

"A human witchling," the Vough said cackling delightedly. "It's not hard to guess what you came here for. What do you want with the Sidhe brat?"

"He's only half Sidhe," she protested. "and he's my cousin. My grandma sent me to look for him."

"Well, you've found him, I'd say." The mad fae woman clapped her hands. "Not that it will do you much good. As long as the wretch calls out of himself, he calls the lightning for me to empower my Behir."

"His eyes don't look right," she said. "Please let him out. I think he might be sick."

"Sick?" The Vough shrieked with glee. "There won't be much of him left by the time your grandmother arrives to claim him. That kind of power consumes and his despair calls a lot of it down on the Sidhe devil. Why should you care? It's not like he's human, you know."

"He's human enough," Leona objected. "He's still my cousin. You let him out of there."

"Okay," the Vough said craftily. "But only for a moment. I want to show you something."

As Leona hung suspended over the floor, the fae woman hefted a stout piece of lumber with a large nail sticking out of one end. It was so strange to see those painfully elongated features wrap those long thin fingers around that beam and heft it in one hand. The woman was obviously much stronger than she looked. With the other hand she reached for the lever at the far end of the panel and pulled it halfway. Three consecutive bars raised up and out of sight on the cell and Johnny stood and looked out the opening. An uncertain smile lit his face when he recognized her. He walked to the opening as if he was not sure of what he was seeing.

"Leona?" He asked. "Is Grandma here too?"

As he took a single step out of his cell, the beam with the nail in it hit him squarely in the forehead, throwing his little body the full length of his cell into the bars and he slumped to the floor between the cot and the bench. There was blood trickling down his face, between his eyes.

Leona screamed in rage at the mad woman and kicked to try and get free of her bonds.

The Vough laughed raucously and moved the far lever back to the up position and the bars returned to their place.

"You think that was a sweet little boy?" The Vough snapped at her. "That would kill a human child, but not that little monster, no."

"You are the monster," Leona growled savagely. "And when Grandma gets here, she'll toss you off that cliff like dumping so much garbage. You crazy old bat."

She struggled to get free but the leather cinch that held her wrists together tightened and cut off the circulation in her hands.

"Now that it's seen you hanging there, child," the Vough rasped nastily, "the Sidhe devil will be all the more frantic to call for help, and the lightning will pummel my collecting rods. While he's asleep, I'll go topside and set up even more of them. My Behir will have the power of a god to wreak our vengeance on them all."

The mad woman crossed the room and vanished behind the moving bookcase. Johnny was beginning to stir in his cell. Even the Vough could not have suspected he might recover this soon. Leona couldn't let him awaken and call more lightning. Grandma had to face the creature his calls would empower. It was time to play her Trojan Horse gambit.

"Gregory, we need you now," she called over her shoulder.

In her daypack, the piskie stirred and struggled to climb out the narrow pack opening they had left for him to negotiate. As he climbed on to her shoulder, she pointed her chin at Johnny and said his name. Taking her cue, the piskie flitted between the bars easily. Leona hoped Johnny could communicate with a piskie as well as he had with pixies. He was moaning now, and the piskie stood on his chest and looked into her cousin's deep black eyes as they opened. Leona could only watch the exchange between her Sidhe cousin and the piskie.

There was certainly some kind of animated discussion taking place. Johnny staggered to his feet and picked up Gregory and held him close to his bloody forehead.

"We'll save you, Leona," he shouted as he all but danced and set the piskie down on the bench gently.

Gregory drew his thorn and brandished it as Johnny cocked his head to one side and considered his new friend. Going over to his cot, he reached under his pillow and pulled out a tiny toy sword and handed it hilt first to the little titan. Gregory tucked his pitiful thorn away and accepted the new treasure as a knight accepting a commission. Johnny pointed in the direction of where he had last seen Leona and the piskie buzzed between the bars like an angry hornet. Johnny danced a merry jig and packed his daypack as if he was preparing to leave.

Leona watched in awe as the mighty little mite sawed away at the cord that held her suspended with a sharpened steel sword. In only a moment, she fell to the floor and ran for the far lever which she was careful to only pull halfway down. Immediately, three bars slid up into the far reaches of the tower. Johnny dashed out of the cell and nearly knocked her down trying to hug her. Gregory perched on Johnny's daypack. His gleaming prize tucked into his belt.

"We've got to get out of here before the Vough gets back down here," she urged her cousin. "She's sure to see the bars have risen from up there." She pointed to the ceiling.

"I gotta get something," Johnny insisted. "It'll only take a minute." He scampered over to a shelf by the door and found a secret drawer and pulled out a polished wooden scepter with an orb in its top.

Leona had her staff and was making the Rune of Opening with its tip on the inside door plate. As the door opened, the far bookcase was beginning to move and the children dashed out into the night heading directly into the forest.

PART TWENTY FIVE

This Will Be The Death of Me

Elvyra worked frantically that day. She grabbed her wand and her obsidian knife and ran out the back door and around through the gate to the front of the house. Crossing out the Sigils of Sealing on all the doors from the porch to the rooms inhabited by Behir and scratching the Rune of Opening in their place, she dashed back to the gate leading into her backyard and the plane of Abred and sealed it from the other side with scratched sigils and rune worked strands of black ribbon. Back inside the house again, she added more runes, sigils and spells around even the doorposts and walls to keep Behir from breaching them into this plane of existence. The entire house shook with the steadily increasing force of his blows upon the doors, but all appeared to be holding for the time.

She sat quietly by the hearth, occasionally stirring her cauldron of acorn porridge, and sipping hot sassafras. She sweetened them both with a little maple syrup. Emma had told her once, that the sassafras on this hill was some of the best and richest to be found anywhere around. She had to agree. The foods and medicines around here were fine and potent, but she rarely left this hill to explore farther into the plane of Abred. There was a noisy, bustling city surrounding this wooded park, with all manner of noisome contraptions racing to and fro up its busy streets, spewing their foul, acrid exhausts in her face. She didn't like the city, but the woods were kind and fair. That was what she cherished most about Abred. Nature was ever so much more sweet and generous here.

The day wore on her. This situation would truly be the death of her, she feared. But shedding her mortal carcass would be preferred than to allow this sweet, shining space to be plunged into death and darkness. The mindless pounding continued, but the intensity was no longer increasing. Emma must have managed to retrieve her grandson somehow and stop the lightning from feeding Behir. This was a good omen. Still she doubted there was any way possible that Emma could defeat the Vough and Behir in his strengthened state. Behir's only weakness could be exploited in moonlight, but it was the rainy season and overcast. It would only be a matter of time before Emma and her grandchildren would be hunted down and killed and the magick of this fine house be used to no good purpose.

The house was the magick that gave the rift between Annwn and Abred its structure and not the other way around. Few there would be who could fathom its design. Many years ago her father had managed to crossover from this point by sheer chance, and built it with wood from both planes for her mother and her. The Vough had sent him help in building it in return for crossing rights into Abred and the adjacent planes on this hill. The last time she had seen her parents, they had been summoned to the Unseely Court and had left that day in a coach that took them down the road in front of her house. They had never returned and she never heard from them again. Try as she might, her great grandmother, the Vough would never comment on this turn of events. She only insisted that she learn the craft of the Wise Women and report to the tower known as Dun Cruachan once a month for tutelage and testing. She never trusted the crazy old fae and determined never to let her get the upper hand. This house and the growing abomination in the next room were the sum total of the Vough's obsession for revenge on ancient enemies, and it didn't matter a whit who got hurt in the process of fulfilling her mad dream. There was no way around it. The house would have to be destroyed.

She had a large shoulder bag in her closet that she used when making the long, monthly trek to Dun Cruachan. She didn't have to worry much about taking food as Emma did, because her hybrid nature could easily metabolize the foods of both worlds. Still, it may be a while, if ever, before she might again taste the sweet abundance of Abred. So, she brought a few fruits and muffins. A hammered silver headpiece and matching medallion, along with her obsidian athame and her wand were the tools she sought to bring with her. She had loaned out her water skins to Emma and Leona, so she would have to find water where she could. She pulled a can of olive oil from under her sink and went outside and covered the wooden fence and gate with rags and soaked them in oil and then returned inside to douse the walls and furniture with the rest. She was careful to set the fire in such a way that it started burning from the very back of the house and worked its way to the front. She left around the back and unsealed the gate and moved into Annwn, putting the gate to the torch as she left. It would not do to have Behir find his way through from there. As the structure began to fail, so would the magick fail that allowed it to be a portal between the two worlds.

The house was still only burning on the Abred side. Behir was not aware of his situation as of yet. She didn't want to be near when he found out and had to vacate, and he had only one way he could go. Tying up her skirts, she invoked the Spell of Swift and ran for the forest in hopes of joining up with Emma, Leona and Johnny. The little Sidhe gate master would be able to return them all to Abred... if they survived this. Still, she had to admit that they had fared a good deal better so far than she honestly expected. Emma was no adept matriarch like her mother, Ella had been, but she was a strong and competent witch. Perhaps being underestimated by her enemies really worked in her behalf. Who would believe that a human witch could pull herself out of a wine bottle, rise and defeat the likes of the Vough?

She found herself quite proud to refer to this woman as "sister." Her spell and her feelings lent wings to her feet as she flew tirelessly through the dark wooded trail towards the flood ravaged valley.

For the remainder of that evening she ran. Fae creatures do not fatigue so easily as the frailer human folk do, and she had her heritage among these here. She noted the runes carved on large stones along the trail. Daylight was gone but then fae also didn't require much light to see. Past Emma's first encampment she fled. Behir would not be too far behind her now. Her best clearing to work her Spell of Moonlight would be where the woods broke for the flooded valley. From there she had a chance of enlisting Emma's aid in fighting Behir, where he would have to slow down to negotiate the flood on his way to the eldritch tower, Dun Cruachan.

Through the shadowy depths of the dark forest she raced the coming of the monster. She stopped only a moment to counsel with She-who-waits. While the giant matriarchal arachnid could not hope to attack such as Behir, still she would do what she could to slow him down. Elvyra tore down the trail, stopping only moments for a bite to eat and drink what rainwater she could get in a cupped leaf. She could hear the trees cracking far behind her as Behir forced his way through the web tangled trail. The sound of a raging river was only a short distance ahead of her.

It was still overcast and drizzling when she reached the flooded valley. The water was more than halfway up the gorge and the current looked very strong. The tree canopy stopped a good thirty feet before the trail broke into a switchback down into what was the wetlands below. She unshouldered her bag and drew out her implements and centered herself for a ritual under the open sky.

Putting on her medallion and a silver headpiece with a large, silver crescent moon on the brow, she drew a large circle in the dirt with her obsidian knife and began the Ritual of Evocation for the Mistress Moon. She had purposely failed to learn to draw the lightning, but she had never neglected Sister Moon. Her night time brightness was the wonder of all Annwn. Raising her wand at the four quarters and then above her head, she cried out for all she was worth. Behir's rasping breath was close enough to hear even with the rushing torrent behind her.

The clouds were beginning to part, and a bare needle of moonlight had found its way into her circle. Behir, for all his ugliness, was no fool. He could not personally breach her protective circle, but that had no effect on the large tree branch wrapped in his tail as he spun back around to face the forest trail he came out from, whipping his tail about.

It effectively knocked Elvyra out of her circle and into the raging river below. With her last breath, she choked out her prayer to the skies before the waters claimed her life.

PART TWENTY SIX

Deja Vu, Sort Of

The night had fallen quickly. In a moment of panic, Emma's old eyes struggled to become accustomed to the profound darkness of the benighted woods. Was someone tracking her in the darkness? Did something just brush against her ankle? She berated herself for acting like a frightened child. She straightened up, set her shoulders back, placed her feet about shoulder's width apart, closed her eyes and breathed in the night air. Her staff stood on the trail before her in her left hand and in her right hand was her athame, with which she tapped a rhythm on the top of her staff. Breathing in through her nose, deeply of the forest air that was privy to all its secrets and expelling it out of her mouth, she blew upon the top of the staff as if to kindle a fire. Calm and purposeful, she tapped her rhythm and stirred a foxfire flame into existence on the top of her walking stick.

Opening her eyes and looking around, she could now see clearly. The night time forest revealed its dark secrets to her in a new light. The Nature of Annwn worked here as Mother Nature ruled in her own world. Nocturnal creatures came out and carried on their duties removing carrion and decay and maintaining an order and balance in the scheme of life. Creatures adapted perfectly to their environment and its particular demands lived their singular and collective existences feeding in stunning efficiency on such bounty as the Nature of this dark world provided for her own. Emma saluted the Mother of this world and continued down the trail, looking for means with which to defeat Behir.

It was nearly midnight when she came to her last campsite. The rainwater still filled the gazing bowl she had scooped out of the rock. Now would be a good time to find out where she stood as she searched the bowl for Elvyra. She had a momentary glimpse of the woman wearing a shining headpiece in the moonlight, holding a wand over her head but a tree appeared out of nowhere and swatted her off a fifty foot cliff in to a raging river. Though it looked different in the limited moonlight, it was not hard to guess what had taken place and where. She choked back a sob. She was really beginning to like the darkling witch. It seemed they had so much in common to share. Her tears dropped into the gazing bowl and another vague image appeared of a huge, dark, serpentine figure fighting its way in the faint moonlight across the swift current to her side of the woods.

Behir was coming.

Realization jolted her and roused her like a splash of icy water. She pulled herself out of her grief and looked about for some kind of trap she might lay for the monster. She had no rope to make a snare, nor any means to dig a pit, so she settled for sharpening wooden stakes and bracing them in along the trail and its sides. Any tree branch along the trail that pointed in the direction of the flooded valley was sharpened to a finely barbed point. Moving farther back along the trail, she found a decent ambush point where a large, cool, stone outcropping would block her from the creature's fae sight. She wasn't sure how tough its hide was, but she could probably stuff a barbed spear or two in his eyes.

Using her witch blade, she cut and sharpened a twelve foot sapling into a formidable lance. As a decoy, she propped her staff a few feet past her hiding spot on the opposite side of the trail. Its glow would draw Behir's attention, and still give her light to see by. When he came close enough, she could pounce on him with her makeshift lance and drive it into his eye. It wasn't the best sort of plan but it was her only hope.

She climbed into the cleft of a large rocky outcropping along the left side of the trail. Both hands gripped her lance in a white knuckled, death grip as she peered down the trail through a small gap between the rocks. The illumination from her staff lit the trail for a good distance in either direction. The sound of wood snapping and a voice roaring in pain that sounded like a cougar screaming from within a large empty box gave its testimony that Behir was on the trail near her campsite and the sharpened stakes had had some effect on him. It seemed like endless minutes of waiting as he seemed to hit nearly every barb on his way up the trail before he came into sight.

What an ugly sight indeed. At first appearance, he appeared to be a six foot tall, scaly black human head, with round black eyes larger than pie plates. From within the depths of those awful orbs came a dull red glow. His mouth was a grimacing gash that cut across the full width of his face. As his hide took another barbed branch, he opened his mouth wider than his body to reveal row upon row of sharp teeth in a cavernous maw that tapered nearly forty feet behind him, as near as she could tell from her perch. He roared out his rage and bit down on the offending branch and tore it out of his hide and spat out the point into the darkened woods off the trail. Then when he caught sight of her staff along the trail ahead, a crafty smile twisted his features as he advanced towards the prize.

Emma leapt out of her stone perch, driving her lance about two feet into Behir's right eye. She held on tightly, trying to use her weight to drive it deeper into the creature's foul head. He raised up his head, about twenty feet into the branches above the trail, taking her with him and trying for all his might to dislodge the spear and the vengeful witch on the end of it. She held on as long as she could, but this wood was not capable of holding the weight a good stout oak of her world might. The pole snapped in her hands and she crashed through the branches to the trail below. It took her a moment to recover her breath after hitting the hard packed clay forest floor. She was fortunate that Behir was currently occupied with his own pain right now, but certainly not for long.

She scrambled to her feet, grabbed her staff and ran up the trail for the tower. The monster had ceased his thrashing and came in pursuit with a vengeance. Branches whipped at her face and her skirt and slip clung to her legs as they pumped like pistons to carry her from danger. As the creature closed on her, his fetid breath bore on her back. Rounding the next bend in the trail, she wheeled around and drove the glowing tip of her staff in the wounded eye socket. She didn't stick around to hold on to it this time. She took off through the darkness for the trail's end.

Her heart pounding fiercely in her breast, lungs heaving like bellows and her legs pumping away to a mad rhythm. A familiar weight slapped on her thigh as she caught sight of a moonlit clearing ahead at the trail's end.

Bursting out from the trees and underbrush into the clean light of the full moon, she came skidding to a halt. The ground dropped away into a yawning precipice and the dark tower was off to her left. Her heart hammered its exertion in her breast and the sweet metallic taste of adrenalin coated her mouth as she drew her witch blade and turned to face the horror that was hot on her heels through those haunted woods. The moonlight gleamed along the length of its rune carved blade like a living thing and extended itself into the gaping maw that crashed through the brush to occupy her clearing.

Behir writhed in hideous agony as arcs of silvery white light danced along his scaly torso. He looked as if he was trying to beat himself senseless as he thrashed about the clearing at the cliff's edge and finally hurled himself over it. His rasping scream echoed until it faded into the distance to be heard no more.

Emma fell to her knees in exhaustion in the clearing, and looked up at the moon.

"You know something, sister?" She panted. "You are every bit as beautiful here as you are in my home world."

"I've always thought so too," said an achingly familiar voice to her right.

The image of Elvyra looked to be made entirely of moonbeams. She was still wearing her silver headpiece and medallion that shined like liquid starlight.

"I'm sorry, sister," Emma said, still gasping heavily. "I'm sorry this has cost you so much. I was hoping we'd get to be better friends someday."

"What I paid, I get back threefold," the specter said as she slowly vanished in the moonlight. "And we were always the best of friends. Look after my woods."

The words hung in the air a moment longer as Emma prayed for the strength to finish the job, collect her grandchildren and go home. She dragged herself to her feet. Her staff lay, still glowing, on the ground near the forest trail where the monster had dislodged it from his eye when he had thrashed about. She collected her walking stick and walked stiffly to the tower door. There was the raised plate that Elvyra had told her about and she traced the Rune of Opening on it with her witch blade. The door opened on a room full of arcane devices, but empty of people.

PART TWENTY SEVEN

A Night Of Darkling Heroes

As Leona and Johnny bolted out the door of the black tower, she plunged into the night fallen woods as quickly as she could, in her haste to get any kind of distance or obstacles between them and the Vough. The trail was nearly a hundred yards off to her left, but she thought it best to get out of sight quickly. From the cover of the trees, they watched for a moment to see if the Vough would chase them. It wasn't long before the elongated hag stepped out the door and shrieked her imprecations into the night.

"You think you can violate my home?" She screeched. "You snub my hospitality and steal my orb like the foul fiends your kind has always been. Curse you, wicked witchling brat and Sidhe devil. Curse you all." She shook her fist and ducked back into the tower door.

Leona released her breath she had been holding. Figuring the Vough might likely be along after them later, she would simply have to move through the woods parallel to the trail as opposed to being found easily on it. The forest was nearly black as pitch, and she couldn't negotiate the darkness quite as easily as her little cousin could. The orb in the scepter he carried glowed a dull orange but it was hardly real light to see by. She barely discerned the pisky perched on Johnny's right shoulder in the dim glow.

"Johnny, I can't see in this darkness," she said. "You're going to have to lead the way through the woods and take us to Grandma. She'll be somewhere in that direction and the trail will be over that way," she said, indicating to her left. "But I don't want to get too close until we're sure the Vough or her monster aren't looking for us there."

"Okay," Johnny said. "It's pretty rocky over this way, so we'll have to be careful. I can feel Grandma a long ways that way." He gestured in the direction Leona had originally told him to go.

For all of their intentions of stealth, they rustled branches, snapped twigs and stumbled over stones and logs picking their way through the darkness. This worked somewhat to their advantage as more than one or two forest denizens utilized the advance warning of their approach to leave the area. What doubts or fears she might have, Leona projected them outwards into the dark, and the dark "scratched its itch" and left her alone.

The night was wearing on and her legs were beginning to cramp from exhaustion. They stopped to rest for a while and shared the rest of Johnny's grape Nehi and some sweet pears as they sat on a log and talked quietly.

"Grandma went back to fight a monster?" Johnny asked incredulously.

"Well, Elvyra is helping us where she can," she said. "She helped us pack and told us how to find you. She's a little snippish, but she's not such a bad lady as I first thought."

"Grandma was alone when I felt her," Johnny said. "What happened to Auntie Vy?"

"She probably couldn't make it across the flooded part," she said. "The swamp flooded while we were crossing it and nothing can get through."

"Then the monster can't get to us either," Johnny said relieved. "Grandma will be okay then."

"You don't think Grandma can kill a monster because she's not a boy," she accused him.

"Leona," Johnny explained, "she is only a grandma with a nice knife, she's not a hero in shining armor with a great sword. Grandpa would have a fit if he knew about this."

"Grandpa Willard is probably worried sick about us being gone so long," she said.

"I hope he's not thinking that we don't love him anymore," Johnny said. "You can't just get a grandpa like him just anywhere. Grandma says he's one inna million."

In the distance, the snap of large branches breaking gave them pause. Through the trees a bright blue light was moving through the forest in the direction of the tower. The sound of something huge followed close behind the light, moving swiftly. Occasionally it would slow and scream like a large cat and resume its chase.

"The monster?" Johnny whispered.

"I think so," she replied. "I wonder where Grandma is, if he made it across the flood."

Johnny was quiet for a minute and said, "That way." He pointed in the direction the blue light had gone.

Leona mused for a moment as the ruckus escalated on the distant trail. For a little boy who had just been knocked ten feet into an iron wall with a timber beam and a nail driven into the front of his head, he seemed a little bruised and bloody, but otherwise just fine. Just like Gregory who had been in rough condition when her and Grandma found him tangled in the giant spider web, but he was okay shortly after. Johnny's 'fae-dar' seemed to be intact as well. All he had to do was want his grandma and he knew instinctively just where he had to go. In the faery tales she had read and heard from her mother, the fae would live extraordinarily long lives, nearly immortal, but they could be killed in battle but live on afterwards in a disembodied form. From watching her cousin and their interactions, she surmised that if they weren't killed outright in such a battle, that they were capable of healing at a fairly rapid rate. How old might Johnny live if something didn't kill him first?

"Grandma is fighting the monster," Johnny broke into her reverie.

"Is she okay?" She asked. "Is she winning?"

"I think she got hurt a little," he said. "But I hope I never make her as mad as she is at that monster. She didn't win, but she sure hurt 'im alot. She's running away now. Towards the tower. We got to go back to the Vough's house. Oh, oh." He finished as the sound of angry buzzing wings approached.

The orb in the scepter Johnny carried, began glowing brightly as if in answer to something in the air. Gregory drew his fighting thorn in his left hand and his new steel sword in his right and crouched on Johnny's shoulder. His sharp little fangs bared in a fierce smile that burned in his eyes.

"How'd you light that thing?" She asked.

"I didn't," he replied, glaring with his strange black eyes into the darkness beyond.

"But I did," the Vough said as she stepped into the light of the orb. She was holding a wicked looking staff with what looked to be teeth and claws sticking out around the top of it.

Numerous piskies, armed with thorns and spears surrounded them on all sides. Gregory crouched as if ready to spring, his tiny wings flexed upwards and ready for a strong downbeat. Johnny glared darkly at the Vough, so intensely that Leona even wanted to be somewhere far away from him. The Vough flinched back for a moment and cried for the piskies to attack.

"Strip the flesh off their bones," the mad fae screamed.

Several of the piskies shook off the wall of fear that Johnny was generating and buzzed in at them with weapons drawn. Gregory leapt at the closest assailant, and twisting at the last instant, avoided the spear thrust. He then whirled around to take off the piskie's head in a backhand strike with his shining sword. Seeing this strange new development, the piskies paused a moment in their attack, seeming uncertain who they feared most, the Vough or Johnny and their outcast cousin.

Leona took the moment's initiative to swing her staff with Grandma's medallion still fastened to its top in a broad swing at the fierce piskie tribe. Most had dodged easily out of its path, but the one it caught off guard, exploded in a shower of blue sparks.

"I want them dead or I will feed your families to the spiders," the Vough shrieked and advanced on them with her wicked staff at the ready.

Johnny, still glaring with one leg propped up on the log, held the glowing scepter in his tiny grip like a baseball bat. His teeth bared in a fierce grimace. Leona had never really noticed before, but her cousin had canines slightly longer than his other baby teeth. She didn't get to look for long as he sprang off the log into the advancing Vough.

Wielding the scepter as a club, he struck down the hag's staff in a blast of green sparks and caught her on the collarbone as he twisted around in midair. The Vough dropped her staff and fell backwards over a stone sprawling in the forest debris. Little Johnny came down on his feet and stood his ground with the glowing scepter cocked for another swing. The dark grin on her cousin's face was not an expression Leona had ever associated with the sweet, blue eyed boy.

A sharp, burning pain shot through her left arm as an attacking piskie stabbed her with his fighting thorn. She wheeled and swung at it with her staff but he dodged her easily and stuck out his tongue at her. The expression melted away almost comically as its head was split by a tiny sword from behind. Gregory smiled his fierce smile and flipped his blade in a cavalier salute and rejoined the fray against his marauding cousins. Not quite the faery prince a young girl could hope for, she couldn't help but admire his panache.

The Vough regained her feet and took up her weapon and stepped back a few paces and raised her staff to the heavens.

"I'll call upon the Dark Power of Annwn to come hither and destroy you Sidhe interlopers," the hag threatened.

Johnny stood his ground calmly with the wand hanging loosely in his hand, never taking those darkened eyes off the mad fae witch, and in a voice that sounded more like a rumble of distant thunder than the voice of a five year old boy he spoke.

"No. You won't."

Punctuating his sentence, the darkness of the night time woods went black on black. A blistering rush of searing frigid air blasted them and the remaining piskies to the ground as the tree branches overhead and the Vough shattered like glass as the ebon lightning crashed through the canopy.

All was black and cold. The sobbing of a broken hearted little boy, somewhere in the darkness, was all that could be heard. The world was still, in expectation of what would come next.

PART TWENTY EIGHT

Moon Dancing And Goodbyes

Lighting her way with her staff as she left the tower, Emma surmised that neither the children or the Vough had come down the forest trail she had traveled. She left in hurry, the monster now dead. It was likely that Leona had taken the quickest route for cover. She walked the straightest line to the woods edge and her suspicions were confirmed by the trampled underbrush that led into the forest interior. The children would likely be as easily tracked by the Vough and whatever minions she might have. Worried, she hastened her pace, being careful not to lose sight of their tracks. She didn't see any traces of the Vough passing this way, but she didn't expect she would. Any witch who lived here long, would know the land intimately.

Ahead in the distance, the sounds of a sobbing child chilled her blood. Had the Vough found the children? She picked up her pace as well as she could in the thick forest and uneven terrain and followed her ears. Whatever evil the Vough had unleashed, Emma was resolved to be her undoing and picked her way gingerly and quickly through the dark woods. No other sounds could be heard, but several hundred yards ahead a moonlit clearing appeared. Her eyes already adjusted to the dim light around, she approached with less caution. The shuddering sobs of her grandson caught her attention. The boy knelt in the dirt next to her granddaughter. Leona blinked up at her a moment and promptly fainted. Littered around the children were the bodies of mutilated piskies, some missing wings, limbs or heads. One lay sprawled on top of another that had a tiny steel sword piercing its chest. The one on top could be none other than Gregory the Peck as it stirred and looked up at her and smiled through the gore caked on his face.

Planting her staff in the soft forest loam, she examined her granddaughter. She was cold to the immediate touch, but an underlying warmth was spreading quickly to her limbs. It was likely she had the breath knocked out of her when the lightning struck nearby. A pink streak showed above her collar on her left side and a closer look shown that Leona had been pierced by one of those fighting thorns and the wound was either poisoned or infected. Emma cleaned the wound with some linen dabbed with a little witch hazel that she had scavenged from the vacated tower and bound it lightly to keep it clean. There was hardly any bruising and it didn't appear to be bleeding much. Her mother's clan medallion was still fastened tightly to Leona's walking stick. She removed it and clasped it back around her neck.

All this time, Johnny never stopped his sobbing, though he was clearly trying to control it, but he never looked up at her. Pulling out some more wadded linen and a little splash of witch hazel. She gently cupped his chin and drew him to look up at her while she daubed at the blood and filth on his face and forehead. Watery, red rimmed, blue eyes looked up at her forlornly.

"I'm so sorry, Grandma," he sobbed. "I was such a very bad boy and I got us in all this trouble. Please don't leave me here. Leona can have my room and I'll stay upstairs and be such a good boy. I promise. Witches' honor." He held his two grubby fingers under his eyes to confirm his words.

"I know my boy is sorry," she said, hugging him. "But I think the trouble was looking for you, and not the other way around, Son. And I fixed your room for you, and Leona's room for her. Why would either of you want the other's room?"

"I like my room," Leona said groggily, trying to sit up. "I really wish I was in it now."

Johnny reached over and hugged his cousin.

"Hey, your eyes," Leona exclaimed. "They're blue again."

"Of course, they are, dear," Emma said, puzzled. "What color were they before now?"

"Oh, Grandma," Leona said in a rambling rush. "They were as black as the lightning here. No white. No blue, just deep dark blackness. It was so scary, all the things that happened. And that nasty old Vough hit him in the head with a huge board and I thought she killed him, and he got up and gave Gregory a sword and we got away and she chased us and... and did you really kill that monster with just a knife?" She asked, looking perplexed.

"My kids are back to me." Emma laughed. "I had some help from some special sisters in killing Behir. He's probably still falling down that abyss right now. Did you kids really take on the Vough and her minions all by yourselves, with those sticks?"

"Well, my stick was magick," Leona replied. "'Cause it had your magick medallion attached to it. Evil faeries exploded into sparks and secret doors would open for me. And Johnny stole the Vough's wand-thing and it lit up the whole place and he smacked her staff right out of her hand and Gregory had a magick sword and he was such a hero and he rescued me a couple times with it and helped fight off the minions. He's the mightiest piskie of them all and Johnny called the black lightning and the whole world exploded and... and then you came and got us. We didn't all die or anything, did we?"

"No, little witch," she said. "We're all very much alive. Though I'm afraid not everybody made it through." She shook her head sadly.

"Auntie Vy?" Johnny asked, holding her close.

"Behir hit her with a tree and threw her into the river," she said sadly. "She couldn't save herself and I was too far away."

"But you said some special sisters helped you tonight," Leona puzzled. "If Elvyra was dead, how'd she help you? Or was there others?"

"Both, sweetie," she said. "I couldn't have beaten Behir without Sister Elvyra and Sister Moon and this wonderful knife our fae friends gave me." She patted her sheathed witch blade under her apron.

"I got an awful lot to learn from you, Grandma," Leona said wonderingly.

"So, you'll be coming back every summer to learn?" She asked. "You know I can't possibly teach it all to you before September."

"Can I?" Leona asked with a grin. "And I want my own, upstairs room," she insisted, glaring playfully at her cousin.

Johnny was on his feet, dancing his little dance in the moonlit clearing and shaking his little fanny to a music only he could hear. The ladies laughed at his antics as he howled his joy to the moon.

"And I get to keep my rooo-OOOOOOMMMM!"

"Hey. Easy, does it, my little wolf boy," Emma said. "We still have to find a way home. There's a terrible flood between us and Elvyra's house and it could be days before we can find a place to cross it. And if you keep making all that racket, who knows what else might find us out here?"

"Ooooh, not good," he said sheepishly and sat down beside her.

"Elvyra, that is, Auntie Vy,—" Leona corrected herself.— "said that Johnny was a little gate master. He got us in to see faeries before. Why can't he take us back?"

"I think there's a matter of where, and when he does that," she said, looking thoughtfully at her grandson. "Do you think you can find a place for us to either crossover into our world or the Sidhe world, Son?"

Johnny closed his eyes a moment as if he was deep in thought, opened them suddenly and pointed in the direction of the trail.

"That way," he said, "in a little while from now."

"You probably mean just before the dawn," she said.

Johnny nodded.

"Let's get to it, kids," she said, getting to her feet. "Your grandfather is waiting and probably worried sick about us. None of this is going to be easy to explain to him or anybody else."

Staves, wands and daypacks were retrieved as they all set off for the trail by the light of Emma's staff. Gregory sat perched on Johnny's pack and was washing himself off with a wet piece of linen that she gave him. She spoke to the piskie and was sure to visualized the things she was saying to him in her mind.

"You take as good a care of yourself," she admonished said. "as you took good care of my family. I send my brightest blessings to you and yours for your help. That sword of yours, keep it oiled well, rust free and razor sharp and it will take good care of you too. We're going to leave you the rest of the fruit and nuts before we leave, and if you're as wise as I think you are, you'll see that the seeds find some good ground to rest in and you'll never lack for their blessings when they mature." She pictured the pear tree sprouting flowers and then fruit.

Gregory nodded and carefully cleaned the blood off his sword blade with a piece of linen and then wrapped the blade in a piece and tucked it into his belt. As they made the trail, Johnny turned off to the right, in the direction of the gazing bowl camp. Somehow, Emma was not surprised.

Arriving at the campsite, Emma instructed the children to leave the treats for Gregory, on the rock slab with the gazing bowl scooped out of it. The piskie was splashing about in the bowl, getting all the blood out of his hair and fur tunic, his precious sword and other treasures heaped around him on the slab. Emma gave him a clean, dry piece of linen with which he toweled off and covered himself as he draped his wet furs over the stone edge to drip dry. In the makeshift, white linen toga, he looked like a dusky, little, sparrow winged angel standing there on the rock and watching them.

"Good bye, sweet prince," Leona said, blowing him a kiss, and he swept her a deep courtier's bow.

Little Johnny left the Vough's staff and wand in the makeshift shelter and faced Gregory. The boy made a fist and held it to his heart and then stretched out his hand, palm upwards to the piskie. Gregory, in turn, reached out his hand, palm downward and made a grasping motion and held it to his heart and they both bowed slightly to each other.

"I'll never forget how you repaid me," she said to the piskie, carefully visualizing her thoughts. "That was high honor if ever I saw it in a full sized man. No silly 'Gregory the Peck' for you, sirrah. I dub thee: Sir Gregory of the Shining Sword. A true hero." She pronounced as she touched each of his shoulders lightly with his own tiny sword.

"I knew it," Johnny said proudly.

Leona clapped her hands and the piskie bowed himself deeply to them all. With all the Sidhe that crossover near her home, Emma was sure he would be happier and safer here in his own world. Still, she would miss the mighty little mite.

The overcast was breaking up in parts, and the beginning of the sun's light was beginning to make itself known. The twilight before the dawn was upon them and little Johnny threw his head back, held out his arms and turned clockwise. No fireflies came out to cover him and fly away but a mist rose up from the ground and when it faded, they found themselves standing by the garden gate in her back yard.

Startled out of a half-sleep, Willard fell off the bench and picked himself up to his knees and hugged the kids as they rushed up to him.

"Oh, I was so worried about you," he said with teary eyes. "I didn't know what happened to you. I waited out here all night."

Emma set aside her now inert staff and came forward. He stood to embrace and she kissed him dearly.

"It couldn't be helped, dear," she apologized. "But the nightmares that plagued our house, won't be returning again."

"I'll fix us all breakfast," he said. "You all look awful, like you've been fighting in the trenches all last night. Why doesn't everybody go inside and clean up. I'll rustle us up some grub for my little cowpokes, and you can tell me all about your adventure. I'm sure it'll be a doozey."

It couldn't be stopped. Nor would she if she could, but she laughed to see it happen. Little Johnny did his dance into the door of her summer kitchen. Turning to her, Leona shrugged her shoulders and rolled her eyes and danced inside behind him.

"You'd think they haven't been home in days," Willard remarked and Emma looked at him oddly.

PART TWENTY NINE

Happy Birthday, Baby

Emma sat reading in the waiting room of the doctor's office. She had cleaned Leona's wound out as well as she could and still couldn't determine if the streaking was caused by poison or infection. Gods knew what else might have been stabbed with those nasty thorns and a good spectrum of antibiotics might be what she needed to beat the infection and keep it from becoming worse. Dr. Julius had been a family friend and physician for a long time, so she wasn't taking any chances with her granddaughter's health.

Johnny sat quietly by her side, and drew circles in his notebook every time the receptionist would reach up and scratch the side of her nose or chin. The wound on his forehead was fading fast and healing well. He'd had his tetanus shot only a couple months ago when he had stepped on a nail in the back yard. His only manifestation of the recent otherworldly adventure was a tiny scar in the middle of his high forehead and an intensity about staying close and trying to please his family. For all he had been through, he seemed very well adjusted. After what she pieced together from the two children, maybe too well.

He was like the cute little unicorn foal she had dreamed of. Cute, sweet, playful and eager to please. But Brother George had the measure of him when he took off his weapons and armor and approached the foal with the utmost respect. That little creature was a good deal more than just a horse with a horn. Everyday with him, she learned a little more about that fact. Where Johnny's differences tended to make most others uncomfortable in his presence, she loved him all the more.

Unlike her daughters, who tended to treat him like a poisonous reptile at times, Leona had demonstrated her extraordinary character in the way she had shown her love for her strange little cousin. What opportunities will be open to this newest generation? Things hadn't happened exactly like her mother had planned, but maybe they were even better. No doubt, she would've been so proud of them all.

Willard, the remarkable old carpenter, had listened to all their stories at the breakfast table when they had returned that morning. In places, he sat back, white faced with horror at what he had heard. He was outraged that anyone would be so cruel to his new family. He could hardly restrain himself from cursing at the Vough's wicked cunning. The fact that the family had been gone for many days and not for just the single day that passed here was no big surprise to him. He told the children tales of people going into fairy land for just an afternoon or an evening and coming back months or years later to find all had changed. He couldn't stop himself from hugging them all, he was so proud. He plopped Johnny's cowboy hat on his head and bounced him on his knee until the little lad was likely to develop saddle sores. Everyone had slept most of that day and Willard had waited on them hand and foot.

When Leona walked out of the examination room only a little worse for the wear, Emma looked up. Dr. Julius insisted upon at least one shot, and a prescription for some pills he wanted her to use up in the next few days. She even managed to obtain an extra sucker for her little cousin from the receptionist. Emma was relieved to hear that everything was alright and that her granddaughter would be going home in a couple weeks time, in the same good health she had arrived in and perhaps a little wiser.

As they were leaving, she could not help but notice a rather hefty, old dowager who was trying to discreetly scratch the devil out of her backside.

"Johnny, stop that," she scolded him quietly. "That's not very nice."

"Not me, Grandma," he insisted. "Hammer-hoids."

Emma put her hand over her mouth to stifle a laugh and ushered the children quickly out of the doctor's office to the street.

Walking down the street about a block, they turned left on North Street and went shopping downtown. She had to pick up a some school clothes for Johnny and thought the soda fountain at Neisner's would be a nice treat for the children. His sixth birthday was a week away, and if his cousin and Skip, the soda jerk, could keep him occupied for a short while, she had intentions of picking up a couple things he wouldn't notice in all the sacks they carried.

She scurried through the store and got him a birthday card with cowboys on it, and a Roy Rogers gun and holster set. Paying quickly at a cashiers desk, out of sight of the soda fountain, she slipped back up to the counter with the kids. Palming three dollars to Leona, she gave her the directions to the ladies room along with a conspiratory wink and her granddaughter did some quick shopping of her own.

They had a splendid afternoon together. Shopping done with Johnny none the wiser, they caught a city bus and got off down the block from her home. Willard had gotten something and was busting at the seams to show her what it was. He had splurged and bought Johnny a Handy Andy Tool Kit complete with a wooden tool box. It had a selection of real, metal, child sized tools. A claw hammer, a ball peen hammer, a saw, pliers, crescent wrenches, t-square, level, tape measure, screwdrivers and the works. Remembering Johnny's craftiness making the little piskie broadsword with a nail and a rock, she gave her approval. This might be his best gift yet. She could imagine the projects Willard and his grandson would begin in the back section of the yard where Johnny had his fort and Willard kept his saw horses. This would also open up some ladies time for her and Leona. This man just had a knack for doing things that complemented her efforts.

***

Johnny was not only surprised by his party, he was shocked that it was his birthday. He had absolutely no notion of time passing. He was overwhelmed at the attention he got. He didn't seem to know if he should cry or do his little dance. She had to assure him that this wasn't the kind of party where he got told someone would be leaving him, but reminded him that Leona was only here for the summer and would leave in a couple weeks to return again next summer. The backyard was filled with balloons, and tables set with punch, soda pop, cake and treats of all sorts.

Geraldine had brought her hoard of children and grandchildren, and they brought a record player and a stack of 45 rpm records. The older girls taught Johnny all the latest dances and he entertained them in return by mimicking their favorite artists. Leona had never met Negro children before and was a little taken aback at first. But the enthusiasm the Smith children brought with them was so infectious that by the second song, Leona was unabashedly in the thick of it all.

Emma, Willard, Geraldine, her daughter Essie and old Ian, all sat in the shade of the pear tree and kept cool with lemonade and paper fans.

"I used to cut quite a rug in my day," Ian remarked to the children's dancing.

"I'll just bet you did," Geraldine said. "But tell me. If the mens in your country wear dresses like that, whats the womens wear?"

"Why, they wear longer dresses, of course," Ian said with mock indignation and they all laughed.

Emma called everybody forward to the tables and she opened Johnny's cards and read them to him. Old Ian's card held a hefty silver dollar, which was downright extravagant for the frugal Scotsman. To Johnny, this was a treasure piece like the "pieces of eight" or a gold doubloon to be stored in his personal treasure crock. He hugged the stoic, elderly Scot with his usual, unbridled affection. Was that a tear at the corner of those wizened blue eyes?

Leona's gift consisted of a composition book for his craft notes, his name written in runes on the cover. As he went to hug her, she discreetly made their "witches honor" sign so he knew what kind of notes went in there. Included in the box were a coloring book, some colored pencils and a box of crayons.

"What kind of writing is this?" Geraldine asked, examining his notebook.

Ian squinted at Johnny's notebook a moment and then his eyes widened in recognition.

"I've not seen the likes of these since I was a wee lad back in the Orkneys," he said. "These are called runes, the ancient writing of the Celtic people. How does such a bonnie lass come by the knowledge of these?"

"I'm learning our ancient history in private school, Uncle Scotty," Leona said proudly.

"Ye do us well, lass," Ian said with a smile. "It must be a fine school, indeed. I had thought that such things would become lost to time before my days ended. Which won't be anytime too soon as dying is far too expensive these days."

"If you wait another fifty years," Essie said with a laugh, "you can probably take advantage of a turn of the century grave clearance and get yourself a real bargain."

"Aye, lass." Ian winked. "Now that would be worth waiting for. I guess I'll get comfortable as I will be here a while."

Johnny was thrilled with his gun and holster set. Willard went inside and grabbed Johnny's cowboy hat and put it on him as he buckled on his gun belt and tied down his holster like a wild, west gunslinger. His little fingers were too small to properly twirl his cap guns, but his hands were lightning fast as he snatched both guns before they could hit the ground when they flew out of his grip trying to twirl them. The crowd "ooohed" appreciatively as he holstered his guns and tucked his thumbs in his belt proudly for pictures.

The finishing touch to the presents was Willard's tool set. The boy's eyes lit up and a million potential projects seemed to cross his mind in the moments he examined these.

"Take care of those, boyo," Willard said, "and tomorrow I'll show you how to use them out in our work area." He nodded past the back hedge row.

There was a little reluctance to not start a project right now, but the rock and roll was playing and a small sea of happy brown faces were moving to its rhythm and little Johnny's pagan soul just had to dance its joy of living to the cosmos.

Somehow, in all this modern rock and roll, a mix of a particularly heathen drumbeat was playing and the six year old imp began leaping and whirling in a circle as the other children watched and then joined in. Stepping along the circle with the rhythm, they stomped their feet, shook their shoulders, wiggled their fannies and resumed the circle dance. None of the children were watching Johnny now, but all of them were caught up in the dance as if they had done it all their lives.

"Where do you suppose he learned a thing like that?" Willard asked.

"Why, all the kids are doing it these days," she replied and hugged him.

PART THIRTY

Ouch.

The third weekend in August came all too soon. Along with it came Evelyn and Ralph, who came for Leona. They had a long drive back to Cleveland and plenty of back-to-school shopping of their own to catch up on. Evelyn was thrilled to tell Emma how well things were going with her marriage these days and thanked her for her sage advice. She didn't really credit herself for Evelyn's epiphany at the start of summer. Her daughter had wanted to talk to her about marital problems, and as she discussed the relevance of the Threefold Law on an entirely different issue, the proverbial light bulb came on. It was delightful to see her daughter and Ralph acting like teenaged sweethearts again.

Without hearing the whole story, at Leona's request, Evelyn conveyed her pleasure with her daughter's progress over the summer. It seems her daughter had been entertaining the notion that Leona might become the clan's next matriarch in the years to come.

"Leona isn't adept as Johnny," Emma told her daughter.

"Perhaps, but certainly there is no way he will be allowed to hold any position of power within the family. Leona, however, might just grow up to become quite the witch in her own right and likely the best choice for a future matriarch," Evelyn declared.

"We will just have to wait and see," Emma replied evasively.

It was hard to say goodbye for the school year, and Johnny was more than a little sad to see his cousin go. His Uncle Ralph shook his hand. His Aunt Evy patted his head and Leona hugged him fiercely, bussed him on the forehead and made him promise to keep some of her things for her until she returned next summer. He was trying hard not to cry, but he managed to hold two fingers below his eyes and nod a yes.

"We are witches of the blood," she whispered to him, and he stood erect and proud as her father's car pulled away from the house.

***

The school year began and Johnny was excited about his second year at Public School #14. He did well in his studies and Emma copied out his report cards to send to Lorry. She was due to have her second child some time in February and wrote regularly and was always sure to include a special letter for Johnny. He, in turn, would send his letter to his mother back with hers. A heavily edited version of the summer vacation was included in her letters to California.

By Christmas time, the letters Emma dreaded most to see, had arrived. Lorry and Dave were doing fine and had just moved into their own house in Riverside. The area was experiencing an economic boom and houses were popping up everywhere like weeds. The new house was a ranch style, with an attached garage and had three bedrooms. One was being set up as a nursery for the new baby, and the extra one was going to be Johnny's. They would be sending for him after the school year. Emma, Willard and Johnny would take two weeks at the end of June to take a Greyhound Bus and visit. At the end of that visit, Emma and Willard would return back alone. She would have Leona to herself for the summer, but after that, she didn't like to think about how empty the house would be.

On February 18th, Johnny's seven pound baby sister, Linda, was born, every bit as pretty as their mother. He was thrilled to hear the news and excited to be going to see them after school let out. He still wasn't fully aware that she and Willard wouldn't be staying long with him there. She had the house here and deep roots in this part of the country. She couldn't just up and sell everything and move out west. Maybe Lorry could be persuaded to send him to visit during the summer months to foster. The boy was undoubtedly going to need those peculiar disciplines that Lorry didn't have. Lorry didn't even like discussing the craft with her or her own sisters. If anything, Lorry wanted to forget anything that brought what happened with Lee to mind. It was understandable, but though Johnny looked like Lorry and not at all like Lee, he was a constant reminder that the human race was not the top of the food chain they liked to think they were. How was Lorry going to cope with that?

Johnny was half human, but all witch, and he would need a master witch to train him. Hollywood had some silly notions about such things. They would have to find a way to work this out for the boy's own good. Willard had tried to console her that Johnny would be happier with his own mother in the long run, but he didn't fully understand. Lorry had very little experience with someone like Johnny, and none of it good, and Dave had none at all. It would have been different had they stayed close so she could help them cope and understand. She tried to convince herself that she was just experiencing a little difficulty in cutting the proverbial apron strings, but she just couldn't picture circumstances working out for him as they stood.

She had to wonder what kind of strain Johnny might represent to Lorry and Dave's marriage. True, Dave went into the marriage without any misgivings about a ready-made family. But Dave came from a completely different culture. All he saw was a fatherless little boy. She had had a good idea of what to expect from Johnny, and what she had learned raising him, surprised and surpassed her wildest dreams. As he got older, his life and his problems would become far more complicated. Who would there be? Who would not fear him, but love him and help him understand himself?

Yes, she loved him and didn't want to let him go. But nobody understood as well as she why it wouldn't work. She had to allow them to learn from their own mistakes and leave her door open to receive him back and help repair any damage.

It was like trying to hold still for something she knew was going to hurt. She prepared herself for it, quietly.

***

The bags were all packed to go to the bus terminal. Old Ian had promised to stop by the house regularly for the mail and to check on things. Johnny was excited at the prospect of a new adventure traveling across the entire country. Emma took a moment to make an impression on him.

There had long been a bardic discipline in the craft, a technique of vocal inflection that had an almost hypnotic quality to those who heard it. The voice was pitched low, so that listeners had to strain to hear it, and so unusual that it stuck in their memory whether they fully understood what was meant or not. It could happen that many years down the line, the listeners would experience something that correlated with this audio post-it note attached to their memory. The light of recognition came on and the message served its purpose. Emma knelt beside her grandson and pitched her voice low and sibilant to accomplish this very task.

"Do you know who's room this is?" She said, indicating his bedroom.

"It's, it's mine. Isn't it?" Johnny asked, looking puzzled.

"Do you see where it is now?" She asked.

"Yes," he replied. "It's right here." He spread his arms wide to indicate the house.

"Don't you sleep here?" She asked.

"All the time," he said. "That's my bed, there." He pointed.

"Then, of course, you understand that your room will always be right here," she said. "And no matter where you are, when you are tired and you want to rest, you will always have your room, right here, with us."

"Always?" He asked, looking into her eyes uncertainly.

"Witches' honor," she replied, making their sign.

Satisfied that her grandson would always have this knowledge, they left the house and began the four day bus ride to California. Two round trip tickets for her and Willard and a child's one way ticket for Johnny.

PART THIRTY ONE

The Dreams of Sunny California

The trip was as close to uneventful as Emma could expect. A hyperactive Johnny, who had tried to take in every mile of America he could, by watching it all race past him out the window of the Greyhound Scenicruiser, got motion sickness the second day out and threw up on a sailor. The young man, so christened to the journey, took it all in good stride, rinsing out his navy jumper in the men's room at the next rest stop and bought some gum for him and Johnny to keep their stomachs settled for the remainder of the trip. Having made a new friend, Johnny sat back and was entertained by tales of mighty warships and stealthy submarines to break up his incessant sightseeing.

Johnny's new Auntie Ginna, Dave's sister, met them at the bus terminal and drove them to the house in Riverside. The house was in a sunny, sleepy little housing development on the east side of the city. Blocks upon blocks of similar looking tracts in whites and pastels continued to Lorry's new home on Randolph Street. Across the street was a wide field giving an unrestricted view of a line of mountains that rose to the east with patches of snow still capping their peaks. Down the block and around the corner was the elementary school where Johnny would be enrolled by the following September. The skies were clear and bright and it looked like a fine start for a reunited family.

Lorry and little Linda Marie were waiting for them inside the house. Emma held her new granddaughter and had Johnny sit down on the couch to hold his new baby sister. He was very careful and overjoyed about his beautiful sibling. When he touched his forehead to hers, she let out a jolly giggle and grabbed his ears and held him there until their mother could pry her loose.

"She likes me," he said with a blush.

"Of course, she does," Lorry said. "She's your baby sister and you are her big brother."

It was comic to watch the range of emotions pass across his youthful face as he worked to assimilate that information. Awe, pride, puzzlement, infatuation, care, responsibility all took their turns rearranging his features. Willard, all too self conscious of the frailty of infants, stepped outside to look at the patio out back.

Lorry and Emma introduced Johnny to his new room with a western theme of bedspreads and curtains with cowboys and chuck wagons in colorful disarray. Together, they situated his belongings into his dresser drawers and closet. A tour of the house came next as her daughter breathlessly described all the benefits of their new home. Linda's nursery was next to Johnny's room and the master bedroom was right across the hall. The walls seemed to shiver and the dishes rattled in the cupboards. Emma looked around, wide eyed, but Lorry seemed to take it all in stride.

"Tremors," Lorry said, in lieu of an explanation. "We get them all the time. You get used to them after a while."

"I'm not sure I ever could," she said. "There's something very grounding about having firm earth beneath my feet, and not moving about as all that."

"We've been here a while now, Mom," Lorry assured her. "They never seem to get much worse than this, and most of them you never even notice."

Dave came home from work a little after five o'clock and all the hugging and chatter picked up all over again before everyone sat down to supper. Emma found all the dishes spiced with citrus fruits and pineapple interesting, but a little too sweet for her taste. Willard, however, let his sweet tooth enjoy the holiday.

After dinner, she helped her daughter with the dishes and clean up. She didn't know how she would say things, in a manner that Lorry was likely to accept, but she was determined to try.

"Mom, look around you," Lorry said in exasperation. "This is sunny California, in modern America. This is not the Dark Ages that Grandma spoke of. Things are different now. There's a wonderful Mexican family that lives across the street and kids all over the block. Different kinds of people are accepted easily here. I'm sure Johnny will have no problem at all fitting right in with everybody else here."

"Johnny will try to fit in anywhere he goes," she said. "But the closer anybody gets, the more they are going to see just how different he is. Are you ready to help everybody adjust?"

"Of course, Mom," Lorry snapped. "You seem to forget that I'm his mother. I love him too."

But, do you know him? She didn't say it. She didn't want to aggravate Lorry and spoil the reunion.

"As for any cultural differences he might have," Lorry went on. "There's a Sunday school bus for a local Baptist church that comes by every Sunday morning and he can get to know how to behave in Christian society through the very best teachers available. If you still want him to foster with Leona during the summers, we'll have to see how things work out."

This was not what she wanted to hear, and not particularly promising. She had plenty of Christian friends in the neighborhood at home, and so did Johnny. Maintaining an easy relationship always meant never relaxing one's guard. Johnny knew there were words and terms he should never use around non-initiates like Christian folk, but he had never learned to deceive people by being anyone but Johnny.

She had never pushed Lorry into accepting the craft. That's not how her family operated. One was either witch born and had an affinity for such abilities and encouraged to develop them or wasn't, and nothing more was said about it. Lorry knew the family's proclivity for the craft in its numerous disciplines. To her, these were silly superstitions, old wives' tales and granny remedies, notions a modern, American woman didn't take seriously. It was a shame she had not insisted that Lorry take more interest while growing up. How was it that she couldn't reconcile what had happened with Lee with the truth of this present world? The reality of her firstborn son was going to be at constant odds with sanity as her daughter perceived it. Emma chose not to argue and left room to help.

She was walking on thin ice.

Her daughter, however, was trying to walk on water.

The week went by all too quickly, and Emma had to return in time for her granddaughter to spend the summer. Johnny walked around in stunned fascination at all the varieties of flowering cacti and strange plants native to the Southwest. It was a very different world for him and he immersed himself in learning all he could. When Dave's sister, Ginna, came to take them to the bus terminal, neither Johnny or herself could say goodbye without tears.

"You be sure to write," she admonished him. "And you come and see your grandma when you're able. Leona's going to miss you too, this summer."

"Her stuff she wanted to keep is in my closet," he said, sobbing. "In case we used the guest room for someone else. I promised her I'd keep it for her."

"She'll be so happy you did," she said. "You're a good cousin. Now you have to be a good big brother. Think you can do that?"

"Oh, yes," he said, smiling.

Everybody hugged and promised to write. The big Scenicruiser departed the terminal and sunny California faded in the distance behind Emma. Her worries for her family loomed before her. She had a few days travel to think about them in depth.

She was a firm believer in the constructive use of "worry." When she could take the time to focus on a problem, or problems, and come up with workable solutions or a reasonable plan of attack, this was time put to good use. When all it wrought was hand wringing and anxiety, then it was time to put that pot on the back burner to simmer on its own and get to work on something productive. She couldn't control all the details of this situation, even at its best, so she chose not to worry over the small points and consider the overview. She couldn't predict exactly what would happen and how it would affect people, but she could be certain that Johnny would be Johnny and as likable and charming as he could be, his very nature was pagan and in a strict Baptist setting, he was likely to find some ardent disapproval. He also had no concept of "tact" or beating around the bush when he needed information. His questions or comments went straight to the heart of the matter that concerned him.

When sitting with her and his aunties as they discussed craft and midwifery, he knew a lot about women's issues for a six year old. He harbored no illusions about babies coming by storks or sprouting in cabbage patches, but he didn't yet have a clue as to exactly how they might have gotten to where they did come from. It had not occurred to him to ask that question yet. As virgin witches tend to wield the most powerful magicks without harm, too much detail about the actual sex act was never encouraged around the youth in the family. She wasn't worried about him being promiscuous, but if certain topics ever came up for discussion, he was very likely going to be true to form and address them in unabashed honesty. This could prove to be a disastrous event in the enlightened America of the 1950's.

In spite of herself, Emma shook her head and smiled. A storm had taken up residence in sunny California in the form of a tow headed, six year old boy. That sleepy little community was about to wake up to more than just their dishes rattling in the cupboards. As long as nobody really got hurt, this could even be quite amusing.

PART THIRTY TWO

Leona's Lessons In Spellcraft

The sun shone through the leafy forest canopy in scintillating emerald hues. Emma strolled the well defined wooded path with her staff in hand and a familiar weight slapping her thigh under her apron. At times, the tall pointed crown of the hat she wore would brush the lower branches and she would have to duck a little to accommodate the extra height.

Coming down to a grassy clearing near a cheerfully babbling brook, she watched a familiar looking, adolescent lioness practice stalking in the tall grass. The beast's hindquarters were much too high and the twitching tail was certain to give her position away. Propping her staff against a tree, she approached the big cat, who cocked her head and watched her curiously as Emma got down on all fours beside her.

"Keep that backside down, and the tail still," she instructed. "It will keep you hidden from view and give you a better point to spring from. Now, you try it."

"Would you care to join us for tea?" Came a familiar voice near the brook.

Standing upright, she turned about. Two women, in tall pointed hats, sat at a table set with a teapot and china cups. They raised their cups to greet her. Her mother and Elvyra waved cheerfully and invited her to sit with them. As in a dream, she walked to them. It was a dream. Wasn't it?

"You're doing wonderfully with Leona, dear," her mother commented while pouring her a cup and indicating a seat at the table.

Emma sat down and accepted her tea and tried not to stare, afraid they might vanish and leave her alone.

"Her mother seems to think we are grooming the next matriarch," she said, sipping her fragrant drink.

"And so you are, dear," Ella said cheerily. "She'll be a fine choice."

"She's no adept," she admitted. "But she learns well."

"Neither are you, dear," her mother acknowledged pleasantly. "But, I can't help but be proud of the way you have filled out my apron. Who, but I would know that you weren't adept?"

"Certainly not I," Elvyra agreed, raising her cup in a toast.

"Johnny's the adept," she said, remembering he was gone.

"And we both know why he'll never be the one to lead this family," Ella pointed out. "He's a male witch and we've never had one before."

"It's not his fault," she replied bitterly.

"It's not a fault at all, sweetheart," Ella assured her. "His role is big enough for one little boy and does not include running this family. Our next adept matriarch won't be born for generations to come. Until that time comes, Leona will be the perfect choice for that job, and she will do it well, as you will see."

"Johnny's not with me anymore," she said sadly. "He's with Lorry and her new husband in California."

As if in response, a distant rolling thunder came out of the west. Though the skies were clear and blue above them, on the far western horizon the storm clouds loomed and brilliant flashes of lightning flickered among them.

"I'm afraid I've got good news and bad news for you, dear," Ella said as she sipped her tea and glanced casually at the distant storm. "The bad news is, that David is not a strong man. He caves in under pressure and Johnny's presence will create a lot of that for him. The good news is that it is unlikely that Johnny will be able to stay with them beyond the next year. You may well have him back, but things are going to get much worse before they get better."

"Will they hurt him?" She asked, not sure she wanted an answer.

"Yes," her mother said. "But he's been hurt before and he's tougher than most children. But he'll need a lot of love to heal, nonetheless."

"But who, better than yourself for that?" Elvyra asked cheerfully, obviously trying to break the glum mood. "Oh, look. Your granddaughter is here to see you."

The lioness was keeping her haunches low in the tall grass then pounced and rolled in the grass near her feet.

"I said, Leona's here to see you," Willard said, trying to shake her out of her sleep. "It's early and Ralph and Evy have just pulled in with her baggage. I'll get some coffee on. Get up, sleepy head."

Emma lay there a moment, collecting her thoughts and recalling her dreams. Pulling on her robe and slippers, she made her way out to the front room. The sun wasn't up yet and all the house lights were on, revealing a pair of suitcases sitting in the living room and Leona coming out of the bathroom to greet her. Evelyn and Willard were talking in the kitchen and Ralph was checking out his car under the streetlight, making sure everything was in working order, and that all the fluid levels were proper. He was meticulous that way.

"Grandma, I missed you," Leona said, hugging her. "I got all A's and a couple B's this year in school. That makes me an Honor Student."

"Johnny did very well this year too," she said. "But I'd expect as much from my two best students." She pulled Leona in by her shoulders and gave her a squeeze.

"It's not going to be the same here without him," Leona said. "But, I'll get to have you all to myself and not feel so selfish."

"Here's your chance to pass up your cousin," she said. "Let's get those suitcases to your room. Johnny has some of your things in his closet for you too. Breakfast will be shortly, so let's hop to it, young lady." She grabbed the larger of Leona's suitcases and started up the stairs with her granddaughter in tow.

Evelyn and Ralph stayed long enough for breakfast and coffee. They had driven through the night from Cleveland to get a jump on the Fourth of July traffic. Leona had slept most of the way in the back seat. It was impossible to miss that she was excited to start her summer studies with her grandmother. Emma smiled to herself as Leona practically rushed her parents off, who themselves were already in a hurry to beat the traffic.

The garden had suffered a couple weeks worth of neglect, while she and Willard took Johnny to be with his mother. Emma and her granddaughter donned gloves and brought out gardening shears and trowels to bring it back to order.

"This tall, lovely lady is called Angelica," she said, indicating the lacy plant. "Her leaves and roots are used in making medicines and the stems and seeds make an excellent confectionery for flavoring foods and teas."

"Grandma?" Leona interrupted. "I really need to talk to you."

"What's on your mind, little witch?" She asked, picking at some weeds at the base of her plant.

"Aunt Lorry doesn't like witches, does she?" Leona said with a troubled frown.

"That's not true, dear," she objected. "She loves us all very much, I'm sure. She was the last of my girls to leave home."

"But Mommy and Aunties say she never liked the craft," her granddaughter persisted.

"Well, no." She paused. "I guess she didn't. She never had much time for it, and had all her own friends outside of the family. She's experienced more than her share of her grandmother's magick while growing up, but you must understand that some of it didn't work out so good for her. Why does this trouble you?"

"Daddy knows almost nothing about all this," Leona said, spreading her arms to indicate everything around her. "So Mommy and me don't talk about these things when he's around. But when I'm with you and Grandpa Willard, I can talk and ask all I want and be as witchy as I like. Does Uncle Dave or Aunt Lorry have any idea what Johnny is like?"

"Not exactly, dear," she said reluctantly.

"I couldn't imagine what it would be like if he lived in my home, with us." Leona went on. "My dad would have a nervous breakdown in a month, and my mom is a little uncomfortable around him too. I can't imagine Johnny being Johnny, anywhere else but here."

"Neither can I, little witch," she said with a sigh. "Hopefully, by this time next year, we'll have our boy right back where he belongs. Then all of us will be happier."

"I've been so worried since Mom read us your letter about taking him out to California," Leona confessed. "Even she was shaking her head as she read it. I feel so bad for him."

"Not too bad, I hope," she said. "He's got a new baby sister that just thrills his little heart, and a whole new kind of Nature to get acquainted with and you know how curious he gets about anything he's never seen before. He has a big field across the street where he can go play and be himself without upsetting his parents. He'll make the best of it, I'm sure. Now, back to this elegant lady named Angelica, dear..." Emma directed the conversation back to the garden work and her lesson in herbology.

In the far back of the yard, Willard was working on one of his projects making a storage shed. Every so often the sawing would stop and Willard looked back over his shoulder at an empty fort and sighed. Emma pretended not to notice.

They weeded the garden and harvested some of the herbs that were ready. After they cleaned up and had lunch, the lessons resumed their pace in the summer kitchen. Here, she taught Leona how to prepare several varieties for decoctions and tinctures for her cabinet while others dried on hooks or in ventilated baskets. In the process of discussing the properties of medicinal plants, Leona also learned the essentials of basic spellcrafting.

"There are warm spells, dry spells, dizzy spells," Emma recited, "fainting spells, sit-a-spells, rainy spells and on and on. What clue does that give you about spellcraft?"

"That it's a period of time where something is happening," Leona answered.

"Exactly that," she said. "For a witch, a spell is a period of time, where a certain influence, or even more than one, is brought to bear, to bring a desired goal to pass."

"But that covers just about everything," Leona protested.

"Yes, it does," she agreed all too gleefully. "A wise woman learns to artfully weave these circumstances to manage her environment."

"But that's hardly magick at all," Leona observed.

"When you know what's going on," she explained, "the less it seems like magick, even if you're calling up faeries. To the aborigines of the South Sea Islands, the airplane was a magickal construct, because they didn't understand the science behind it. If you were to ask most people how the airplane flies or how their television works, they couldn't tell you. The best of them might say it was something to do with wings, or use some words like volts, amps or ohms. But because they still didn't understand the principles that caused them to operate, these would be little more than magickal mumbo jumbo, but to those wizards of engineering and electronics, those words would explain so much more."

"So, the more you know, the less it seems like magick," Leona concluded.

"Oh, there's more than enough real magick happening everyday," she said. "People often refuse to acknowledge it. They couldn't explain it and don't understand it, but to them it happens, just because..."

"You mean, like the forces of nature?" Leona asked.

"In general, yes," she said. "But don't forget the forces of their own nature. People often don't understand even themselves. To a witch, all of these things and more serve as tools. Here's a good example: Your Grandpa Willard often forgets things, like he forgot to mail this letter today. He doesn't like to be nagged about things. He's a grown man and he likes to think he's his own boss, so he'll resent you if you remind him."

"So, what do you do?" Leona asked. "Mailing it yourself is hardly a worthwhile spell. You've got enough to do already."

"True," she said. "But Grandpa Willard has a nature that I can rely upon."

"To forget to mail a letter and get mad if you remind him?" Leona asked.

"Oh, he's not all that bad, really," she said. "Most men feel that way and are forgetful of domestic chores, but there's a point that influences him, and I can make use of that to help him remember, so that he thinks it's his own idea. He has a sweet tooth."

"How will that help?" Leona puzzled.

"Watch this, and then watch how everything turns out." Emma took the unmailed letter and placed it on top of the candy dish of pastel mints that Willard kept on top of the television cabinet near the front door. She and Leona went about their business, saying nothing, as Willard came in from the front porch and absently stuck his hand in the candy dish and found the letter. Popping a mint into his mouth, he looked at the letter a moment.

"Honey, I'll be back in a few minutes," he called out. "I've got an errand to run." He grabbed his hat and started walking for the corner.

"Amazing," Leona said, giggling. "Just like magick, how that worked."

"It's so much more than that," she told her granddaughter. "Not only did the letter get mailed. He feels good about himself as a man, and his sweet tooth and his sunny disposition are going to combine to buy us all a treat for tonight while he's down on the corner."

"What man has a chance against the wiles of a wise woman?" Leona remarked.

"Say that quietly, dear," Emma informed, "they like to think it's their world, we live in. We mustn't spoil it for them."

The witches cackled gleefully, rubbing their hands together in anticipation of a fine snack. Willard was not a man to let them down.

PART THIRTY THREE

A Bad Boy's Virtues

Johnny was beginning to think the faeries of California were an unfriendly lot to humans and Sidhe alike. The bright, rainbow hued, winged one that darted about his mother's flowers would not stop so much as a moment to speak to him. It's wings buzzed like a large insect, but it looked like a beautiful little bird... but no bird he ever knew flew like that. It had to be a faery creature. Plant life here was as pretty as it was hostile and covered in all manner of thorns, needles and prickers. The tarantula that climbed up the patio arbor was the largest spider he had ever seen in this world. Not as big as She-who-waits, but this place was sunny and bright and not the shadowy darkness of Annwn. It certainly wasn't the sweet, fae brightness of Gwynydd either. Just what was this place, anyway?

He had been here for several weeks now. He turned seven years old at the end of July and would be starting second grade at a new school in September. A lot of things took a little getting used to. His new baby sister didn't speak much faery, but she loved her big brother and he could play with her for hours and neither of them got bored. Dave was now called "Daddy," and that seemed good. He recalled the happy families on television like in "Father Knows Best." Now he would be a part of a fine American family and they could all do fun things together, and Daddy could teach them wisdom. He tried to convince himself that life was good, but something prevented him from really feeling it.

He missed Grandma and Grandpa Willard, but now he had Mommy and Daddy and Linda and Auntie Ginna and Uncle Lynn. He even had Sunday school, and they would sing and learn the Bible and everything. Jesus was a wonderful person who loved all the different children of the world, and they said that Jesus even loved him too. Jesus could do the very best magick and heal people and even put them back in their bodies and raise them from the dead. But he wasn't a witch because witches were bad, at least that was what everyone said out here in California. He suspected that Jesus was a witch but didn't tell anybody because they wouldn't like him if they knew. It was smart to keep quiet about such things and then people would like you. Some people had had enough of the magick and did bad things to Jesus, but he was as powerful as he was good and didn't stay dead. Maybe he and Jesus could be friends someday.

Most of the kids were pretty nice, but Jessica was a spoiled snot and Buddy Green, the deacon's son, was a very bad boy. Even so, Sunday school was a nice place. He'd never had anything like this before. Why hadn't Grandma ever thought of this?

Still, he always had the feeling that he was standing on the very brink of trouble. Trouble only came when he wasn't looking for it. So he remained vigilant.

He had made friends with the girl next door. Ted and Patty Kraft had a little girl his age, named Diana. Ted worked as a deputy sheriff, and he and Patty used to invite Mommy and Daddy to all their parties on the weekends. It seemed that only a few adults ever went to Sunday school. It was just for kids. He and Diana would start second grade in school next September. Her breath always smelled like vitamins and she liked to play house with dolls a lot, but girls were like that, and he didn't have any qualms about girls being girls. She was nice, but sometimes just a little too bossy.

"Let's play 'house,'" Diana said, pulling out her dolls and crib. "You can be the daddy and I'll be the mommy and this is our baby and I'll make us dinner on this pretend stove and then you have to eat it and say, 'This is great stuff, honey.' And then I'll say, 'It's just a little recipe I got from my mother.' And then you kiss me and the baby and go to work and..."

"Going to work" was a great way to avoid being excessively scripted. He wondered if real daddies felt the same way. He wandered into the field across the street and pretended he was a world famous explorer in the wilds of Africa. The Kraft's Great Dane, Duchess, often followed him on such forays. Duchess played the part of all the wild animals and he was careful not to over script her part. Which usually meant he was going to be covered in lion slobber instead of being eaten. By the time he remembered to come back, Diana was right where he left her and still chattering away at him.

"Where have you been all this time?" She said, wagging a digit in his face. "I've been worried sick about you. Then you have to say: 'I'm sorry, honey. I've been out drinking with the boys.' And then I'll say: 'You gotta sleep on the couch.' And then..."

Johnny laughed. It often went just this way. Diana insisted that it wasn't funny, but then she laughed too. Then they pretended to be a team of world renown scientists, studying the dinosaurs in the wilds of deepest, darkest Africa, in the field across the street. Of course, their studies hadn't gone very far before Duchess, the fierce allosaurus chased them down and covered the intrepid scientists in dinosaur drool.

When Johnny played with Diana, her mother, Patty, always insisted that they check back in with her every so often. This usually meant treats like Kool-Aid or popsicles at check in time before being allowed to return to play in the hot sun. Both of their skins tanned a deep, golden brown and their hair bleached pale blond in the California sunshine. Diana almost looked like she could be his sister, and insisted that they should grow up to become movie stars. Then they could go and star in monster movies and see real dinosaurs that didn't slobber all over them. To Johnny, this was preferable to actually being eaten, but then, as Diana would point out, he was just a boy.

It was Saturday afternoon as they were returning from safari in the fields, they were confronted by Deacon Green's black sedan in the Kraft's driveway and Buddy waiting alone for them on the front lawn. Johnny got more than enough of Buddy in Sunday school. For a boy who's dad was on a first name basis with Jesus, Buddy sure could be bad. The grownups were having drinks in the backyard patio and as kids they had to occupy themselves and stay out of everyone's way.

"Wutcha guys doin'?" Buddy asked.

"We were exploring and hunting big game in the jungle," Johnny said.

"We caught Duchess, the ferocious, man eating lion, " Diana said, holding onto the big dog's collar to avoid being slurped.

"That's just a dumb ol' dog," Buddy said, "and those are just tall weeds."

"Duchess is a good girl," Diana insisted. "Aren't you, girl?"

Duchess agreed with a wet doggie kiss.

"We were pretending anyway," Johnny said. "So, what did you want to play?"

"I can't leave the yard," Buddy said. "My dad won't be staying long. We've got church tomorrow. Maybe we could make a tent with a blanket on top of those bushes over there," he suggested, pointing to the blanket in the shade that they had been playing on earlier in the day.

"We can use the tent as our base camp," Diana suggested, "and send out our scouts to map the jungle from here."

Johnny liked the idea. If Buddy was any where near as bad as he behaved in Sunday school, he could put some distance between them by leaving to explore the jungle.

They fastened one end of the blanket on a low hedge and held up the other by propping a pair of plastic flamingos under the remaining two corners. In no time, the base camp was established and they enjoyed popsicles under their new tent.

Being the biggest of them, Buddy insisted upon assuming the role of party leader. The first order of business was that they should bed in for the night. They lay down in the grass under the tent, and Buddy sidled over to Diana's side and began rubbing up against her.

"What are you doing?" Diana asked.

"Yeah," Johnny said. "We're supposed to be sleeping."

"None of your bees wax," Buddy snarled, kicking Johnny in the face. "You're supposed to be out hunting lions or somethin'."

It wasn't a very hard kick, but Johnny's nose smarted a little. However, hitting Buddy back would only get him into trouble. It seemed like a good idea to take Duchess and leave for the jungle a while.

He found Duchess laying in the shade by her water dish. The big dog was ready for the big hunt at an instant's notice. Passing the tent on the way out, Diana cried out.

"You keep your hands off of me," she insisted.

"Then you pull them down and let me look." .

"I don't know," she replied, "We're not supposed to be doing stuff like this.

"I said pull 'em down or I'll hit you good," Buddy snarled.

Johnny looked inside at Buddy standing over Diana as she lay in the grass frightened.

"No," Johnny commanded.

"Are you going to stop me?" Buddy sneered.

"Yes," Johnny said, as he fought down the rumbling thunder in his soul.

Buddy advanced on him with his fists balled and ready to fight. As he got within arm's reach, Johnny balled his little fist and planted it, stoutly on the end of the larger boy's nose. Buddy fell backwards, holding his nose and howling for all he was worth. In short order, the parents came out to investigate the ruckus.

Deacon Green tried vainly to console his son, whose nose was bleeding profusely. Diana's mom brought Buddy a towel with some ice wrapped inside, and Buddy's dad whisked him away home, all the time threatening to sue if his son's face was damaged.

Patty grabbed Diana aside, who seemed confused at all that happened.

"I didn't do anything wrong," Diana insisted. "The boys were fighting."

Johnny's mom looked at him fearfully, as his dad tried to console everybody else that it was just boys being boys. He couldn't bear the look on his mother's face and stared down at his feet until his father snatched him away.

Daddy was very angry and dragged him by the arm, marching him to his room faster than his little legs could follow. He received three sound licks on his fanny with the belt and was scolded for fighting.

"You can just stay here in your room," his father said, "and forget about supper, young man." He had committed the unforgivable sin of embarrassing his parents in front of the deacon of his church.

He sat sobbing, hating himself for the trouble he caused. At the time, it all seemed like the right thing to do, but the circumstances proved him wrong. He was no hero. He was a bad boy, and a worse one than Buddy.

Brother George came by and tried to cheer him for saving his friend's virtue. But Johnny didn't know what a 'virtue' was, and evidently, it was nothing that grown ups cared for very much either. Like faeries. Johnny was very upset.

"Will you just go away," he shouted. "I've been trying to be a good boy, and all your stupid ideas just get me spankings. Just leave me alone. I don't want to get into any more trouble over pesky faeries, or dumb old 'virtues' either."

The party at the Kraft's broke up early as a sudden summer thunderstorm caused everyone to run inside. Johnny sat scowling on the edge of his bed as his father looked in on him and just shook his head in disgust and staggered a little on his way to the bathroom. His mom looked in and came and gave him a hug and slipped him an oatmeal cookie.

"I'm sorry, Son," she said. "You just can't go around hurting people you don't like. That's bad. You should learn to talk to people about things nicely. Your grandma says you're a smart boy. Smart boys use their heads and not their fists. You think about that, and don't let your dad see that cookie, sweetheart."

Johnny hid the cookie in his sock drawer. He didn't think he deserved any treats after the terrible way he had behaved. He still didn't like Buddy, but then Buddy didn't get a spanking, and he did. Who was worse?

He was not allowed to go to Sunday school when the bus came by for him the next morning. Was that an indication that maybe Jesus didn't like him very much either? He cried bitter tears into his pillow and promised he would be better behaved.

PART THIRTY FOUR

Elvyra's Altar

Before she even opened the letter, Emma knew she wasn't going to like it. Lorry's letter went on to relate how Johnny had managed to get himself kicked out of Sunday school for fighting.

"Our little Johnny?" Willard asked incredulously. "To think of him fighting at all, much less in a Sunday school is more than I can imagine."

"It goes on to say that the fight started at a party the day before." Emma adjusted her reading glasses and continued, "It was something between himself and a bigger boy who was the son of the church deacon. He broke the boy's nose. The deacon is threatening to sue and Lorry thinks he's showing all the earmarks of his father's cruelty."

"Not Johnny," Willard declared with surprising vehemence. "Boys will be boys, they say, but I don't care what anyone says, that boy wouldn't even dream of hurting a fly unless something really bad was in the works. And you say it was a bigger boy? Hardly the actions of a bully, wouldn't you say?"

Emma recalled the children's account of the Vough's demise. Even then, threatened with an awful death at her hands, Johnny did not actually hit the woman. He struck her staff out of her hand and the black lightning finished off the mad witch. Undoubtedly, there were some important pieces missing in this story. If there were any real threat at all, the older boy was lucky to have escaped with his life. No, she remembered how he hated himself for allowing that to happen. That night in the woods, he couldn't even bring himself to look her in the eyes. Somehow, he must have thought it was the lesser of two evils to actually hit the boy. But what happened to make him think so?

"Yes, dear," she said. "Our boy is no bully. And boys being boys as they say, I have to wonder about the kind of Christian charity this deacon manifests with the talk of lawsuits. It seems like a whole lot of social embarrassment has clouded the issue of what had actually happened, and nobody cares to know."

"What's Johnny's letter say?" Willard asked.

"It says he's sorry and that he'll try to be good," she replied, stifling a sob. "It says that over and over again and not much else. He's obviously very upset about all of this. It doesn't even occur to him that the grown ups could be wrong. He blames himself for the turmoil he caused, and they don't understand that they are the most important people in his world. I want to think about this some more before I write a reply. We won't mention this to Leona either. Maybe if we all drop him a line, and send him a picture or something..."

"There's a photo booth at Neisner's," Willard offered. "Four photos for a quarter, and it only takes a few minutes. How about the three of us do that?"

"Just what the good doctor ordered, dear." She kissed him.

The next day, she, Willard and Leona stopped in at Neisner's and each sat for an individual portrait and then all of them crowded into the booth for a group picture. They had fun clowning around. Emma included the day's photo strip in Johnny's letter with some words of encouragement. Leona had an idea that Johnny was not doing well in California, but Emma avoided the issue by simply stating that he missed them all, which was true enough.

The next day, Willard had some work helping a friend with a contracting job, and Emma fixed a daypack for her and Leona to go up to Cobb's Hill. Leona had asked about what might have happened to Elvyra's home after their adventure last year and the best course of action was to examine it firsthand. She had been putting off visiting the house herself and it was about time for a little closure. Besides that, her larder was getting a bit low on a few items that she harvested at the park.

It was a lovely day for a stroll down the wooded pathways. They stopped here and there for a bit of this leaf, a bit of that root and a couple of good fungus shelves. A vision of Elvyra, standing in the silvery light of the full moon, telling her to look after her woods, gave her pause. The city of Rochester might argue with her as to whose woods these were, but city officials never made this place one of their stops. Most people preferred the part of the park bordering the reservoir with its trimmed lawns and flowering bushes, trees, tennis courts and baseball diamonds. Few people found any comfort at all trekking the few acres of hardwood forest at the southern end.

"What do you think we might find left of Auntie Vy's house?" Leona asked.

"I'm not sure, dear," she said. "She destroyed it to break the connection it made between here and Annwn, so it's safe to assume that the ruins will either be wholly in this plane or that one. There might not even be anything to see at all. There's some shaggy mane mushrooms that grow over that way, that your grandfather likes in his omelets. We'll see then. The trail forks off to the left from there, to where her backyard used to be."

"It's strange, not seeing her roaming around here with that basket of hers over one arm," Leona said as she brushed the dirt off some roots and tucked them in her sack.

Arriving to where Elvyra's house used to be, half in this world and half in Annwn, it was strange. There were no charred ruins or well tended backyard or even a part of a foundation to show a house was ever there at all. Peering through the ivy covered oaks that used to border the yard, a tangle of overgrown bushes and shrubbery occupied the grounds that broke into another yard in the distance by the private drive.

Almost obscured, between two large oaks and in a tangle of climbing ivy, was the marble table that used to sit in the far back of Elvyra's yard near the trail. Emma and Leona cleared some of the vines away for a better look. Tucked away, underneath the table was a medium sized, rusted, iron cauldron with some leaves and debris in it. Leona emptied it out on the table top to find two disks. Both were about an inch and a half in diameter. One was hardened clay and the other was silver with a crescent moon on it and a loop for a chain. The clay disk held only a tiny handprint, about a half inch wide and a large X inscribed beneath it.

"This cauldron looks in good shape with a bit of scouring," Leona said. "Look what was inside." The girl blew away debris to reveal better detail.

"The cauldron would certainly have been Elvyra's" she said. "The silver piece is a medallion I think I remember her wearing the night we fought Behir. That would have been lost with her in the flood. How did it get here?"

"Maybe this clay disk is a clue," Leona said. "It is either an X or Gyfu, the Rune of Partnership."

"Or Gyfu as in the G sound for Gregory," she said, indicating the tiny handprint. "Gregory must have found this in the valley when the flood subsided."

"Now, we'll have something to remember her by," Leona said. "I've even got a memento of Gregory."

"I'll get this medallion cleaned up and store it away in my jewelry box," she said. "And we'll clean up that cauldron and I'll show you how to burn it and use it. We can use it to make a brew to toast our sister from these very woods. She would have liked that. We'll melt some wax to coat that clay for you and you can keep your memento of Gregory for years to come."

Emma drew out her witch blade and invoked it to cut an inscription into the edge of the marble table in a memoriam. She kept it simple as there were very few who would understand:

"Elvyra's Altar"

Drawing the vines back over the table to keep it hidden, they left the park for home with their prizes.

Making good on her promise, Emma helped Leona scour the cauldron. Then she dried it off and coated it with a thin coat of lard, inside and out and set it in the stove to burn itself black. All the windows were open to aid the exhaust fan over the stove and keep the house from getting uncomfortably warm. After the cauldron was allowed to cool, they rinsed it out again and then filled it with cold water and added some freshly cleaned sassafras roots to the pot. After a good rolling boil was accomplished, the brew was left to simmer and then cool to a rich reddish brown broth.

Emma prepared some acorn muffins with honey and bits of sweet pear, while Leona set the table for three, for tea and muffins. Together, they celebrated their friendship with Elvyra and recalled their adventures with the dark witch. After the festivities, Elvyra's cup of brew and muffin were removed to the garden for Nature's own to enjoy in her honor.

They heated paraffin wax to seal Gregory's clay note for Leona's pisky keepsake. This got wrapped in wax paper and relegated to Leona's box of treasures. Emma treated the amulet to a bit of silver polish, remembering Sister Moon that night. It was decided that the cauldron would be Leona's personal tool for her craft studies. Elvyra would have, no doubt, approved such use. She would always be remembered as a true sister.

PART THIRTY FIVE

California Apple Banger

"It must have been the booze," Lorry told herself again and again.

She and Patty Kraft had gotten together and put on the Halloween party to end all parties. They put up loads of decorations and a huge, paper mache, witches' cauldron full of candy for the itinerant ghouls and goblins. The neighborhood adults came in costume and the party moved between the Kraft's spacious living room and the ever popular, backyard patio, strung with Tiki torches and paper lanterns. Being a Friday night, the kids were all up much later than usual and everyone had a good time bobbing for apples, playing games and spooking all the trick-or-treaters that came to the front door.

There was a party nearly every weekend since she had moved out here. She loved to socialize but Dave had taken to drinking more and more. Dragging him home early and drunk out of his mind was becoming a weekly ritual. If he wasn't crying over some long past social slight, then he was getting belligerent over some presently perceived insult. He doted on his lovely daughter, but he was becoming less and less enamored with Johnny.

Johnny's fight with the Deacon's boy hadn't helped things at all, as Dave bemoaned that the social embarrassment and disapproval this engendered had probably cost him his promotion at the plant. Deacon Green was a floor supervisor in another section of the factory. The deacon had been persuaded not to sue them by Ted Kraft, who had a little conversation of his own to add to the story of what happened in his front yard with his daughter. The Krafts thought Johnny was a perfect little gentleman. But really... fighting with other boys, over girls at only seven years old? What was he going to be like when he was actually old enough to date? He could be such a charmer, like his father was. She didn't like to think about that.

She had dressed up Linda as a little clown and Johnny as a little devil and they played well with the other kids until eight-thirty when she took them back to the house and had her niece, Beatrice, baby-sit for the remainder of the party. With the kids home, in their pajamas and Beatrice pouring over her homework at the kitchen table, Lorry returned to the party next door.

Ted, dressed as a pirate, and Dave, dressed as a cowboy, were arguing over by the barbeque the merits of gentlemanliness in today's society. Most of the discussion was the liquor talking through both of them.

"You're too hard on the boy," Ted insisted, punctuating his point with a stentorian belch. "S'far as I'm concerned, he did the right thing by my Diana. You should be proud of him 'stead of bein' all upset over what stinkin' Dinkin Green's gonna think about you. Your problem is that you are too thin skinned about the damnedest things, Dave."

"I'm not thin skinned," Dave slurred. "That kid could give Bela Lugosi the heebie jeebies. I don't even trust him 'round my little girl, and you shouldn't either. But I'll tell you what," he said, hitching up his pants and trying to stand a little straighter. "If you want the little bastard, you can have 'im. 'Cause I'm not gonna be the guy they blame when he ends up in a instatit...institooter... a goddamn boy's home." He waved an imperious finger and stormed out of the yard for home in a zigzag sort of way.

"Sheesh," Ted exclaimed with a burp. "What a grouch!"

"The older boys, behaving like much younger boys," Patty sagely observed, waving her highball at the retreating cowboy.

"Maybe he'll get home under his own power this time and sleep it off," Lorry replied.

Twenty minutes later, a very worried Beatrice crashed the party to see her.

"Aunt Lorry," Beatrice said sobbing. "Uncle Dave is out of control. He came in all drunk and angry and started taking it out on me and Johnny. He started yelling bad things at Johnny and kicked him hard. Then he picked up the baby from her crib. He's so drunk, I was afraid he might drop her, but he yelled and told me to get out of his house."

"You want any help, Lorry?" Patty asked, glancing dubiously at her inebriated husband.

"No thanks," she said. "I can usually manage his tantrums. Beebee, you stay here and I'll go look in on things. It'll be alright, sweetie."

Lorry dashed for home, the front door was still ajar from Beatrice's flight. Inside, the baby was crying and David was roaring at Johnny.

"See that, ya little bastard," he yelled. "You made my little girl cry."

Something thudded and crashed, as Lorry neared the front room.

"See, baby," Dave crooned to the squalling infant. "Daddy chased away that little bastard."

For a moment, it looked like there were two Johnnies in the ravaged living room. Dave was tossing the baby up in the air and catching her to try and stop her crying. Surprised to see someone else in the room, he missed his catch and Johnny bounced off the couch and caught his sister before she could hit the floor and dashed for Lorry's legs, pushing her back down the hall to the front door. In the living room, Dave was livid with Johnny for stealing the baby and began hitting the boy on his head and back with a golf club. She all but fell backwards out the front door as Johnny kept pushing his baby sister at her.

Regaining her wits for the moment, she took her daughter from her son and moved out the front walk from the house.

"Boy, is your father ever mad at you now," she said, still trying to reconcile what she saw.

"Apple banger," Johnny said, rubbing his hip.

"Was that a cuss word, young man?" She growled.

Johnny just shrugged his shoulders. Dave was still inside trashing the house with a golf club and swearing at Johnny. Patty came over to see if they needed any help and escorted her back to her house where the party was winding down.

Ted had made a pot of coffee and drank it black to try and clear his head. Beatrice took Linda, who was none the worse for her adventure and rocked her to sleep in Patty and Ted's bedroom. Patty was dabbing a washcloth at some of Johnny's bruises as he sat quietly, staring at the wall as though he could see through it, to what was happening at home.

Lorry had Ted walk with her back to the house to check on Dave. As they walked up the front walk to the door, Dave burst out the door with a mangled golf club in hand, wailing like a baby then threw himself on the front lawn face first.

"I killed him," he sobbed. "I killed the little bastard. I really did it."

Lorry looked on in horror as Ted knelt down beside him and gently removed the golf club.

"Who'd you kill, sport?" Ted chided him jokingly. "Everybody is safe at my house and you're behaving like a wild man here. C'mon, get up and show me what you did tonight."

"I've really done it this time, ol' buddy," Dave said. "He wouldn't stop staring at me with those spooky eyes of his and I let 'im have it good. He hurt my baby and I lost my temper and killed him." Dave led the way back into the house.

Ted and Lorry exchanged looks, and followed him inside. The house was in shambles and the living room was lit at a crooked angle by a fallen lamp. Lorry put it back up on its end table, the hot light bulb had already begun melting a spot into the carpet. Dave tossed aside cushions and debris looking to uncover the body he swore was there. Ted looked throughout the entire house and finding nothing, calmed him down.

"If you had hurt anybody that bad," Ted said, "there would be blood all over the place, or even on this golf club. You didn't kill anybody, sport. You just had too much to drink. You need to slow down on this stuff, Dave, and dry out for a bit. Too much juice will ruin your life, my friend."

Dave sat on the floor sobbing, while Ted went into the kitchen to brew coffee for them. Lorry began picking up the mess as he continued feeling sorry for himself. Over and over, she played it all back in her mind. She had seen him hit Johnny with that club too. But it couldn't have been Johnny, because he was pushing her out the door carrying his baby sister in his arms. He was with her at the Kraft's' house and he only had a couple bruises. It must have been the booze that had them all confused. Somehow, Johnny was responsible for all of this insanity. Dave was going to end up in a padded cell, or worse, and leave her and Linda to fend for themselves. Her mom knew how to handle the boy; he was all her idea anyway. A carefully worded letter to her mother was in order, but how was she going to explain this?

With Ted and Patty's help, Dave stopped drinking himself into a stupor the next few holidays. Even so, by Linda's first birthday the following February, the rift had seemed to grow between Dave and her son. Johnny would not speak to him at all, which was fine because she had no idea of what Dave might do if Johnny had called him an "apple banger" to his face. She had no idea what that meant, but it probably had something to do with his golf swing.

The worst of it was that when Dave was in the general area, Johnny never took his eyes off him. The silent stare was all the emotion Dave could evoke from the boy. He would never turn his back on Dave, even if it meant he had to leave the room walking backwards to do it. He would play normally with his sister all day, and then when Dave came home, he would back away and go to his room. He would stubbornly not so much as blink as long as the man was in the room.

Psychiatrists probably had a word for this kind of behavior, but whatever it was, no doubt it would be as expensive as it was hard to pronounce. His schoolwork wasn't suffering. He was at the top of his class with straight A's. It was more likely the boy's way of getting back at Dave for calling him a bastard and kicking him. It was scary to think of how long he would carry a grudge.

On a good note, her mother's letters indicated that she was all for the idea of Johnny's return. Could she really give him up again? She had to save her marriage. Little Linda needed her daddy and Johnny didn't have one. This family couldn't long survive that kind of tension. She had to make a decision, and soon.

PART THIRTY SIX

Dark Visions

Emma rode the great bay stallion, and together they rode the winds. Soaring high above the mountains and valleys, she watched below for the herd with the lovely gray mare and the unicorn foal. On a windswept western prairie, the sound of a screaming stallion caught her attention and she wheeled about to investigate. The scene unfolded in a box canyon, where a wild Appaloosa stallion reared to attack and attempt to chase off a silvery white colt. A gray mare huddled to the back of the canyon with her nursing foal and the stallion stood between them and the unicorn colt.

The colt had suffered numerous bites and hits from the larger stallion as evidenced by the marks on his silvery hide. No longer did the silvery nub appear on his forehead, but it had the beginnings of a fine spiral horn. The colt made no aggressive action, nor did he attempt to defend himself from the stallion, but the intermittent flashing in his eyes attested to the anger and fury brewing within. The Appaloosa was in a terrible lather and insane with rage and although the unicorn was doing its best not to present any threat, the colt had but three choices. He could leave the herd and fend for himself in the wild. He could stay and be crippled or killed by the crazy stallion or he could lower his horn and charge the larger beast in defense. The colt was the smaller of the two, but by no means was it defenseless.

The storm clouds gathered over the box canyon and lightning flickered ominously in the skies. The furious stallion's hooves pummeled at the colt whose eyes flashed in defiance, mirroring the stormy scene above. The wind knocked Emma from her steed and she came tumbling down to land on her feet between the enraged Appaloosa and the very surprised unicorn colt. Stretching her arms forward...

She steadied herself by gripping the kitchen counter with both hands and leaning heavily, trying to catch her breath.

"Are you alright, hon?" Willard asked, gently gripping her shoulders.

"Just a bit over tired, I suppose," she said. "I seem to be dreaming as much standing up as lying down these days."

The letters from Lorry were becoming more and more troubling. She rubbed her temples trying to loosen up the tension between her eyes. Her grandson was withdrawing from human society, and who could blame him? He wasn't seeing humanity at its best by any stretch of the imagination. Lorry's assertion that her son was the evil shadow of his father had all the earmarks of becoming a self fulfilling prophecy in the way she rejected the boy. Johnny wasn't communicating much in his letters anymore. Had he given up trying to fit in? Her hopes rose with her daughter's hints of sending him back east for the summers and possibly longer. Lorry feared for her marriage.

Emma feared for Johnny. It was a shame she could not pull him out of school in mid-year and get him back before worse happened. June was still four months away and she could sense the tension building from three thousand miles away.

"Our boy isn't doing so good out there, is he?" Willard asked in response to her worried silence.

"Not for any lack of trying," she replied. "Lorry means well by him, but he reminds her of Lee, and there's nothing he can do about that. No matter what he does or how hard he tries, she sees Lee, and poor Johnny is invisible to her. I'm thinking Dave sees another man in the house, though I fail to see how a seven year old boy could fit that description. My mother said he was not a very strong individual. Perhaps his drinking has become his primary problem."

"Your mother?" Willard asked. "She passed on years ago. How would she have known this?"

"She passed on the morning Johnny was born," she said. "But every so often, she shows up in my dreams with sound advice concerning him. I can't explain it any more than I can explain the sunrise, but I've learned to accept the fact and I've always been blessed for it."

"I think I understand," he said. "I had a dream I was visiting with my mum a few years ago and in the dream she had given me some good advice."

"Really?" She asked. "What advice did she give you?"

"It's kind of embarrassing, really," he said, blushing.

"Oh, come on," she prodded. "What did she tell you?"

"She told me I needed to consider getting a good woman in my life again," he said. "That was about a week or so before I replaced those front steps and that banister on your front porch."

"Mothers never seem to stop caring," she said. "I wish I could have met yours."

"But, if Dave's as bad off as you say," Willard pointed out, "won't Lorry and the baby be in dire straits as well? What can we do that will help everybody concerned?"

"I'll look into it tonight, dear," she said, "and then we'll make our plans to straighten out this mess."

"You're not going to take off on a broom or something, are *you*?" Willard asked.

"No, dear," she said, laughing. "If witches were supposed to fly broomsticks in modern America, God would never have told us to leave the driving to Greyhound. Now, would he?"

"I didn't know God so favored Greyhound," Willard said smiling, " though, I imagine the seats are a lot more comfortable."

***

Willard turned in for bed early. He had taken on some extra work with a contractor down at the union hall and needed to get an early start. The house was quiet, and Emma could work undisturbed. She munched a few hazelnuts while she set up her mother's old gazing bowl on the coffee table in the living room. A single candle lit the room, its lonely, flickering flame reflected in the surface of the water in the bowl. She centered herself and slowed her breathing and let her eyes relax on the water and searched for her grandson. A dark scowling visage was all too quickly replaced by another of wide eyed wonder that leapt at her out of the bowl, giving her a start. She lost the image for a moment and calmed herself to try again.

"Grandma, it's *you*," her grandson insisted.

"Yes, of course it is, sweetheart," she returned. "You about scared the life out of me jumping in my face like that."

"Sorry, Grandma," Johnny said. "I'm wishing I was home with you so bad."

"Honey, what's going on out there?" She asked.

"Everything I do is wrong," he said. "I try to be good, but it always comes out bad. I don't think Dave likes me anymore, and Mommy thinks I don't belong in her new family. I want to come home."

His last words came out at her with an overwhelming depth of longing that made her feel it as a physical burden. Along with it came a rush of painful memories so vivid that she feared she would be poisoned by the venom in them. It was as if Dave's tirade was directed towards her and his brutal kick hitting her in the stomach. It didn't hurt nearly as much as the names he called the boy. Johnny's panic for his baby sister's safety made her heart hammer in her breast, which then grew woefully heavy seeing the disapproval on Lorry's face. Of all the scenes that played before her eyes, underlying them all was that scowling, dark visage she saw in the beginning of her session.

Things could get a bit strange around Johnny at times, but somehow this seemed all blown out of proportion. He would not be imagining that kind of behavior from Dave. He would never expect that kind of treatment from people. Something was happening beyond too much alcohol to influence the situation to this degree. Johnny's actions with the deacon's boy were no indication of any deep seated problems on Johnny's part, nor his actions in behalf of his baby sister. What stood out, was that Lorry and Dave were completely blind to any good in her grandson. Whose face was that, scowling at her from the bowl? And how were they involved in this?

"Listen to me carefully, baby," she instructed her grandson. "Grandma, Grandpa and Leona all love you very much, and we know you belong with us. Your mommy had to learn that for herself. Your mommy and Dave have both got some troubles that are bigger than they can handle, and they don't know it's not you. So, you've got to promise Grandma something, sweetheart. Are you ready?"

"Yes, Grandma," he said. "I'll do anything you say."

"I know you will, sweetie," she said. "Do you have any good hiding places or friends you can run to if trouble comes?"

"I can hide in the field," he said. "And Deputy Kraft likes me too."

"Good. That'll be fine." She said. "I want you to promise me. Witches' honor. That when things start to get bad in the house or with Dave, that you will not get mad and not interfere in any way. I don't want you to hurt anybody and I don't want anybody hurting my boy. I want you to run and hide or run to Deputy Kraft's house when it gets bad. Om biggun tu?"

"I think so, Grandma," he said. "I'm to run and hide or run next door if things get bad. But, what if he tries to hurt Mommy or Linda?"

"That's the hard part, sweetheart," she said. "I didn't say it was going to be easy on you, dear, but you've got to trust your grandma. No matter what happens, you've got to promise me that if anybody hurts anybody, that you will have nothing to do with it at all and get away from it as fast as you can. Somebody is trying to do bad things and blame you, sweetheart. If you're not there, then that can't happen. I will come and bring you home as soon as school lets out for the summer. Now, do I have your word?"

"Yes, Grandma," he said, placing his fingers below his eyes. "Witches' honor."

"Your Grandpa Willard and I are very proud of our boy," she said and closed the session.

The scowling face in the background lingered a moment longer in the bowl and then was replaced by her mother's face.

"You're learning well, my dear," Ella said. "There is always more to life than what immediately avails itself to meet the eye."

"Who is doing this to them?" She asked.

"Surely, you didn't think the boy's dragon would be so easily defeated," her mother replied. "Now, did you? The Vough and Behir were only minions. The good news is that if you can get Johnny away from there, and clear David's head a bit, their problems will alleviate, though, as I said before, he is not a strong man. Remove the boy, and the dragon will have no further use in meddling with their lives."

"We've got a few months before I can get him back," she said. "But why is this dragon such a problem? And what can I do about it?"

"Dragons and unicorns are ancient enemies, dear," her mother replied. "The symbolism shouldn't have been lost on you, there. And what witches have done for centuries beyond counting, is give sage advice and wait for all things to come together as they should. I believe you have done that, dear. Trust him as much as he trusts you. After all, he's our boy. Dave and Lorry are motivated to the actions they have taken by fear, and Johnny, by love. I'll put my money on love every time. In fact, I've bet my life on it." Her mother smiled and winked and disappeared as the water shown only the flickering candle in its gentle mirror.

Blowing out the candle and emptying the bowl and drying it, Emma went to bed to sleep on it all.

PART THIRTY SEVEN

El Brujo

It was Friday night and David sat nervously waiting in the cantina after work. The jukebox alternated between Hank Snow, Johnny Cash and some Mariachi tunes from South of the Border. He lit a cigarette and ordered another beer to calm his frayed nerves. The big man frightened him, but he was glad that "Big Mig" was on his side. Miguel Casteneda was not the kind of fellow he ever wanted to meet in a dark alley at night. He had to be the tallest Mexican he had ever met, and spooky too. At well over six foot tall, the muscular Latino was also known as "El Brujo," a shaman or witch doctor of some local renown. He had his own booth at the cantina, where special customers came to consult with him in occult matters.

Dave had met Miguel here at the cantina some months ago. He and some of the guys stopped here for a few drinks after work and Miguel had taken their money in an arm wrestling contest. Being a gracious winner, he offered to tell their fortunes. Some of the guys wanted to laugh it off, but "Big Mig" was not the kind of guy that anybody laughed at and expected to go home in the same condition they arrived in. So, they all sat quietly as the giant did his hoodoo act for them.

Miguel had told Scoop that his wife was cheating on him with his cousin, Bill. Lo' and behold, it turned out to be true. Scoop had left the bar that night and caught them in the act. He shot cousin Bill in the pants and was currently serving time for it. The big Mexican had revealed to Todd, that he would get promoted up to the design department, where his machining skills would be used to make prototypes. A week later, Todd was crafting wing components for supersonic jets at a hefty pay raise. Maybe Miguel had connections in the aircraft company and could get him promoted too. He'd listen to any kind of mumbo jumbo to get an advancement. Dave had a rapidly growing, new family to support and a new mortgage to consider.

He had excused himself from the guys, to go to the men's room and dropped by Miguel's booth on the way back. Miguel had some strange things to say. The first was that Dave's career was jinxed by a child with a devil for a father. If allowed to go on, this child would not only nix his chances of ever getting promoted, but usurp his wife and baby daughter's affections in the home. The giant sized shaman had taken off his own obsidian arrowhead charm and gave it to him to wear under his shirt for good luck and protection. It was uncanny how much Miguel knew about him.

That very next weekend, Johnny had gotten into a fight with Deacon Green's son and broke the older boy's nose. The deacon had threatened legal action and if that wasn't bad enough, Green was a manager in another department at the company. His chances of ever being promoted were drifting completely out of reach. What was worse, his daughter seemed to prefer Johnny to playing with her own father, and even Ted and Patty were beginning to express a preference for Johnny's company. They called the boy their little hero. He was desperate.

The bone jarring slam of a tequila bottle on the table next to him, startled Dave out of his reverie.

"Jeffe, you asleep or what?" The big man said smiling. "The night is still young and you want to nod over a beer?"

"No, I was just thinking, is all," Dave said. "I've got a lot on my mind these days."

"I would have a lot on my mind too," Miguel agreed, "if I had such a devilish creature living under my roof and eating my groceries. Si, I would be very worried."

"But what can I do?" He implored the big man. "I have to be careful, he's my wife's son by a previous marriage. I've got to keep my family together."

"She was never married to the boy's father," Miguel said. "That was a lie. But what's done is done, as they say. Si, you should keep your family together. However, the boy is not yours, and should not be your problem. Now, should he? I have here, a little something that could help you." He held up a small, green glass bottle of powder in his big fist.

"You...you can't expect me to poison him," he stammered.

"No, no," the giant said with a smile. "This will drive the devil right out of him. The local Indians use this stuff for conjuring spirits. It won't poison him, but let's just say, he won't want to stay with you for much longer. Your problems will all be taken care of and you can get back on the right track with your family. I see some big changes in your future with Rohr Aircraft Company. But you need to see that this ends up in the boy's food and milk. A little here, a little there, until it's all used up. Comprendo?"

To make his point, Miguel poured a little of the powder in his tequila and drank it down.

"This stuff will give him the heebie jeebies until he has to leave?" Dave asked, accepting the bottle.

"More or less, that's what it does to the devil's children," Miguel agreed amiably.

"My friend, you have saved my family's future," he said. "What do I owe you for this?"

"Oh, Senor Dave, I couldn't accept any money for this," Miguel replied, shaking his head. "Under the circumstances, it is my sacred duty to help you rid yourself of this devil in your very midst. I am sure you would do the same for me if the situation were reversed. Please, accept my humble gift to bless your family."

Dave pocketed the bottle, paid the tab and left the cantina in much higher spirits.

Arriving home a little late and reasonably sober, he kissed his wife and daughter and brought Johnny some milk and cookies with a discreet dash of Miguel's powder added. The boy was sitting on the couch, wearing an imitation coonskin hat and watching Fess Parker as Davy Crocket on the television.

"A peace offering?" Lorry asked, watching the display.

"It's not that I don't love the boy as my own," he said. "I just have some serious concerns about his behavior. With his violent attitude, will our baby girl be safe around him? Did his father have a family history of such behavior? As parents, we have to consider these things, hon."

"Well, I didn't know his father's family," Lorry admitted. "In fact, Lee and I weren't married at all. He was my first real love and it didn't turn out very good. It was pretty bad. I try not to think about it."

"You still miss him?" He asked.

"No. Of course not," she said. "He was an evil man. Charming, but very brutal."

"I'm sorry," he said. "I didn't mean to draw up bad memories. What's done is done, as they say. The past is past and we have a bright future together as a family now." He kissed her and stepped outside to have a cigarette and clear his head for a while.

Miguel was right again. Lorry and Lee were never married, and Lee was a devil of a man if ever there was one. If the big man had been right about so much, then it stood to reason that he was right about this too.

The boy would be gone soon, and his future with the company would change for the better. He might even be able to buy a pool and a wet bar and host a few of his own parties. Life would be so good.

It wasn't until Davy Crocket was finished that he began noticing a change in Johnny's demeanor. He had lost interest in the television and was looking about the room and the walls, as if seeing them for the first time.

"Why don't you go fix yourself a bath," Lorry told the boy, "and get yourself cleaned up and ready for bedtime."

Johnny looked at his mother oddly and then wandered into the bathroom and ran the water in the bathtub. About ten minutes later, Dave jumped up off the couch at the sound of Johnny's screams. Throwing open the bathroom door, he was greeted by a billowing cloud of steam. As it cleared, it revealed the boy standing in the tub with the hot water tap turned up full, his feet and ankles beginning to blister in the scalding water. Snatching the boy out of the tub and setting him on the toilet seat, he grabbed a towel and soaked it in cool water from the sink and wrapped it around the boy's burned feet.

"What happened?" Lorry asked worriedly.

"It seems he tried to boil himself," he replied. "He was standing in the tub screaming with only the hot water on when I found him."

"Is he alright?" She asked.

"Those are second degree burns," he said. "We're going to have to take him in to the hospital for treatment."

"He's run his own bath water before," she said. "I can't understand what's gotten into him to pull this foolish stunt."

"Who knows what goes through kids' minds these days?" He replied. "You're going to have to stay with the baby and call Ginna to give us a ride to the hospital. Don't worry. This is not life threatening. He'll be okay once we get those feet treated."

Ginna came quickly with the car and everybody made a fuss and remarked on the boy's strange and self destructive behavior. Dave was being made out as quite the quick thinking hero for once. It would not be long before he had one less mouth to feed and his jinx would be gone. As he sat in the waiting room at the hospital , he hummed to himself a happy tune.

PART THIRTY EIGHT

Coyote Dreams

Emma could only follow at a distance, as the unicorn colt wandered aimlessly across the barren prairie. Gone were the wolves she had seen when he was just a foal, but the new terrain had no lack of hostility of its own to offer. The smoke of a fire on a distant mountain shown itself in the serpentine column of a great, writhing, black wyrm.

Coyotes, Gila monsters, tarantulas, sidewinders and scorpions watched the progress of the colt's dazed ramblings with undisguised interest. Buzzards circled lazily overhead and ravens flew from perch to perch, checking on the colt's progress. The herd was nowhere in sight. He has no friends to look after him or instruct him. Oh, Danu, this should not be the destiny of such a beautiful and noble creature. A large raven detached itself from the circling birds and perched on a rock in front of her.

"Do you know me?" The bird asked her plainly.

"This land is different," she said. "If I were to go by what I know, you would be Morrigan, the Battle Raven."

"One of many names," the bird replied. "Here, I am known simply as Raven, but for our purposes, that is not important. What is important is that you will need allies, or the lone warrior is crow bait."

"Will you help us?" She asked.

"I always do," Morrigan answered, "but always in my own way. You see those coyotes following the colt? Their nature is to tear him to ribbons when he becomes too weak to defend himself. The others will do nothing of themselves. They feed on smaller prey and are only curious. You will need the help of the Chief Coyote to save your colt."

"Who is he, and where can I find him?" She asked.

"The Trickster is as clever as your colt is unique," Raven replied. "He will likely be watching, even now."

"And so I am, Sister Raven," said a voice behind her.

Emma turned about. A lone coyote sat calmly, attending the discussion between her and the raven with a detached interest.

"The wise woman seeks an audience with you about the strange colt," the Raven said.

The coyote arose to all fours, circled around her and sniffed at her.

"The smell of the Good Red Road is on your feet," he said, "and something else from a far place. This is mixed medicine, which always has unexpected results."

"Will you help my grandson?" She asked pointedly.

"It depends on what you mean by helping," Coyote replied. "If a warrior's heart is pure and his mind is single, I will help him find himself and he will become stronger and wiser. If his heart is corrupt and he is foolish, I will help him to feed the buzzards and the people of the prairie. Such mixed medicine in this one, I find. Who knows what such can bring? Mischief? Entertainment? The deep wisdom of the stars and the moon?"

"I have this," she said, pulling out Elvyra's lunar medallion.

Coyote gazed upon the silvery crescent on the medallion a moment and sat back on his haunches, raised his head and sang to the skies. The coyotes who were following the unicorn colt withdrew to a high place and sang to the silvery crescent moon that hung in the sky.

"That has only bought him time," the Trickster confided. "Remember how I help. It is in my nature to be so. If you have raised your young warrior in the ways of this mixed medicine, and if it is strong to stand we will do well by each other. If not, compose for him a death song to sing on the desert wind. He is much too young to know his own."

With a twitch of his left ear, Coyote faded from sight as the colt meandered towards a shady arroyo to rest. Finding him at peace, she rested too.

***

"You're looking like you've gotten a good night's sleep for a change," Willard remarked at the breakfast table that morning.

"Yes, I'm feeling a little better about some things," she said. "I still want to make it a point to waste no time getting there to bring Johnny home, though."

"You'll have to travel alone this time," Willard said, "but you're a big girl now, so I doubt you'll get into any mischief." He chuckled as she batted him playfully on the arm.

"I'll get a round trip ticket for yourself and a one way ticket for our boy," he said. "I'll work some extra jobs that are coming up and keep the home fires burning for you both and be here if Leona arrives early this year."

"We can afford all this?" She asked.

"Oh, the money's in no great danger," he said, "besides, I don't think we can afford not to do all this. What good is money if we're miserable without our boy. I miss him something awful. He was a part of it all when I married you, and he's not here. I love you more than I've ever loved any woman, Emma. I never had any children of my own, but even if I did, none could replace the part of my heart that this little boy owns. You go get our grandson, Emma, and I'll put the finest roof over your heads that these old hands can build, and I'll love you both forever. Carpenter's honor." He held two fingers under his eyes, and somehow she didn't think he was joking.

The next day, the news came in the mail, that Johnny had scalded his feet in the bathtub. Dave had rescued the boy from himself and had taken him to the hospital for treatment. He would be fine when the blisters healed, but there was some concern over his self destructive behavior. Johnny wouldn't purposely hurt himself. There had to be another influence to bring this about. As the Vough was the evil behind what the children thought was Elvyra, Emma wanted to know the unknown scowling face behind Dave. She wearied of the evil that lashed out at her boy from its hiding place in the shadows.

As she reviewed her dreams, it did seem as if the colt's mind was a bit addled. Originally, she attributed this to walking too long in the hot sun or just plain weariness. Now, she wondered at what was being used to hold her boy in its cruel grip. Perhaps Coyote could advise her on this type of magick. If something was not done soon, he would not likely last until she could fetch him home. She had no desire to compose anyone's death song. She would initiate a dreamwalk tonight.

***

The unicorn colt lay sleeping the day away in the shade of the arroyo. Coyote sat high on the opposite bank and watched over him.

"Some kind of magick is being used on my grandson," Emma remarked to the uncanny animal.

"I've seen this before," he said. "The Mescaleros use this medicine to seek the spirit world. They get their visions and find their path. Your little warrior is much too young to be on this kind of path, and I think he won't need the peyote to find his way on the path of dreams and spirits."

"What do the Mescaleros do to shake this off when it happens?" She asked.

"It's simple enough," Coyote replied, his eyes never leaving the colt. "They dance and they sweat. I've been wondering why he hasn't danced."

"He hasn't been happy," she said. "He misses home."

"There is his quest," Coyote said. "He must learn to live well, even when it looks bleakest. He must learn to celebrate life in the face of death. It is the quest of a spirit warrior. He's very young for such a thing, but he is already on that path and I see no other way but to travel down it. He will have to find it in himself to dance this out and he will survive and grow from it. Otherwise, it will kill him. You have made him a death song, haven't you?"

"No, it will not be necessary at this time," she said. "You said that if I had raised him well in the ways of our medicine and it is strong to stand, and if his heart is pure and his mind single that he will live and thrive. I am confident that I have given him all I could in his few years and that there is no magick stronger among our people than the magick of the unicorn, whose heart is the purest of beasts and whose horn is the single focus of his mind. My grandson will know pain and suffering, but he will grow strong where lesser creatures fall. Your words to this effect have given me this confidence. No death song is needed, only sage advice."

"I've never seen such a thing as this creature on the whole of this island," Coyote said. "I will watch and learn a new thing for my people. I hope you are right, old woman. I will have another tale to tell beside the bonfires."

Emma gazed down at the sleeping colt and willed herself into his dreams. The prairie scene melted away to be replaced by her grandson sitting forlornly on the side of his bed. An oversized pair of white socks covered his bandaged feet. Dark circles formed under eyes that were much too young to be so tired. His eyes brightened when he saw her specter standing in his room.

"Grandma, you came," he said.

"Yes, I had to check up on my boy," she replied cheerfully.

"I was bad again, " he said regretfully, "and did something stupid and hurt myself. I'm sorry, Grandma. I didn't know what I was doing. I was trying to be a good boy. I don't know how this happened to me." He pointed at his feet.

"I know, dear," she said. "There is someone out here, like the Vough, who doesn't like you and he is doing things to hurt you."

"What can I do?" He said in despair. "I'm only a little witch, even smaller than Leona."

"There was a man, not so long ago," she explained, "that said that the bad things that happen to people, that don't kill them, only serve to make them stronger. Well, you've always wanted to be a real hero like Davy Crocket or the Lone Ranger and all those guys, right?"

"Oh, yes," he said with a bit too much enthusiasm, his eyes lighting from within.

"Well, my boy," she said. "If you can get through all this mess in good shape until I can come and bring you home, you can pretty much bet that you're going to grow up to be some kind of strong man. Don't you think?"

"I will?" He asked with a note of wonder.

"I promise," she said as he faded from her view and her own dreams rushed in to overtake her.

PART THIRTY NINE

Iktome's Dance

Johnny woke up with his head feeling clearer than it had for a while. His feet were healing well and itched as the blistered skin dried and shed itself for the newer layer beneath. His bandaged feet fit his slippers alright, but it would be a couple more days until he could get them back into shoes again. He looked over his book work that Diana had brought him from school and he was appalled at the stuff he had written there. He crumpled up the paper and began his assignment afresh. He was going to show his grandmother how good he could do. School work was easy and he liked to learn new things. The more he could read, the more he could learn. He just couldn't get enough.

He worked quietly in his room, until Dave looked in.

"I hope you're hungry, kiddo," Dave said, cheerfully, "I made you breakfast."

A bowl of Maypo, a glass of orange juice and a couple slices of toast and jam later, the world around Johnny shifted into a subtler gear. By this time his mother looked in on him.

"Hey, Sonshine," his mother said, "Why don't you get something on those feet and get out to the patio for some air for a while so I can clean your room and make this bed." He put his slippers on over the bulky white socks and went out into the backyard.

"Aren't you a little young for this?" Asked a small voice in the leaves climbing the patio trellis.

"Who are you, in there?" He asked, trying to peer through the leaves.

"I am Iktome, the Spider," said a handsome, fat tarantula, stepping forward.

"What am I too young for?" Johnny asked, standing back a little ways.

"You are too young and too pale to be a Mescalero brave," Iktome said. "Or of any of the other tribes I can think of. What tribe or clan are you from?"

"I'm a Celt," he said, "of my grandma's witch clan."

"I've never heard of them," the Spider said. "Still, far away tribe or not, you are much too young for this quest."

"Quest?" He asked in amazement. "I love quests. Our most famous heroes did quests. I want to be a hero someday. Grandma says I will be a very strong one if I live through all the bad stuff."

"Then you must dance," said the Spider.

"Dance?" He asked. "Dance for what?"

"Yes, dance," Iktome said irritably. "Didn't your medicine man explain to you how any of this works? Braves older and stronger than yourself have died on vision quests, and you get left out here with no instruction on how to dance? What kind of witch clan do you come from, boy?"

"We're good witches," he insisted, "and I can dance good too. Everybody in my neighborhood says so."

"The little sun headed brave is a witch too?" Iktome asked, laughing.

"I'm still learning from my grandma," he said defensively. "She's our clan matriarch."

"Hoka hey, a witch warrior," the Spider exclaimed. "and so young and small. It is too much what they expect of you. You probably don't even have a death song. I shall sing you one, myself."

"You sing for me," he commanded, "and I will dance my dance. I will live and I will be strong as my grandma said so. You sing, Spider, and you will see."

He danced as Iktome sang. First, the Spider sang in the pulse of a beating heart, and as Johnny's dance swelled with his zest of life, the handsome arachnid quickened the pace until he was dancing a merry, eight legged, jig along with Johnny under the patio trellis. Stomping, whirling, leaping and strutting, no brave had ever danced with such a wild medicine.

***

Dave watched Lorry put the finishing touches on Johnny's bedroom. It was good he got outside, as the room was beginning to smell of a boy cooped up too long. She brought the tray with the empty bowl and juice glass into the kitchen to put in the sink.

"Did he eat all of his breakfast?" He asked.

"It looks like it," she said. "I sent him out back for a while. He could use some fresh air and his feet seem to be less tender for walking."

"I'll say so," Dave said, peering at the spectacle out the back window.

"What's happening out there?" She asked, moving closer to see.

"The idiot is dancing his fool butt off out there," he said.

"This can't be good," Lorry said, pushing her way out the back door.

Dave watched from the window, as Johnny continued dancing energetically and completely oblivious to his mother's abrupt presence in the back yard. As she approached the patio, the sight of something scurrying in large circles on the flagstones gave her pause to return with all speed to the safety of the house.

Upon seeing the instantaneous conversion of a concerned mother to a wild eyed, thrashing harridan on a collision course with himself, Dave threw open the back door and stepped back to allow her in. He continued backing up, as her forward momentum remained unchanged upon entering the living room and both of them tumbled over the hassock onto the couch as he struggled to calm her down.

"My God, woman," he shouted. "Get a hold of yourself. What has gotten into you?"

"Spiders!" She said breathlessly. "There's huge spiders dancing on the patio."

"What?" He said, looking about for any sign of arachnid activity. "Have you been eating the boy's Maypo?"

"No, I haven't," she said in exasperation, "and what does that have to do with anything?"

"Nothing," he said, a little too quickly. "Nothing at all. I was just wondering if you were becoming as loony as he was?"

"Listen, there are tarantulas all over the patio," she said, with a shiver of disgust, "and he's out there dancing like a maniac. He may have been bitten. Now, you go out there and get him."

"What?" He asked incredulously. "Oh, you've got to be kidding me. The kid boils his feet and I take him to the hospital, and as his feet get better, he dances in a nest of tarantulas and I have to go get him. That kid is going to be the death of me."

"If you don't get out there," Lorry screamed hysterically, "and get him away from those spiders, I'm going to be the death of you!" She emphasized her point by hefting a table lamp as a club.

Dave swallowed hard, grabbed a golf club and headed out the back door into pandemonium. The back yard was rapidly filling up with tarantulas, snakes, ravens and all sorts of vermin. Johnny was still dancing about like a little maniac. When the boy whirled and locked eyes with him, standing with his golf club in hand, his whole world shifted into another gear. A strange music filled the back yard and the spiders were stomping to its rhythm, and the boy continued his wild dance, never once losing eye contact. Dave's knees began shaking and he moved his feet forward to try and get control of his terrified joints. Looking down, there were spiders dancing about him and he high stepped, picking his feet up higher to avoid contact with the arachnids. The music was taking him in its rhythm and his hips and shoulders began moving of their own. He forced himself to stop and not move in spite of his fears. He was not going to get caught up in this strange dance. Then he looked down and away from Johnny's eyes. His clothing was covered with spiders. He shook, leapt, whirled and danced in terrified abandon. There was no stopping him as he crashed through the wooden slat fence and down the street. It was a little over a mile to the cantina, but the spiders would be shaken loose by then.

It was well after the bars closed down when he got home that night. He was more than a little drunk. His clothing was unbuttoned and one of his shoes were missing. He looked about the house and violently shook his clothing out whenever he thought he might have seen something moving in the dark. The little bastard had gotten him good this time. The creep had turned his house into a friggin zoo for vermin and had run him off. He was going to lay low for a while and then... pay back. He'd give that kid a dose so large that he'd never come back again. There's only one man in this house.

PART FORTY

The Good Red Road

Coyote sat alone on the mesa, staring long into the west from his perch on top of the world. The unicorn colt was nowhere to be seen. Emma looked about, noting his absence.

"He danced," Coyote replied to her unvoiced question. "He danced a wild medicine, so very different from here, and he counted coup on his enemy in a way that even Crazy Horse would have envied him. He even made Iktome dance, and that fat, old Spider is known for his fine dancing. It's what makes him so attractive to the ladies."

"I knew he would dance, eventually," she said. "My ancestors on both sides of the ocean have it in their blood and bones, and my grandson as much as the best of them."

"Things are quiet now," Coyote said. "But his enemies are licking their wounds and dreaming of tasting his blood. It will not stay quiet for very long."

"His stepfather is not that enemy," she explained. "He is not strong enough to carry this out on his own. There is a dark, angry face behind him. Do you know of whom I speak?"

"Yes, a mestizo witch, a brujo," the Trickster replied. "He is a mixed blood witch of Spanish and Mescalero ancestry, with a touch of your Otherworld in his veins. He is the colt's ancient enemy."

"A male witch?" She asked.

"Don't be so surprised," Coyote said. "They are not common, but they can be very powerful and dangerous. Your grandson would have no chance at all without some kind of help. The colt is full of surprises, which is why I love watching him, but he has not yet come into his own. The brujo is wise to see that this does not happen. He has every reason to fear this pony of yours when it is full grown."

"So, this is to be to the death?" She asked.

"Eventually, it will end up so," the animal replied. "The brujo has just learned to respect the power of the little warrior's dance. His medicine ran back to him in fear. Now, he will wait and find the right moment to strike and he will not show mercy. He will not allow his enemy to strike back. His fear and respect has made him doubly dangerous."

"I will come and bring my boy home," she said. "Perhaps then, things will quiet down for my daughter's family, and I can continue raising him in the ways of my people."

"A wise, temporary solution," Coyote acknowledged. "El Brujo will have no need or interest in your weakling kin, if the colt is gone and not reachable there. His power is found in this arid land and not in your moist, eastern woodlands. At best, you will postpone their meeting until your own warrior has reached his full age and power."

"They have to fight?" She asked.

"You've seen the smoke signals on that far mountain,—" Coyote nodded to a writhing column of black smoke, "—haven't you?"

"For a long time now," she replied.

"That is your enemy, announcing his presence and his intention," the Trickster explained, "Your unicorn and that dragon are destined to clash. The only real question here is, where and when the battle will take place. The nature of that beast is such that if it can murder the young colt to avoid facing a more formidable foe later, it will do so. It seems that there are a great crowd of spectators watching to see how this turns out. Some wish him well; others do not."

"What do you wish?" She asked.

"I wish him well," the Trickster said. "He makes me laugh, and will give me many stories to tell around the fire, and the people will feed me well for them. Iktome and Raven like him too, but that means nothing. It is not our battle. We have lived to see many proud braves in the Ghost Dance. We will live to see his contribution as well. I only hope he joins it in the kind of joy he brought Iktome. He is such a spirited boy. I would cut off my own paws to see him and Crazy Horse dance at the same fire."

"I gather the two of them would raise some eyebrows," she said.

"In so many ways," Coyote said, with a smile that shone in his luminous eyes. "But now, I need something from you. Do this for me, and I will do what I can for our little, yellow haired friend."

"What would you like?" She asked, cautiously. "If it is within my power to do, I will deny you no good thing."

"I will have to insist," he said, solemnly, "that you teach him more of the Good Red Road."

"I hear you well, friend," she said. "But, I myself have been taught so little of it to teach him. I didn't grow up with my people on a reservation. I grew up in my mother's house and learned her ways. She loved and respected my father, and I learned as much as he taught me. He made my first knife for me." She showed the Trickster her witch blade.

"I am concerned," Coyote said, "that he watches our people portrayed in these western movies and would lose his respect for his own people. He does not look redskin, with his cornflower eyes and yellow hair, but it is in his blood along with your other clans, and must not be denied. When the time comes, I will send him teachers, but he will not respect them if the whites poison his mind about our people. He must not close himself off from his full heritage. We own a small piece of this boy too."

"I give you my word as a witch of the blood," she said, raising her blade to her palm.

"Don't cut yourself needlessly," Coyote said quickly. "We are already in each other's blood. There is no need to mingle more than that. I accept your word as given. Do your best. I could ask no more than this."

"He is my best," she said. "And at this very moment, it is only your mercy that protects him, and not my own. Let me bring my boy home alive and we will never forget you. Ever."

"Such iron words," Coyote said, his amber eyes growing large and hypnotically luminous. "Don't you think this coffee smells good?"

"Yes," she said as the huge amber eyes transformed to pale blue as Willard gently wafted the steam from her cup towards her face.

"And if you don't get up and drink it, sleepy head," he said with a chuckle, "it's gonna get cold on you."

Emma smiled, stretched and sat up to accept her coffee. Willard sat on the side of the bed with her.

"You, ah, check up on him in your dreams?" He asked. "Isn't that what you do sometimes?"

"As best as I can," she admitted. "Why do you ask?"

"Well, sometimes you talk in your sleep," he said. "And I catch a few things of what's going on, and I want to know how our grandson is doing. I know he's different. Remember the automatic candles from our wedding?"

"I'll bet the good pastor is still trying to figure that out," she said, smiling. "Our boy has a knack for having deadly enemies, and equally strange friends. He'll be finished with school in a couple weeks, and I hope to be there to collect him when he's ready."

"Then you should write a letter to say you're coming for a little visit," he said. "Take some pictures of our new granddaughter. Spend a week or so, and get our boy home so I can teach him a good trade with a hammer and nails. He's wasted far too much time in the land of frivolous movie stars and palm trees. Palm trees just don't make good lumber. Y'know what I mean? Here's the tickets to get you there and back." He slapped a pair of Greyhound envelopes down on her bedspread in front of her.

"I'll write that letter today and let Lorry know I'll be on my way soon," she said, toasting him with her coffee cup.

She wanted to give the letter a few days of a head start on her before she left for the bus terminal. This would give them time to prepare for her and maybe a little confidence that Johnny won't be their problem for much longer and take a little pressure off everyone concerned. She had packed her bags for the trip and remembered she wanted to check up on something before she left. There were promises she didn't want to forget to keep.

That afternoon, she strolled down East Avenue for the Rochester Museum and Science Center. There had been a newspaper blurb about their natural history exhibit and she wanted to see if there was anything she could use in it.

Arriving at the imposing white stone structure, she walked up to the central information desk. There were few visitors besides a school tour looking at stuffed panoramas behind glass on the main floor. The woman at the desk had a friendly smile and was glad to answer questions.

"Do you have any exhibits or information here on the local landscape two or three hundred years ago?" Emma asked.

"We'd be a poor museum if we didn't," the woman said cheerfully. "On the second floor, a large section is devoted to the Iroquois and Seneca people of this region, complete with artifacts, dioramas, and a full sized longhouse. Would you like a map and a brochure?"

"Why, yes, thank you," she said, accepting the brochure.

"Just take that elevator over there to the second floor." The woman directed her.

The second floor proved to be a treasure trove of Indian life before the white man settled these parts. She was sure it would be a pleasant field trip for Johnny and Leona one day this summer. The longhouse was an actual log cabin with wax manikins of an Indian man, woman and baby in native dress going about daily life. Behind one glass display, was a gruesome recreation of a local burial site, complete with the bones of someone's long lost ancestor and the artifacts found with the skeleton. While she could understand the academic interest, she wasn't sure that this would be the kind of respect Coyote would approve of. Taking a cue of the Trickster's methods, maybe she could use them as a good example of what is not appropriate. Nonetheless, this gave her what she would need to educate her little cowboy about the other side of his roots. She would keep her promise as best as she could. The Trickster, himself, would help with the rest.

She was beginning to note a growing list of the boy's helpers. First, were the nuns of St. Brigit's. Then Brother George, the dragon slayer imaginary brother, who was not imagined. There was Geraldine, who had more mouths to feed and care for than either of them cared to count. The woman would take Johnny in with her own brood and watch over him when she had appointments or such. Old Ian, the neighborhood skinflint, could not maintain a dour look on his face when Johnny was present. There was Elvyra, whom even the children never suspected was a friend. Brave Gregory, the piskie hero of the woods of Annwn, who was most instrumental in rescuing him. The boy was Irish, which was a strike against him in certain white circles, and Sidhe, which could work either way depending upon the company kept. The Indian side was never discussed, even among the family. By rights, Johnny was at least one eighth Native. Here were Coyote, Raven —who could be of any culture— and Iktome the Spider going to bat for him, and the boy making friends and dancing with them as if it were only natural that he should do so.

Emma so missed her father at this moment. He could have told the boy the stories he needed to hear to find himself. Her father had been a chief. He could have taught the boy to dance like an Indian and make him as proud as she was to be his daughter. She just never thought of him much as "Indian." He was simply "Daddy." Somehow, in all of this, it was not just Johnny. She would find a piece of herself. Was it her imagination? Or did that raven mask on the totem pole just wink at her?

It was time to leave.

PART FORTY ONE

Rite Of Passage

Dave didn't know whether to rant or rejoice. Lorry had received a letter that his mother-in-law would be on her way to bring the boy to stay with her for the summer, and possibly forever. He would be free of the brat at last and his luck would change. But deep in his darkest depths, he still had a score to settle with the little bastard for humiliating him in front of so many. Before that old crone would get here, he would empty the rest of Miguel's powder into the boy's food. Then maybe the brat would try to boil his own head, and Emma could take back what was left of him. Yes. Now he was feeling decidedly better about himself.

Opportunity knocked when Ginna came and took Lorry and the baby for a Saturday doctor's appointment. That would leave him in charge of making Johnny's breakfast and getting him out and away from the house so that he could not be affected by the boy's weird magic. Also, if the kid was as far across the fields as he liked to play, he could not be expected to know if anything was wrong or have to rescue him. Miguel's hoodoo gods were smiling upon him.

"Up and at 'em, kid," he said cheerfully. "Get dressed and ready for breakfast. You've got a full day's work ahead of you and I'll have you a lunch packed and everything."

"Work?" Johnny asked, excitedly. "I've got a job too?"

"Yep." He said. "It seems those fields across the street stretch on for miles and miles and no one has ever explored them as far as they go. Seeing as it is such a beautiful day, I think we should pack you a lunch and set you to exploring the outermost reaches of them for science. You'll need an early start if you expect to get them explored before suppertime."

"Yes sir," Johnny said, dashing about his room looking for his socks and sneakers.

It was almost too easy. The remainder of the bottle went into the boy's oatmeal. The biggest single dose yet. The kid finished all of his breakfast and grabbed his sack lunch, which was free of any potentially incriminating evidence, and out the door in minutes. Now, it was time to put on his favorite Tex Ritter album and do a little house cleaning to please the missus.

***

Johnny made excellent time getting out into the field. The sunshine was warm and friendly on his shoulders and the tall grass smelled sweet. This would be a great day for exploring and adventure. He didn't even have to go back home for lunch, so he could explore much farther. Perhaps today he would make it all the way up to the base of those mountains. It had always appeared that the field ended there, but he could never be sure. Today, he would find out.

He found an old wooden mop handle in a pile of junk that someone had left in a gully. Twisting off the mop head between two large stones, it made a serviceable staff for his journey. As he turned back to face the eastern mountains, the world shifted gears on him again. He was almost beginning to get used to this happening, but somehow, this was different. In the distance, a fire burned on the slopes of the mountains and a single plume of black smoke rose above, looking down on him as if it were alive. The adventure was about to begin. Just in case, he sharpened the end of his staff and prepared to deal with anything that tried to stop him from exploring his field.

He was scraping out a fine point on a granite boulder when he noticed the blood on his hands. As he examined his palms, another couple drops of crimson landed on his fingers. His nose was bleeding. This was a fine predicament. Wiping his bloody nose on his sleeve, he continued his hike towards the far side of the field with his spear in hand. He was going to be a mighty hero some day and it would take more than this to stop him.

The world went topsy turvy for a moment when he plunged through the tall grass and fell into a gulley. He got back onto his feet and nothing seemed to be hurt, with the exception of the bloody nose, but that wasn't hurt, that was just a nuisance. He picked up his spear and his lunch and set off to explore the gully. The walls were twisting and undulating and making him a little queasy when a loud buzzing hummed near his feet. A large rattlesnake was coiled to strike and angrily buzzing its rattle at him.

"Back away, man thing," it said. "Don't make me hurt you."

"Why do people always want to hurt me?" He insisted angrily.

"I never said I wanted to hurt you, man-child," the reptile replied testily. "You almost stepped on me and I wanted you to leave me alone. If you leave me be, I will not hurt you at all."

"I'm sorry," he said. "I'm just a little bit dizzy and didn't see where I was going."

"I can taste your blood in the air," it said. "It's a wonder you can even stand with all that medicine in you."

"Medicine?" He asked, confused. "Isn't that stuff supposed to make you better? I don't feel so good." He promptly fell on his face, narrowly missing the rattler.

"Wake up," a voice commanded out of the darkness. "To sleep now, is to die."

He opened his bleary eyes. The rattler had moved a way off and lay relaxed in the sun. Nearer to his face was a familiar dark form.

"Wake up, wake up," Iktome said. "It's time again to dance."

"Oh, I don't feel like dancing," he said, rolling over. "Who else is here?"

"A good friend of mine has joined us," the Spider said. "He will teach you an Injun dance. But you have lost a lot of blood. Did you bring anything to drink with you?"

"Oh, look, a doggie," he said, as his clearing sight revealed the canine form at the top of the gully looking down at him. "C'mere, doggie. Here, boy!"

"I am not a dog," the animal declared indignantly. "I am Coyote, the Trickster, and I am here at your grandmother's request to teach you our ways."

"Grandma's here?" He asked, sitting up.

"She said to tell you that she is coming," Coyote said. "But that won't help if you are not alive when she gets here. What do you have in the bag?"

"Lunch," he said. "But I'm not really hungry just now."

"You have lost blood in the hot sun, boy," Iktome said. "and you reek of peyote. You need food and drink more than anyone I know. Is there anything juicy in that bag?"

"Here's an orange," Johnny said, sorting through the sack, "and a peanut butter sandwich and a baloney sandwich."

"Then you should eat the orange first," the Spider urged him. "Eat all of it now."

Johnny sat and bit into the orange, devouring rind and all.

"Did you say there was baloney in there?" Coyote asked, licking his chops.

"Yes," he said, slurping the juice out of his orange to quench his thirst. "Would you like some?"

"You are too kind," Coyote said. "Don't mind if I do. Perhaps Iktome would like the bread."

"No," the Spider said. "I prefer my food a little juicier. Besides, I ate earlier this morning. How about you, Brother Snake?"

"Ugh," the snake said with a shiver, "no bread for me. I was sleeping off a fat rat when the boy disturbed me."

"I'd like a crust of that bread," a raven cawed, "if you don't mind. But you should eat all of that other sandwich yourself. You're going to need your strength to dance again."

"Is that a spear you have there, little warrior?" Coyote asked.

"I thought he was going to pierce me with it when he surprised me," said the snake.

"I made it when I saw the dragon on the mountain," Johnny said through a mouthful of peanut butter and jelly.

"You were prepared to fight a monster like that?" Iktome asked.

Johnny nodded.

"Then it seems we should dance a full warrior's dance today," said the Spider. "Don't you agree, Raven?"

"Indeed, if he lives," Raven said. "I believe it is his time."

"Then it is decided," Coyote concluded. "You will take up your spear and dance with us as a new warrior. Iktome will make your circle in the sand, and Brother Snake will sit in its center and provide us a rattle. Raven, when this is under way, and it looks like the boy will live, you know what we will need for him. Go, fetch it."

The raven took to wing with a cry. The rattler slithered into the center of the gulley and Iktome danced a wide circle in the sand around the serpent. Coyote's tail beat a rhythm in the sagebrush as the snake rattled counterpoint and the Spider began to sing. Johnny took his first steps hesitantly as he willed himself to keep his balance.

"Come down on your heel," Coyote instructed, "and not so much your toe. Now raise that spear like you intend to use it, boy."

Johnny danced. His heart pounding stronger and stronger to the beat of drums echoing in the distant past. Dancing. Step down heel, step down heel, side step, side step. Raise that spear. Shout! Iktome singing. Brother Snake buzzing in rhythm and tracking his every step with interest. Coyote coaching and beating time with his tail in the sagebrush. The sun danced in the sky. The stars moved in their spiral dance in the heavens. The shimmering forms of ghosts danced the circle with them, but he did not stop. All of nature danced and he belonged to that dance.

***

The taxicab dropped Emma off at the house on Randolph Street. She paid the cabby and hefted her suitcase for the walk up to the door. Before she got very far, Lorry came dashing out to greet her.

"Mom, you're here early," her daughter exclaimed hugging her.

"Didn't you get my letter?" She asked.

"Well, yes, but I figured you'd be at least another week," Lorry said, taking her suitcase from her. "But I'm glad you came. Linda is getting bigger and sweeter every day, and you know how your grandson misses you."

"I brought a camera with me this time," she said. "I'll take some pictures to share with friends and family back home. How are you and the baby doing?"

Dave appeared at the door smiling and holding the baby for her to see.

"Aw, how beautiful she is," she said. "Let me set this stuff down and hold her for a little while."

Dave handed off the baby and took up her bags and set them inside. She would be sleeping on the hide-a-bed in the living room sofa during her stay.

"I don't see my grandson around," she said. "Is he out somewhere playing."

"Well, it's past lunchtime," Lorry said. "But sometimes he gets caught up in whatever he's playing and shows up a little late. It's not too unusual."

"Oh, I packed him a lunch today," Dave said. "So, he'll probably be back sometime closer to supper today."

"Packed a lunch?" Lorry asked. "Where did he go?"

"He's probably just across the street in the field," he said.

"Then go call him," Lorry said, "and tell him his grandmother's here. He'll be so excited to see you, Mom."

Dave glared at his wife, and went out the front door and let out with a loud whistle and called for Johnny. Certainly, that would carry for some distance. But twenty minutes later and the boy still hadn't shown up. Emma had the distinct impression that something was wrong, and Dave seemed to make every effort never to look Lorry or her in the eyes when he spoke.

"Here, Lorry," she said, "Why don't you take this little sleeping beauty from me and Dave and I will go surprise Johnny."

"We will?" Dave said with a start.

"See?" She said, smiling. "Some of us are surprised already. Let's you and I take a stroll through the fields and find our boy."

She went through her suitcase and found an apron and belted her witch blade underneath.

"I can't just let my good skirt get all dirty and frazzled out there," she explained.

Twenty minutes, forty minutes an hour later, they continued walking the fields and Dave whistled and called without an answer. He would still not meet her eyes when he spoke.

"So tell me about your Mexican witch doctor," she said, "this 'brujo' you've been talking to."

Dave did a double take at her and looked away again.

"He warned me about you and the boy," he said. "He told me you were witches, in league with Satan."

"Satan's house must be divided," she replied evenly, "if you would consult one witch against another. And what of yourself, holy man? I can't seem to recall ever seeing you set your righteous foot in a church of any kind. You even got married by a justice-of-the-peace. You who are so eager to bring down judgment upon another. Tell me, by what god do you poison my grandson?"

"It's not poison," Dave said. "El Brujo ate some of it right in front of me. It won't hurt him, just drive the devil out of him."

"What devil is that?" She growled. "Would it be the one who would passionately defend a little girl's virtue? Or would it be the one who would boil a little boy alive in his bathtub? I'm not sure. Which side of this devil are you on?" She caught his eye and locked her gaze to his.

"You,.. you can't hurt me," he said, eyes darting about wildly. "Miguel gave me this for protection against you and the boy." He showed his obsidian arrowhead pendant.

"So, that's how he's controlling you," she said. "Listen well, you idiot. You are my daughter's husband and my granddaughter's father, and while I am not particularly impressed with your actions of late, that makes you 'family,' even as my grandson is family. I am not the one who will hurt you. You'll do that without any help from me at all. To me, you are a bent nail to be straightened out and made useful. Take that pendant off and bury it in the dirt at your feet."

He tried to resist for a moment. He struggled with himself a while longer and then the pendant's cord fell away and it dropped into the palm of his hand. Looking up at her, he kneeled in the dirt and buried it.

"We will have a longer talk later, as a family," she said. "But meantime, you should go see about getting us some help searching for the boy out here. There's no telling what kind of shape we'll find him in."

"I'm sorry, Ma," he said.

"I never thought you were behaving like yourself, Son," she said. "Now, you get us that help, and I'll keep searching out here."

She reached into her deep apron pocket and pulled out a little packet of salt, which she sprinkled over the spot Dave buried his arrowhead. The ground smoldered beneath it.

"What is that stuff you're using?" He asked.

"Just simple table salt," she said. "It has that effect on fighting corruption and decay. This thing was to rot your brains and make you see and think what the brujo wanted. Now, get going and call for help."

Dave dashed back for the house. The sun was sinking in the direction of the neighborhood, and night would be falling soon. Emma stilled herself to feel for her grandson. Breathing in, she could smell the sagebrush, and blood. The sound of distant drums and Native voices chanted and sang. He may be wounded, but he was dancing somewhere out there. Sage kept bad spirits at bay, so he would be with friends, no doubt.

Night had fallen, and a full moon rose quickly to light her way. The sound of drums and singing filled her mind as she moved ahead, towards the distant mountains. Far behind her, the lights from numerous flashlights spread out across the field. A lone coyote sat in the moonlight, on the edge of a gulley.

"You wouldn't happen to be watching a young colt dance, now would you?" She asked, walking forward to the edge.

The coyote winked its pale eye at her and trotted off looking for game. At the bottom of the washout, a boy sized figure danced around a large rattlesnake, shaking a lance with an eagle feather attached near the tip. A fat tarantula looking like an animated shadow in the sand, danced a comic counter beat to the boy.

"It's long past time for all good boys to pack it in and return to their families," she announced to the bizarre spectacle below her.

All motion stopped for a heartbeat. The spider scurried into the underbrush for cover. The snake slithered away to its hole, and the boy leaned heavily on his lance and looked up.

"Grandma," he said, and slumped to the ground in a dead faint.

***

It was nearly noon before Johnny awoke in his bed, surrounded by his step dad, the deputy sheriff, a doctor who insisted upon shining a flash-light in his eyes and more importantly, his grandma.

"It seems as if the effects of the peyote has worn off with no apparent side effects other than a little dehydration," the doctor said. "Keep him away from that stuff, and I'm pretty sure he'll live to be older than all of us."

"I'm sorry, Doc," Dave said. "I really thought it was something that would help him. I didn't mean him any harm."

"Well, let that be a lesson to you," the doctor said, not unkindly. "Don't go accepting hoodoo cures from witch doctors without first check-ing with a real doctor."

"Hey, what's this?" Ted asked, looking at the eagle feather clutched in Johnny's hand. "Where'd you find an eagle feather, buddy?"

"Raven gave it to me," he said.

"Well, I hate to tell you this, my friend," Ted said sadly, "but the law says you can't keep this. It's an endangered bird. Only Indians are al-lowed to have them."

"I'll take that," Emma said, "I am the daughter of an Iroquois chieftain. I will keep it for my grandson, who is the great grandson of that same chief."

"That will do just fine then." The deputy smiled and handed her the feather.

They kept Johnny filled with soup and fluids the rest of that Sunday. He would be up and about for his last few days of school before summer vacation. Meanwhile, Emma took a little time to get re-acquainted with her new family. Dave sat in attendance as she spoke with them both.

"Sweetheart, you know I've always loved you," she said to Lorry. "Never once did I ever insist that you be anything that was not in you to be. When you chose not to follow your sisters in the craft, I loved you no less for it and respected your choices."

"Dave, I was impressed that you could walk so boldly into a ready made family and take on that kind of responsibility," she said. "Dave, Lorry is no witch, and what you think of witches is not particularly flattering to those who are. Hurting a little boy in ignorance is still hurting him. But in all fairness to the both of you, Johnny is a little beyond your experience, and he needs to be loved and respected for who he is too. He surprises me all the time, but I'm a bit better educated about him than either of you would be. I can deal with him on his own terms, while you two now have this very lovely, very normal daughter who will need every bit of your undivided attention. Willard and I feel almost lost without our boy. His cousin, Leona, misses him too, along with all his old friends in the neighborhood. How about he stays with me, and I raise him and teach him even as I have with you and your siblings? You visit him, he visits you and we are all one happy family and nobody gets stressed beyond the measure they can bear. I want all of us to have a happier future."

"I would have asked you, Mom," Lorry said. "I just felt like I was failing as a mother."

"What would you think," she said, "of a mother who had sent her son to the finest boarding school money could afford, to secure him a solid future? You know, if little Linda starts showing any witchy traits, she can foster during the summers like Leona does now, and her big brother will be there to help her through it."

"Point taken, Mom," Lorry replied, smiling.

"Ah, Mom?" Dave interjected. "About that powder out in the field, that was really just salt and nothing magickal?"

"Oh, my son," she said laughing. "Who ever told you that salt wasn't magick?"

END OF BOOK ONE OF WITCH CLAN SERIES

Printed in the United States
214241BV00001B/5/P

9 781554 046607